S0-DQW-293

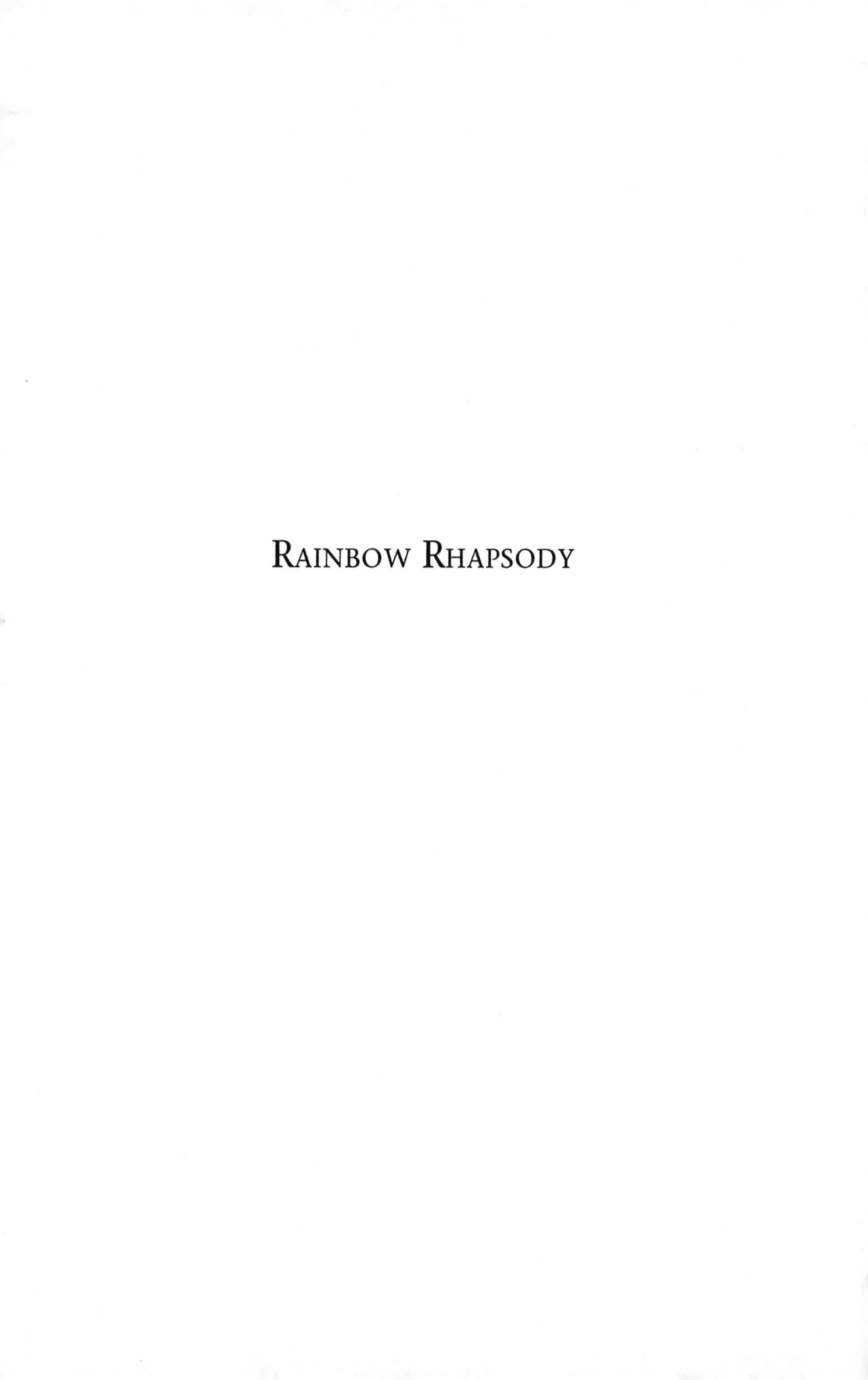

Rainbow Rhapsody

Also by Rick Borsten

The Great Equalizer (The Permanent Press, 1986)

Rick Borsten

RAINBOW RHAPSODY

Breitenbush Books Inc.

First edition: 2 3 4 5 6 7 8 9

Library of Congress Cataloging in Publication Data

Borsten, Rick

Rainbow rhapsody.
I. Title.

PS3552.07554R3 1989 813'.54 88-22294
ISBN 0-932576-68-0 (cloth)

"Save Our Planet" and "The Reaper" © Neal Gladstone.
"Country Cliché" by Neal Gladstone, © Kaleidoscope Records.

Lyrics to all other songs by the author.

Breitenbush Books, Inc.
P.O. Box 82157, Portland, Oregon 97282
James Anderson, Publisher
Patrick Ames, Editor-in-Chief
Text design by Ky Krauthamer

The publisher acknowledges the support of the Oregon Institute of Literary Arts.

Distributed by Taylor Publishing Company,
1550 W. Mockingbird Lane, Dallas, Texas 75235

Manufactured in the United States of America.

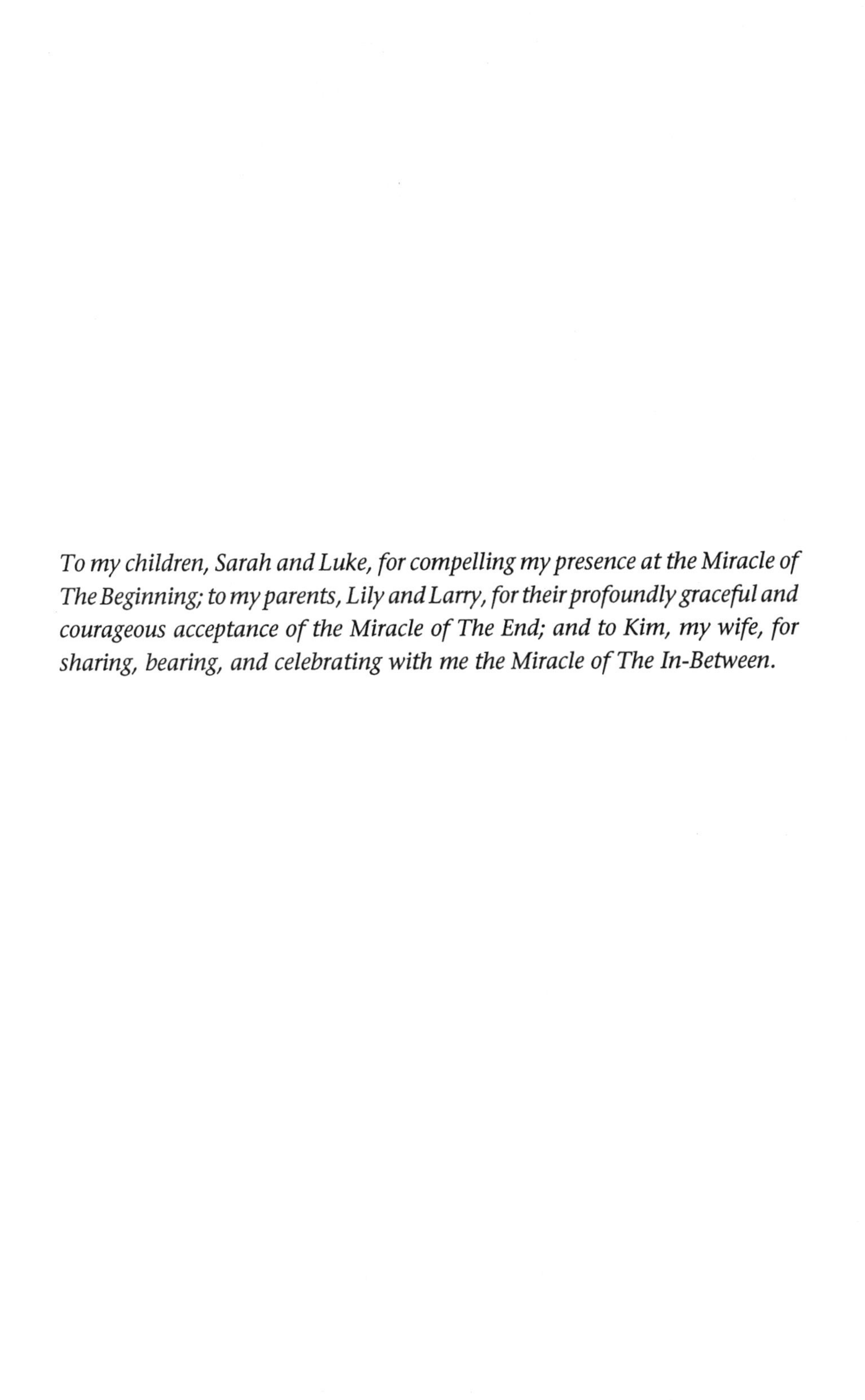

To my children, Sarah and Luke, for compelling my presence at the Miracle of The Beginning; to my parents, Lily and Larry, for their profoundly graceful and courageous acceptance of the Miracle of The End; and to Kim, my wife, for sharing, bearing, and celebrating with me the Miracle of The In-Between.

Acknowledgments

I gratefully acknowledge the important assistance of the following people: Carol Paulson, for her invaluable information regarding the White Train and the philosophy of the protestors who have tried to stop it; Drs. (and friends) Mark Jacokes, David Grube, Dave Cutsforth, and Bruce Byram, for providing me with some critical medical information; Dick and Rose Clinton, Rick Cooper, and Kim Crane for their editorial suggestions; and Neal Gladstone, for his music.

The brief nuclear scare scenario is patched together from at least two sources: *The Fate of the Earth* by Jonathan Schell and a broadcast of "Consider the Alternatives" on National Public Radio. The quotes attributed to David Walker are, indeed, taken from his pamphlet, first published in 1829, entitled *Walker's Appeal, in Four Articles, together with a Preamble, to the Coloured Citizens of the World, but in Particular and Very Expressly to Those of the United States of America.* My source of information regarding relaxation and breathing techniques for childbirth was *Natural Childbirth the Bradley Way,* by Susan McCutcheon-Rosegg with Peter Rosegg. Dizzy Gillespie's astonishing one-fingered A-flat was taken from *To Be, or Not . . . to Bop: Memoirs of Dizzy Gillespie,* with Al Frazer.

Rainbow Rhapsody

. . . in the end, it is the threat of universal extinction hanging over the world today that changes, totally and forever, the nature of reality and brings into devastating question the true meaning of man's history. We human beings now have the power to exterminate ourselves; this seems to be the entire sum of our achievement.... If we do not now dare everything, the fulfillment of that prophecy, re-created from the Bible in a song by a slave, is upon us: *God gave Noah the rainbow sign, No more water, the fire next time!*

—James Baldwin

Part One

Landings and Takeoffs

As usual, autumn has descended upon western Oregon like a gray fog upon a festival of color and light: muddy skies broken by bursts of sunshine, double rainbows, and kaleidoscopic leaf storms—swirling mosaics of magenta and gold, crispy death and summer history tumbling through the soft rains before surrendering to the grass and earth or rotting on the city streets and sidewalks, sticking like wet paper to the hissing tires and gritty shoe soles.

Beyond the Portland city center, in all the residential neighborhoods and out into the suburbs, wooden fences are slowly rotting—returning splinter by soggy splinter to the earth—with the last of the petunias, marigolds, and chrysanthemums. Step on any of the waterlogged lawns even a trifle too indelicately and you will surely leave a permanent smear of mud in place of the green.

At the eastern boundary of Portland lies the airport, surrounded not by soggy lawns, but concrete roads and runways. And yet the rain is at work even here, plunking and gurgling as it seeps into the tiniest cracks and fissures, feeding the subterranean micro-flora and -fauna, and slowly forcing apart the white concrete, making way for the water-fed, light-seeking, bloom-dreaming life below.

However, as the small jet touches down at the Portland Airport, it is not life that the superstar is contemplating. Rather, he is—as he stares out the rain-streaked window with his usual intensity of terror—envisioning a great explosion of metal and flame, an instant inferno with him at the center, the jet wreckage skidding, tumbling, and twisting off the runway and into the rain-swollen Columbia River.

But this is really nothing new. Ever since the day his mother was hurled from her car to *her* final crash-landing on the hot white stretch of interstate, the takeoffs and landings have petrified Rhapsody Walker, for they always force him to consider the possibilities: takeoffs and landings, beginnings and ends. Possibilities that could forever nullify *the in-between*—his mid-flight superstardom.

But as the front tires settle and the jet slows with a burgeoning roar, Rhapsody Walker's death vision begins to dissipate. He fingers his seat belt and, almost smiling, attends to the sound and feel of his breath.

At last the tour was almost over. A show tonight at the Portland Coliseum, tomorrow night at the Seattle Kingdome, and the fourteen weeks and thirty-nine performances would be history. In fact, the "Black and Blue Tour," as it had been billed (the name deriving from Rhapsody's most recent best-selling album, *Rhapsody in Black and Blue*), was going to go down as the most successful, or at least the most lucrative, in the history of rock and roll—the most successful in the history of music. In thirteen and a half whirlwind weeks and thirty-seven performances the tour had thus far netted twenty-three million dollars, excluding the considerable proceeds from sales of posters, t-shirts, albums, tapes, discs, and videos. The album, out less than a year, had long since—within weeks of its release—gone platinum and was presumably on its way to some wholly new category of sales.

There were those who supposed the secret to Rhapsody Walker's success was his hard-edged, dynamic voice. Others believed it was his ability to write a catchy, uncomplicated tune with clever lyrics, and rhythms that could take over your feet and, against your will, set them to tapping. Some even argued that his on-stage performances were the key to his fame: his ability to thrill an audience with his rapping and dancing and feisty presence. And at least part of the appeal of his latest album must have been the wide variety of music it offered: everything from reggae, jazz, rock, blues, and soul, to a country-western parody called "Roses for My Keen-Nosed Gal," which Rhapsody had written one morning when the woman who'd spent the night with him wouldn't allow him to kiss her, after they awoke, until he'd brushed his teeth and gargled. Then, after his morning turn at the commode, she'd actually had the audacity to strike a match to cover up his, Rhapsody Walker's, most intimate odor before *she* would venture into the bathroom; thus he wrote, and later sang, with a flawless white country intonation, the now familiar refrain:

Now I know you were blessed with the keenest of noses
So I'll gargle for you, but I can't poop roses.

But none of this could have accounted for sales of forty-seven million records worldwide in less than a year. It was his charisma, his sassy-souled black magic, the mystique of his planetary fame. And, as he surely would have pointed out, the hunger and desperation of the forty-seven million record buyers.

Man, I've got more power than you can even imagine. So much power it's crazy. Almost scary. For instance: Before I had the money for a hip reduction two years ago, I used to hate my hips. They were wide, sorry hips that poked out every inch as wide as my shoulders. Back in high school, if I tried to wear a nice tight shirt to show off my arm muscles, that shirt would just cling to my sides and make my hips look even wider and sorrier. Gave my body a shape like a pear with the fat side down. Loose shirts helped some. But I finally figured out that if I wore a t-shirt underneath my regular button shirt it filled in my sides—gave them some padding—so that my hips didn't poke out so far. And then, by accident, I saw that if I unbuttoned my outside shirt from the collar all the way to my belt, I could actually have me a "V" from my shoulders to my waist. Like magic. Made my shoulders look wider and my hips skinnier.

By the time I cut my first album the t-shirts I was wearing for padding were wild-colored: purple, lavender, tangerine, pink, or turquoise; or a rainbow swirl of all of them. And pretty soon I couldn't look out in the crowd—any crowd, anywhere in the world—and find a man or a woman or a four-year-old girl who wasn't wearing a wild-colored t-shirt underneath a shirt unbuttoned all the way to the belt.

One day I'm worried about hiding my hips, and the next day—serendipity, Jack—there's ten million women of every size, shape, color, religion, and country who would not only pay a hundred dollars for a front-row view of my hips, but who are dressing same as me and hiding *their* hips. And that's the kind of crazy power I've got!

Power like nobody else in the world.

Power that lets me lift my microphone and, like some black electric Moses, part a sea of people. I just wave my microphone, my magic rod, and the crowds swell and ripple any way I want. Crowds so desperate to see something in me that they *give* me all that crazy power, and then *that's* what they see in me. And they don't even know it's all an illusion. A tilting of mirrors. Black Magic and nothing else.

On the way from the hotel to the Portland Coliseum, lights flash through the dark, the traffic slows to a crawl, and the limousine finally stops halfway across the bridge, the highest in a network of crisscrossing highway bridges, major arteries running through the city's heart, spanning the northward-flowing Willamette River.

"What the hell's going on?" Rhapsody Walker demands of his chauffeur.

"Don't know," the chauffeur says. "Must be a wreck or something."

"Damn!" The superstar stares hard through the windshield, all light and color through the rivulets of rain. "How bad? Man, I hate this shit."

Sitting beside Rhapsody Walker in the back seat of the limousine, Russell Kirkland, the bass player, shrugs. "I wouldn't worry about it, Rhap Man. We still got plenty of time." Smiling, he pulls his golden nail file from his shirt pocket. "And they ain't gonna start without us, anyway."

The hell with *us*, Rhapsody thinks, then, suddenly desperate for fresh air, kicks open his door, steps quickly out, and, taking a deep breath, leans over the cold steel of the bridge railing to stare almost two hundred feet down into the Willamette.

"What the hell you doing?" Kirkland shouts through the opened door. "Man, you letting in all the rain and cold."

"So what," Rhapsody whispers to the river, drawing together his unbuttoned shirt at the collar, his face already wet from the drizzle. With a shiver he spits as far out as he can, watches for half a second, then hunches his way backward into the car. "Spit in a river," he tells Kirkland, not bothering to look at him. "That's all any of this shit amounts to."

♪♪♪

His entrance that night is spectacular as always: the customary great leap over the drums and ducking drummer, out of nowhere and into the spotlight, a moment of black magic. The right leg of his pants is black and the left leg white. The left side of his buttoned down shirt is black and the right side white. And underneath he wears a t-shirt with wide horizontal stripes the color of the rainbow.

"You know the difference between black and white?" he screams into the mike as he prances across the stage, not even a hello, just those dazzling black and white legs lifting high, sending out jolts of energy that spark through the coliseum and ignite the crowd. "You remember your fucking science books?" Hands clap above heads nodding everywhere, the collective scream so loud that individual screams are simply swallowed, unheard. "Now think about it! Because if you remember your science books then you can give me a pro-per sci-en-tif-ic answer." He enunciates with exaggerated precision, here, before modulating right back into his standard lingo. "Let's take white. What does white do when it see another color coming?" He holds up a warning hand and, taking four quick slide and glide steps backward, plants his back foot, then points his mike straight out like a gun. "White say, 'Get back, Jack, because I am white.' You remember now? Oh yeah! I ain't gonna lie to you. Just check your science books. Study up on your facts. White *reflects* other colors. Don't want no other colors. Uptight with other colors. Wants to stay pure. 'GET BACK!' "

The audience is ninety percent white—it's been the same throughout the West—and yet they cheer him eagerly, applauding as they roar, their smiles almost frenzied, all plugged into the same group fever and soul.

"But what about black?" he screams into his mike. "What does black do when *it* see another color coming?" He gestures as if inviting the entire audience on stage with him; flashes his sweetest down-home smile. "Black say, 'Come on in, now. Nice to have y'all.' Ain't that right? You remember now, don't you? In-tro-duc-to-ry Phy-sic-al Science. Black take on *all* colors. Pure acceptance, Jack. The whole rainbow."

Sanchez the drummer and Kirkland the bass player lay down a funky beat, and Rhapsody dances and skitters his way to the front of the stage, every part of his body jiving and juking in rhythm, until, suddenly, he stops and cries, "How about you?" His arm sweeps expansively over the crowd. "Are *you* ready for the whole rainbow?" He cups his hands behind his ears and his fans respond with a collective howl of assent.

A tight, syncopated slap of the drum, and the rhythm suddenly shifts down as the Black and Blue Band launches into Rhapsody's popular new reggae rendering of "Over the Rainbow." The crowd is his. He can feel his power, direct and absolute; knows he controls these people, inside and out. And yet he cannot forget that in less than three hours he will be leaving them just as starved as they were before the concert; just as starved as he, Rhapsody Walker, planetary superstar, is before and after every concert.

♪♪♪

The limousine, tires hissing, sped along the old Banfield Freeway en route to the airport. The Portland concert was already history. But not the drizzle. The drizzle, as far as Rhapsody Walker could tell, had neither let up nor intensified. He found it hard to believe—ludicrous almost—that his grandparents, Curtis and April, would even consider moving to Oregon. After nearly half a sunny century together in South Florida, this rain would rot them to the bone in a week.

In the back seat he now turned from the window to look at his friend, the bass player, who was busy filing his nails with his twenty-four-carat gold nail file. In general, Russell Kirkland was an easygoing young man. But when it came to his fingernails he was an obsessive-compulsive. Insisted that if they weren't manicured properly—at least twice a day—the perfect tone of his bass would be thrown off.

"Hey," Rhapsody said. "What's happening after Seattle? You going straight home, or what?"

"That's right." Kirkland answered without looking up from his nails. "You?"

"Back to the city," Rhapsody said. "Good music every night. Good food. Action with the ladies. And then soak in the jacuzzi until I look like a prune." He stared at Kirkland's long fingers, street light glinting off the golden file. Jesus, why did he even bother faking it. Here he was, talking to his closest friend in the band—maybe his closest friend, if there was such a person, in the world—and all he could do was lie about his jacuzzi. He was sick of his jacuzzi. And he *couldn't* eat at a restaurant—couldn't even leave his L.A. mansion; his fans kept an ongoing vigil—without causing a mob scene. Total hysteria. Disguised or not. And women! God, they were hardly worth the effort. Even the classiest ladies he met were nothing but trouble. He feared he was not a real person to them, but a fantasy, and after sex he nearly always felt vulnerable and inadequate. He wasn't all that bad a lover. Just a human one. No way in hell, he was sure, could he live up to their expectations. (Expectations, he feared, that his stage persona and the lyrics to many of his songs did little to dispel.) He protected himself—got the upper hand—by turning cold. Becoming unreasonable. Telling them they were lousy lovers and driving them off in tears. He wanted an ongoing relationship—trust and intimacy—but that seemed to be impossible. He had no one to turn to. Nowhere to go. This was, he felt certain, a kind of slavery that his ancestors could never have envisioned.

"Man," Rhapsody shook his head, scowling, and with a thumb gestured out the window. "Can you believe my grandparents would even think about moving from Florida to a place like this? Nothing but rain, Jack. Nine months of cold and drizzle. And old Curtis tells me *I'm* crazy for living in L.A.; tells me, 'Why, you nothing but a lemming, boy. A big-city lemming just racing to the edge of the cliff, fast as you can.'"

"What the hell he got against L.A.?"

"Not just L.A.," Rhapsody smiled. "New York, Atlanta, Chicago. It doesn't matter. He says, 'Listen to me, boy. If most of the buildings is taller than most of the trees, a place is got to be evil. Just use your nose,' he says, 'and you can *smell* the evil. White Plans and White Poison. The White Machine.' "

Kirkland stopped filing his nails to look up. "Didn't you tell me he used to jam with Bird and Diz on Fifty-second Street? Wasn't *nothing* white about *that* city street back then."

"Yeah, but I don't think he lasted a week. He says he couldn't keep up with those guys and was glad he couldn't. Because when he finished playing or listening he would step out into the street, and when he looked up he couldn't see any trees or stars. Nothing but buildings. Says it made him shake all over."

"Shit," Kirkland said. "All that shaking must have messed up his mind. What the hell does he think? We all supposed to spend our lives at some Little House on the Orange Grove, like him, so we can count the stars at night? Memorize the fucking constellations?"

"That's right," Rhapsody said. "You better keep your eyes on the stars because if you live in the city and *can't* see the stars, then boy, you nothing but a lost lemming."

He laughed with his bass player, though only for a few seconds, then turned away sharply to stare through the window at the rain-blurred smudge of city lights.

The Grove of Eden

♪

RHAPSODY WALKER WAS FOUND BY HIS GRANDFATHER, CURTIS WALKER, early one morning in the late summer of 1970, on the front porch of his, Curtis's, twelve-acre South Florida orange grove and farm, wrapped in a blue checked blanket and set in an empty orange crate atop a stack of cloth diapers, with a blue plastic baby bottle beside his tiny right ear. The sun had just risen, and Curtis, a thickish, almost bullish man, was bare-chested and barefooted, wearing only his boxer undershorts, but already beginning to sweat.

He'd stepped out for the morning newspaper, but when he found the infant on his porch instead of the *Miami Herald* he halted in mid-breath. "God damn," he said, then shouted for his wife, April, through the open front door.

Seven months earlier, Curtis and April's only living child, George Gershwin Walker, had been killed in a freak tractor accident; and now, here was a baby on their doorstep who bore a striking resemblance to George Gershwin when *he* was an infant seventeen and a half years earlier. Curtis's memory had been reinforced by dozens of baby photographs, so he was certain he could not be imagining the resemblance.

The complexion, the features, the hair, the shape of the head. All nearly identical. Enough to spook him.

He knelt, shivering in spite of the early morning heat, to carefully lift the taped, folded note from the top edge of the crate. The baby's eyes were opened wide, and he was intently studying the porch ceiling. Curtis looked up to where the baby was looking and saw the quivering rainbow refracting through one of the small, heart-shaped crystals that April had hung from a hook beside some wind chimes. The infant was calm and quiet. Not a squeak or a murmur. A rarity, as Curtis would soon enough learn.

By the time April, with a gasp of shock and delight, had lifted the baby and the empty baby bottle from the crate, Curtis was reading the note, which was typed, it seemed, almost professionally.

To the parents of George Gershwin Walker, the note began.

> *You don't know me, and I regret that I never had a chance to meet you, but I was your son's girlfriend. We'd been seeing each other for only a few months, but our relationship was so intense and private that he was afraid to tell you about it. (We already loved each other very much and had spoken several times of marriage.) We were careful. We took precautions. But two months before he died I became pregnant. He didn't know I was pregnant until the day before the accident. The baby—this baby—is not just my baby, but George Gershwin's baby, and your grandson. I love the baby—I touch his skin and feel like I am touching a part of George Gershwin—but the circumstances are all wrong. I want to finish my education—as I know George Gershwin would have wanted me to—and find a very good job so that I can make enough money to provide my baby with all the advantages. My mother is a widow, but is too young to receive social security. She has worked some, but has been fired from every job due to her incompetence. She had a poor education and, since my daddy died when I was eleven, has not made or kept much money. She is a loving mother, but, as I said, I want this baby to have all the advantages. George Gershwin always spoke of you with the greatest respect. He said you have, all your life, been very wise about saving and investing your money, and living thriftily. I believe that until I can finish my education and*

begin to make money, you can and will provide the best possible home for my baby. I will miss him terribly, but feel better knowing that he is in caring and loving hands.

Please do not try to find me. Even if you do try you will not be able to, for I am leaving the area. I'm sorry to burden you this way, and look forward to the day I can meet you face to face. I will return for my baby as soon as I have completed my education, begun working, and earned enough money to raise hwim properly.

The letter was signed, *George Gershwin's girlfriend, and your grandson's mother.* And there was a postscript: *Of course, I will write to you regularly to let you know how my education is progressing.*

"God damn," Curtis Walker said, then showed the letter to April.

"She writes a lovely letter," April said when she'd finished reading. "And she's absolutely right to want to finish her education." She gently jiggled the baby, who had at last begun to cry.

"That's all you got to say?" Curtis said. "That she write a *lovely* letter? Here I am, almost forty-four years old, and I'm supposed to be a brand new daddy all over again? After working so hard to raise two boys who didn't even live to be men?"

"Hush now," April said to the baby.

"I will not hush!" Curtis said. "What if I don't want to raise another baby? And what if his mama decide she don't want to come back for him? What I'm supposed to do then?"

April sniffed the top of the infant's soft head, and smiled. "This baby," she said, "is your grandson. And his mama *will* be back for him. Just as soon as she's finished her education. Now if she was George Gershwin's age, that will be next year. One year of taking care of your own grandson!"

"One year without a good night's sleep," Curtis moaned. "One year of feeding him and changing his diapers. One year of letting him drool and spit up all over us and listening to him cry."

As if to prove his grandfather's point, the baby suddenly began to cry more loudly.

"God damn," Curtis said.

April held the bottle to the baby's mouth. "The way I recall it, you never changed more than ten diapers. And when there was crying at night you seemed to sleep right through it just fine."

The truth was that Curtis had never minded the rigors of baby raising. It was the risks that he was no longer willing to tolerate. The unspeakable thought of enduring a third loss.

"Just one year," April said. "I know we aren't as young as we used to be. And it might not be easy. But we'll manage."

Five minutes later they were gliding on their wooden porch swing, trying to pacify the crying baby with motion, when Curtis pointed out that they didn't even know his name.

"It's the least I got coming to me," he said, and by the end of the day had settled upon the name Rhapsody in honor of his dead sister—and closest childhood friend—Feyla, whose favorite composer was George Gershwin, and whose favorite composition (after "Summertime," from which no good name could be taken) was "Rhapsody in Blue." Feyla was a long-limbed, gangly rail of a girl who, back in the 1930s, before she died, had helped Curtis emotionally endure the terrible beatings inflicted upon him (upon them) by their drunken and depressed father.

To sanctify the memory of his relationship with Feyla, Curtis had named his first son Porgy and second son George Gershwin. And so it came as no surprise to April when Curtis now announced that he was naming this baby Rhapsody.

For the next year Curtis and April waited for young Rhapsody's mother to return, or at least to send the letters she had promised. They waited through crying and soiled diapers, colic and midnight feedings, sickness and tantrums, drooling and diarrhea, spilled milk and spilled food. And thrown food. And mashed food. And spit food. And smeared food. Food spread and dried in the hair and eyebrows. Food crusted in the neck lines and behind the ears.

Through all this they waited patiently, but heard not a word. Not a note or a phone call. And they waited longer. They waited through the terrible twos (a misnomer of an affliction, which struck their grandson at eighteen months and left him, gradually and grudgingly, sometime during his fourth year). They waited through "Captain Kangaroo," "Mr. Rogers," and "Sesame Street." They waited through the endless digressions of whys.

"Why," Rhapsody asked his grandmother, "don't I have a mama?"

"You *do* have a mama," April told him for what seemed to be the hundredth time. "But she is not going to come back until she's finished with school."

"Why?"

"Because she is smart enough to understand that if she wants to find a good job and take good care of you she will have to be well-educated."

"Why?"

"Because a good education is the key to success."

"Why?"

"Because that's the way it works."

"Why?"

"Never mind."

"Why?" Rhapsody asked his grandfather. "Why don't I have a mama?"

"Because," Curtis growled, "I'm your mama."

"No way." Rhapsody, who was almost halfway between four and five, shut his eyes tightly and shook his head.

"It's the truth," Curtis said, scooping his grandson up in his arms. "Now come here and give your mama a bear hug." It was the way Curtis preferred to deal with such questions as he awaited the return of Rhapsody's mother.

They waited up to Rhapsody's fifth birthday, and they waited through his year of kindergarten. It was some time that year they gave up waiting. Gave up happily. An unspoken, cautious, and gradual surrender. The boy was theirs, they were at last certain, to raise until he was raised.

When he was in first grade and still burning with curiosity, Rhapsody asked April why it was that on the TV show "Sesame Street" it didn't seem to matter if a person was black or white, but it did seem to matter everywhere else: at school for instance, especially with the older kids; and at the park, where he noticed that before and after school the black children played basketball on the west court, and the white children on the east court.

"Does it matter?" he asked.

"That's a question you'll have to answer for yourself," April said. "When you're older and more experienced."

Unsatisfied with his grandmother's equivocal answer he found his Grandfather Curtis in the rocking chair on the front porch, and asked him the same question.

"Now who you say it was been telling you that it don't matter if you black or white?"

" 'Sesame Street.' "

" 'Sesame Street?' "

"On TV," Rhapsody said.

"Oh, on the TV. Well, that explains it." Curtis lifted his grandson and set him on his lap. "Now listen up. It *does* matter if you black or white."

"Why?"

"I'll tell you why, if you listen. Now, what color is the dirt?"

"Brown," Rhapsody said.

"And what grows in the dirt?"

"Trees, " Rhapsody said, pointing to the rows of orange trees.

Curtis nodded. "Trees, flowers, grass, plants, shrubs, bushes, weeds. Anything you want. Right?"

"Right."

"Now how about the beach?" Curtis and April drove with Rhapsody to the beach—fourteen miles to the east—half a dozen times a year. "What color is the sand?"

"White."

"That's right. And what grows in the beach sand?"

"I don't know," Rhapsody said.

"*Nothing* grows," Curtis said. "You can build a sandcastle, but that white sand don't grow nothing."

"Nothing?" Rhapsody said.

"Nothing," Curtis said. "And what happen if you go back to the beach the next day after you build the sandcastle?"

"I don't know."

"It's gone," Curtis said. "The ocean take it back. Because the ocean is alive. Fish grow in the ocean. And plants and seaweed."

"Sharks!" Rhapsody said.

"Sharks too," Curtis said. "The ocean can grow sharks because the ocean got some color to it. Like the dirt. Like you and me."

Rhapsody didn't understand this, and said so.

"It's like the difference between the city and the country," Curtis went on. "Now in the city there is more roadways and pavement and buildings than there is dirt and trees. But in the country there's more dirt and trees than roads and buildings. More color. More things growing. More life."

"More life," Rhapsody repeated, once again looking at the orange trees.

"That's right," Curtis said. "So tell me now: what's going to happen to the city one day?"

"I don't know," Rhapsody said, befuddled by the complexity of the world.

"What do you mean, you don't know? What did I just finish telling you about what happens to the sandcastles?"

"Oh yeah, " Rhapsody said. "The ocean takes it back."

"Same thing with the city," Curtis said. "One day the trees and grass and dirt gonna take it back. And *that's* the difference between black and white—it's the difference between the country and the city; between the soil and the concrete. You understand now?"

"No," Rhapsody admitted.

"No!" Curtis cried. "Then, boy, you better go pick yourself an orange. And if you bring a big one back for your grandpa he'll give you a bear hug."

"How about a quarter?" Rhapsody said.

"A quarter!" Curtis rubbed his chin. "How about a quarter *and* a bear hug?"

"Deal," Rhapsody said, and dashed into the grove of trees.

Rhapsody loved his life on the orange grove; loved the overwhelming fragrance that wafted through and saturated the air at blossom time; the incredible sweetness of an orange, fresh-picked or fresh-squeezed. Every day after school he spent hours climbing the trees, and picking—and gorging himself on—the oranges when they were ripe.

Often, he rode up and down the aisles of the grove on horseback with Curtis, who, every month until the fruit set, sprayed the leaves of each tree from his saddle with his homemade brew of foliar fertilizer—fish meal, bone meal, blood meal, horse, cow, and chicken manure, and

April's compost, all diluted into a sprayable solution. And though the oranges he grew were not particularly impressive to look at, they were among the sweetest, juiciest oranges grown in the state.

"When you eat an orange you got to eat it slow," Curtis instructed Rhapsody. "One section at a time. Then you can tell which sections was facing the sun, because they're the ones got the sweetest juice."

And it was true. If he ate slowly, a section at a time, and paid attention, Rhapsody really could tell the difference. It was all terrifically magical to him: the trees growing out of the dirt, the fruit growing up through and out of the trees, and the juice—sweetened by the sun—filling all the fruit.

After dinner, before sunset, Curtis often took Rhapsody into the grove with him on his horse, and played his saxophone as they rode slowly among the trees. "Your grandma believes the trees like the music, too," he told his grandson. "She says they take it in like water."

And it was easy for Rhapsody to imagine that the trees did somehow absorb and enjoy the music. In fact, it seemed to him that saxophone music must have been intended for the out of doors: the way the sound would rise, floating, then spread out in waves, dipping and hopping, giving new life to the air, filling it with a sort of auditory shape, texture, and color.

Every morning before school he helped April with the chores: milking the cow, collecting the chicken eggs, feeding all the animals, and taking out the kitchen scraps to the compost heap, which always began to steam—like a small volcano—when it was piled high enough, and was always, eventually, transformed into a rich, loamy soil, the ingredients mysteriously homogenized, crumbling, if squeezed, into a fine, consistent tilth, which Rhapsody then helped April spread over her ever-thriving flower and vegetable garden.

"I don't care," Rhapsody told April, "if my mama *never* comes back."

He meant it, of course. With all his heart. And yet as he grew older his Eden ineluctably began to lose its lustre. His grandparents—whom he'd always worshipped—eventually became an annoyance to him, and worse, an embarrassment. Particularly his grandfather, Curtis, who had singularly strange ideas, and who, compared to the fathers of the other kids in his class, seemed old and senile—from another century of another world. He had plenty of money but hated to spend it: wouldn't wear anything but his old bib overalls; wouldn't get rid of his old clunker pick-up truck and buy a new car; wouldn't even replace his ancient black-and-white TV with a color TV, or buy a decent stereo, or new records. (All he had in his dusty old collection were tinny recordings of Charlie Parker, Dizzy Gillespie, and Thelonius Monk—weird music you couldn't even dance to—and a few equally undanceable recordings by George Gershwin that popped and crackled all the way through.)

And God, his grandparents (particularly Curtis) were so overprotective that he felt smothered by them. For instance, they wouldn't allow him to play basketball at the Banyan Park courts, where most of his friends hung out after school. Instead, Curtis put up a makeshift plywood backboard and hoop in the dirt driveway and told Rhapsody he could have his friends come *there* to play.

When Rhapsody was seven and a half, Curtis started giving him weekly piano lessons. But Rhapsody hated the piano. The scales and piano books were a bore, and his back and bottom ached when he sat for more than ten minutes on the hard walnut bench. His daily half-hour practice sessions were like torture. Slave labor. A ball and chain around the neck of his youthful ebullience. He learned, but slowly and grudgingly. Against his will. And by the time he was nine, as soon as his daily half-hour was up he would grab his portable radio, tuck it under his arm like a football and run with it deep into the orange grove, where he could turn it up full volume—the tinny speaker rattling against the radio grill; blessed distortion—and sing and dance his way through the trees, slapping irreverently at the leaves, or plucking off oranges and, like Fred Astaire with his firecrackers, zinging them at the ground to explode into juice as he danced triumphantly. (The oranges that exploded most spectacularly were the overripe or rotten ones that had already fallen from the tree. Even so, Rhapsody preferred to snatch the fruit from the branches and set the entire tree to shaking—quivering with fear, it seemed—in his intimidating presence.)

He loved to sing and dance because it came from within, instead of being forced upon him from without, and felt so good, the perfect antidote to the rock-hard piano bench and the boring grind of scales. When he sang or danced he didn't even have to think about it or work at it. Like a bird, he thought. Free and easy. Effortless. Black Magic.

Two months after he'd entered the fifth grade, when he was ten years old, Rhapsody Walker didn't come home after school for his weekly piano lesson.

From his rocking chair on the porch, Curtis watched the school bus drive by without stopping. "God damn," he said, coming to his feet, his heart shifting into double time as he hurried in to tell April to call the police.

"He missed the bus!" she said. "Why should I call the police?"

Curtis shook his head. "Not on the day of his lesson he didn't miss the bus."

"It's a *perfect* day for him to miss the bus," she said. "He *hates* his piano lessons."

"But he respects *me,*" Curtis said, heading for the door. "Something happened."

As he slammed the door of the pick-up truck and slid the key into the ignition, he felt himself shudder. It was happening, he was sure, all over again. Another son, another death. Three for three. Divine symmetry.

He sped into West Coconut Beach scanning the roadsides, staring through the windows of every passing car while he squeezed the steering wheel, his fingertips gone numb from the pressure. With an unsettling vividness, he remembered stepping onto the porch and finding the baby in the orange crate, peacefully staring at the quivering rainbow on the ceiling. Blinking away the memory, he cursed the girl—a woman now—who, ten years earlier, had left them this bundle of pain.

As he passed the Banyan Park basketball courts he suddenly veered to the curb and screeched to a halt, hoping that someone among the crowd of boys would have seen Rhapsody. The moment he stepped from the truck he spotted his grandson racing off the court and toward one of the huge banyan trees that surrounded the park.

Curtis hustled past the basketball court, ignoring the stares of the boys and keeping an eye fixed on his grandson, who was scrambling up the tree.

When he reached the above-ground root network of the great banyan, Curtis yelled to his grandson, "Come on down, boy. We're going home now."

Young Rhapsody, who was twenty-five feet above the ground, squatting upon a joint of thick limbs, yelled back, "No way. I'm through with the piano."

"Fine," Curtis said. "Come on down, and we'll go home and talk about it."

"I ain't coming down," said Rhapsody. "But when I do I'll be playing basketball. So you can take your sorry old truck and drive it home alone."

Curtis felt a great rage pushing up slowly from his chest, spreading into his neck and shoulders, and down his arms. He balled up his fists and shouted, "Boy, you better get down here, and I mean *now*!"

Behind him, Curtis could hear laughs and taunts from the boys on the basketball court. "Climb the tree, old man. Whup his ass good."

"That's right," Rhapsody shouted. "Why don't you come on up and get me!"

"You better hope I don't have to, boy."

"You're too old to climb a tree," Rhapsody said. "And too scared. A scared, sorry old man."

Curtis was halfway up the huge trunk before he knew it. Like riding a bicycle, he tried to convince himself as he climbed higher.

The pursuit did not last long, for Rhapsody—startled by his grandfather's will to climb, and by his quickness—had trapped himself on a dead-end limb. He was too high up to jump, and there were no limbs or branches near enough for him to grab hold of.

"Easy," Curtis said to Rhapsody as soon as he knew he'd trapped him. "Come on down now and we'll go home."

"Come get me," Rhapsody said, and then, miserably ashamed, started to cry.

"God damn, boy," Curtis said. "If I have to come get you I might drop you."

But Rhapsody would not move, so Curtis shinnied along the limb until he could grab his grandson by the elbow.

Rhapsody offered no resistance and the two of them climbed down together.

When they reached the ground Rhapsody tried jerking his arm free. But Curtis was ready for him and held tight to his elbow, guiding him roughly away from the tree and past the jeering crowd of boys, while

Rhapsody hung his head, as humiliated by his weakness as he was astonished by his grandfather's strength.

They rode home in silence, Rhapsody staring at his hands in his lap, wishing he'd jumped from the tree and killed himself.

The moment Curtis pulled into the driveway, shifted into neutral, and set the hand brake, he turned sharply toward his grandson, the engine still rumbling, and slapped at his cheek, backhanded. Rhapsody ducked and threw up his arms, and Curtis wailed away at the arms—at anything he could reach—pummeling the top and back of his head and neck, his shoulders and forearms, all the while shouting, "I'll show you who's too scared and sorry. Why, you nothing but a punk, boy. A crying little punk with no respect for no one."

He didn't stop until April opened the truck door, screamed his name, then pulled Rhapsody from the seat. Curtis sat back, winded and trembling, and set his hands on the steering wheel while April glared at him, before leading her sobbing grandson away from the truck, up the porch steps and into the house.

A few seconds later, Curtis realized his hands were still trembling because the truck motor was running. He switched off the ignition and stared through the windshield, remembering with horror the many times he'd been brutalized by his own father, and all the vows he'd made to himself—and until now, kept—that he would never raise his hand against a child of his own.

In the house, Rhapsody was lying face down on his bed, sobbing into his pillow, his grandmother sitting at his side, stroking his heaving back.

"I'm sorry," Curtis said to him from the bedroom doorway.

"I'm sorry, too, " Rhapsody sobbed back, half lifting his head.

"You were right," Curtis said. "I'm too old to be your daddy. Yours or anybody else's. From now on if you want something you can come to me and ask for it. Otherwise you on your own."

It was three months later that Dr. Theresa Brown, her education at last completed, dialed the Walkers' Florida home, long-distance.

While April listened, flabbergasted, Rhapsody's absentee mother explained that she was ready to come get her son; that she was now an obstetrician with a new but already thriving practice in Charlotte, North Carolina, and thus with the financial wherewithal to at last be an effective mother.

"Why in God's name didn't you let us know?" April demanded, not bothering to hide her bitterness. "We gave up on you a long time ago."

"Gave up?" Theresa Brown said, "What about all my letters?"

Ten years earlier, the night after she left her infant son on the Walkers' front porch—the night before she caught the train for North Carolina—Theresa Brown had carefully copied the Walkers' address from her mother's old West Coconut Beach phone directory, which, unfortunately, had been printed four years before Curtis's farm and orange grove were annexed to the rapidly growing city and the address changed. All along, then, Rhapsody's mother had been sending her painstakingly composed letters to the wrong address. And because she'd been so single-mindedly and stubbornly determined to carry through with her grand strategy of completing her education before trying her hand at motherhood—a strategy she was certain would be jeopardized if the Walkers ever found out who and where she was—she'd sent her monthly letters in envelopes without a return address; thus, each of her 123 letters had been both undeliverable and unreturnable, and all her meticulously forthright explanations and justifications, deliberations and ruminations, updates and progress reports, had been for naught. The past ten years of her life—her triumphs and failures, revelations and transgressions—had remained as much a mystery to the Walkers as their lives had remained a mystery to her.

When, a week later, Theresa Brown drove to South Florida to meet and take back her son, she was afraid he would hate her; afraid he would, quite understandably—given the unthinkable fact that he had never in his life heard a word from her—respond with the same bitter resistance that April had responded with.

But she needn't have worried.

To Rhapsody, Dr. Theresa Brown was his savior, his deliverer from the evils of the most insufferably boring life imaginable. Not only was his mother a doctor, she was a goddamned obstetrician, a deliverer of babies. It thrilled him to think that white people had to trust her with what was, to them, surely more precious than anything in the world. The very course and pulse of their future resting entirely in her competent black hands.

What's more, she was from the big city, with all its hustle and bustle, glamour and excitement. No more acres of stillness surrounding him. No more oppressive silence. No more chicken shit and pig slop.

And his mother was, he immediately decided upon meeting her, not just good-looking, but classy-looking. (He was embarrassed to be seen by her in this creaky old house, with its musty curtains, ancient appliances and furniture, and obsolete TV and hi-fi.) She dressed sharply and stylishly, and carried herself with obvious pride and confidence. And there was a playful spunkiness—almost a mischievousness—about her dark eyes. But best of all, she was young. Blessedly young. *His mother!*

She moved young, talked young, looked young, and smelled young. When she drove him around the streets of West Coconut Beach in her sporty car—which still smelled brand new inside—she played cassettes on her stereo: wonderful, funky, tight, contemporary music, turned up so loud that it took over your whole body; forced it to jump and jerk and jive with every beat. And she drove fast and aggressively, bobbing her head to the music as she insouciantly switched from lane to lane, dodging in and out of the flow of traffic, her hand never leaving the stick shift. Driving with purpose, Jack. As though she had places to go. Nothing like Curtis. It was almost always a major embarrassment for Rhapsody to ride with his grandfather, who lumbered along in his old pick-up truck, perfectly content to follow—at a good safe distance—the car directly ahead, changing lanes only to make a turn, and then only after checking the rear view and side view mirrors three or four times each, and finally, peeking back over his shoulder to absolutely convince himself there were no cars lurking in the blind spots. And while Rhapsody slumped deep into his seat, hoping he wouldn't be seen, Curtis remained unfazed by the inevitable stream of cars honking and tailing behind him, or roaring past, angry faces, fists, and fingers flashing behind windows.

And yet, tired of and embarrassed by his grandparents as he was, young Rhapsody nevertheless felt badly for them now, particularly for

April, who, next to his spry surgeon mother, seemed pitiably old and infirm—as much of a relic as her dusty old books of poetry and literature, her dreary houseware and homemade dresses.

During the three days of Theresa Brown's visit—and the entire week before she came—April kept hovering and fawning over Rhapsody, touching him and staring at him lovingly and longingly, crowding him until he felt suffocated and had to retreat into his bedroom, close the door, and turn up his music. (He loved her and felt sorry for her, but she sure as hell wasn't making it any harder for him to leave.)

Curtis, on the other hand, seemed to be avoiding him. He spent most of his time on his horse, inspecting the orange grove, his old sax strapped around his neck. But the distant music that came wafting up from the trees seemed to Rhapsody noticeably more plaintive than usual: the same kind of music Curtis played whenever he remembered his long-dead sister, Feyla, whose love of Gershwin Rhapsody had been named for.

When Rhapsody was packed and ready to leave, April and Curtis suddenly reversed roles: April touching his shoulders then kissing his cheek with the lightness and quickness of a butterfly, before disappearing out the back door to putter about in her garden; and Curtis startling him with a long, tight, almost desperate hug. "A bear hug for the road," he whispered.

"Don't worry, Grandpa," Rhapsody said, surprised by the love he felt in Curtis's hug, as well as the love he suddenly felt for Curtis. "I'll be back every holiday."

"I ain't worried about holidays," Curtis said. "I'm worried about the city. About you. I want you to be careful."

"I'll be careful," Rhapsody assured him.

But Curtis pulled back from the hug to look him in the eye. "Because if you live in a place where there's more buildings than trees, and more pavement than dirt, then boy, you in big trouble."

Uncomfortable, Rhapsody tried to look away, but Curtis shook his shoulders and pinned him with a disturbingly intense gaze. "I know I already told you you were on your own, but I want you to do one more thing for me. I want you to go pick yourself an orange to take with you. Just keep it in your hand the whole drive up, and smell it as often as you need to, and if you ever forget the way it smelled when you snapped it from the stem—then boy, you'll know the evil has worked its way inside you, and that you nothing but a lemming, and the cliff is coming up fast."

As he listened to his grandfather's farewell sermon, then dutifully hustled into the grove to pick his final orange, Rhapsody felt jubilantly lucky to be escaping with his sanity, to be starting his life anew. And four hours later, just outside of Jacksonville—farther from the grove than he'd ever been—Rhapsody peeled and shared the orange with his young mother, neither of them noticing the sweet difference between the sections.

A Crash Landing

♪

SEATTLE WAS READY FOR RHAPSODY WALKER. THERE WAS THE RAIN, of course—the same clouds that would drench Portland tomorrow—but a little rain would never diminish the enthusiasm of the crowds. The day the tickets became available at the Kingdome box office all thirty-five thousand seats had been sold. Within twenty-four hours scalpers were getting a hundred and a half per ticket. And now, the day of the concert—the grand finale of the Black and Blue Tour—if you had a ticket you could name your price. Never mind the rain. Never mind that housing and lumber were down and that unemployment was up. Somehow, there were people willing to pay five hundred dollars, six hundred dollars, eight hundred dollars, for a seat to a two-hour show. People eager to be scalped. Happy to brag about it afterward. Seattle was ready for him.

Rhapsody, on the other hand, was anything but ready for Seattle. Here it was, his last concert of the tour. He should have been psyched. Revved up, yet loose. Instead, he felt fatigued and languid. Practically anemic. And he found the Northwest damp to be unbearably oppressive. A glance out his window at the relentless drizzle was enough to make him shiver. But you don't let a touch of malaise stand in the way of a million-dollar engagement.

"One more show," Rhapsody moaned to Kirkland. "A dozen songs and I can put my ass to bed for a month. Bake my bones in the L.A. sun."

They were sharing the penthouse suite, twenty-eighth floor, overlooking Puget Sound to the west and Mount Rainier, buried under the rain clouds, to the east. Rhapsody was sprawled on a couch. Kirkland sat in an easy chair, filing his fingernails.

"That's right, Rhap Man. After tonight you just soak in the jacuzzi. Soak the sickness right out of you. The new songs will come when they come."

"No songs!" Rhapsody slumped deeper into the couch cushion. "I got nothing to say, Jack. I'm through. Not a goddamn thing."

"Hey now, it'll come," Kirkland said. "You can't keep it from coming even if you want to."

"All I want," Rhapsody sniffled, "is the fucking sun. All I want is to get my ass outa here."

"Right," Kirkland said. "Tomorrow morning you'll be on your way."

♪♪♪

Backstage I wonder if I can make it through half the show. My energy is gone, and you can't create energy, Jack. Law of Thermodynamics. Our percussionist and all-purpose instrumentalist, Mookie Perry, wants me to try some of his pills. Amphetamines or some shit, and vitamin B-12.

"Hey, for three hours you won't remember what tired is," he tells me. "Guaranteed smooth flying."

"You can't create energy," I explain. "It's the law, Jack. Thermodynamics. You better study up on your physics. Remember your schooling."

"Okay, hero. It's your stage."

I've tried every drug, but they're all poison. They fill the hole for a few hours, then leave it bigger. Emptier. Harder to climb out and harder to fill. Sometimes I think my music, my performances, are a drug. Every concert fills the hole, then leaves it bigger. Like a sugar high. Empty calories. A mirage of energy. Thermodynamics, Jack. You can't escape it.

Hermanos, the warm-up band, is into their last number. A soprano saxophone is blazing. We could use a sound like that. After the show I'll tell him I want him. *If* I can make it through the show. My knees are so weak I can hardly stand. No way I'm going to dance across the stage for two hours tonight.

Finally I give in and find Mookie Perry. He slips me a few pills and tells me I'll grow wings on my feet in ten minutes. Just in time. I swallow and wait.

Kirkland already has his bass strapped around his neck. But he's still filing those goddamned fingernails. Afraid if he doesn't get them just right—honed to the nubs, smooth and rounded—his tone won't be perfect. He sees me watching and flashes a thumbs up. Then back to the filing. Serious business.

The audience is clapping and cheering. The musicians of Hermanos file past us, accepting slaps on the back and congratulations. When they started the tour nobody knew who they were. Now their album is climbing the charts. The power I've got is crazy. Obscene. I can turn their sax player into a king, or let him slip into oblivion.

In twenty-five minutes the stage is set, I'm ready to fly, and the audience is clapping and stomping in unison. I've got the power to keep them hanging, screaming, for hours. Overnight, if I want.

I signal the band members. No need for instructions; this is our thirty-ninth performance. In seconds the mass scream of the audience reaches a new level because the lights have been turned out. They're a community in the dark, anticipating, ready for the explosion. The band is on stage, everyone in his place, and the music starts up in the dark, Kirkland laying down a funky, syncopated bass line, the tone perfect, vibrating through every breastbone. Sanchez joins him on the drums, then Billy Davis on the keyboards, Shadow Jackson on the guitar, and Willie Veal on his alto sax.

I'm ready, thanks to old Mook. My energy is restored, the laws of physics suspended. I could leap a mountain if I needed to, no problem. I make my way to the spot, fifteen feet behind Sanchez, for my running start. The lights flash on and my legs are pumping; the crowd are on their feet, arms waving everywhere, shirts unbuttoned to the belts. I take off perfectly, flying over Sanchez, lifted by the screams of thirty-five thousand, a floating cushion of sound, higher than I've ever jumped, *even the Law of Gravity suspended.* Feels like I've been up for thirty seconds—don't want to fly off the edge of the stage—so I let my feet down for the landing. But right away they catch, and I'm suddenly horizontal; and when I look down, Sanchez's tom-tom is rushing at my face. A crash landing. *Isaac Fucking Newton, Jack. You can't escape it. The apple's got to fall.* The rim of the tom-tom catches my throat, and I tumble to my knees, dazed, the world closing in around me, the screams of the audience smothering me so that I can't breathe. Can't filter the screams from the oxygen. I clutch at my throat, but the air won't pass through. My lungs and my head have become a single point of awareness. No pain. No panic. Just a calm. And a blackness closing in around me, taking the place of the light, as if I'm moving backward into the dark at high speed, the light already far below, shrinking to a pinpoint. An irreversible course. "*Real* power," something whispers, and I hear It with my single point. My lungs and my head. The center of the enfolding blackness. "The Final Landing," It hisses. "You're already gone."

Kirkland is the first to get there and he knows right away it is bad, because Rhapsody's eyes are wide and confused, and his chest is heaving crazily. "Rhap, come on now, Bro, you're all right." But Rhapsody's hands are at his throat and his eyes seem to be inflating, getting ready to explode from the sockets.

"Shit, man!" Kirkland screams to Sanchez, who is kneeling beside them now, still rubbing the back of his head where Rhapsody's foot caught him. "Get the fucking doctors. The paramedics. He ain't even breathing."

Sanchez takes off to find the paramedics, though he saw the superstar's eyes and knows there is no time to fight the crowds. But he goes anyway, pushing his way through the throng, feeling utterly powerless and sick to his stomach.

Rhapsody has slumped to one side. His eyes are closed. Kirkland cradles his head, crying for somebody to help. He sees Shadow Jackson and Mookie Perry hurrying toward him, with a round-faced, chunky little man in a cowboy hat. He wears jeans, cowboy boots, and a western-style shirt with pearl white snaps and small red and white checks. There's a beeper on his belt, two pens and a pad in his shirt pocket.

"He says he's a doctor," Mookie Perry screams to Kirkland, the crowd pressing in on them.

The man throws down his hat, then kneels, cocking an ear to the superstar's face and feeling his throat. "Get me a knife," he orders. "Any kind, but fast. And keep everyone back, for Christ's sake!"

"He ain't even breathing," Kirkland shouts. "He need CPR."

"His heart and lungs are fine. Just find me a knife, and give me some breathing room." He pulls one of the pens from his pocket—a ball point with a clear plastic body—and begins to disassemble it.

And while security guards are wrestling back the crowd, and Shadow Jackson is screaming for a knife, Kirkland suddenly remembers his gold nail file and rips it from his shirt pocket. "It's plenty sharp," he tells the doctor.

"Fine," he says, taking it and testing the point against his finger. He feels Rhapsody's throat again, then, using two fingers as a guide, sets the point of the nail file against the superstar's flesh.

"Jesus," Kirkland cries. "What the hell you doing? You gonna kill him!" He would punch the fat little cowboy out, but his movements are so purposeful and at such crosscurrents to the pandemonium that Kirkland can only stare in disbelief, gawking when, seconds later, he sees the golden nail file poking from Rhapsody's neck like a stick from a popsicle. And yet there's no blood. Not a drop. Not even after the doctor has pushed the hollowed-out plastic body of the pen into the incision, and removed the nail file.

Kirkland shakes his head. "This is not happening," he whispers to himself. "Not real. No way, man."

The doctor puts his lips to the end of the hollowed pen and blows. Slowly, Rhapsody's chest lifts. His eyes flutter open. "Breathe," the doctor tells him. "Easy does it."

Déjà vu, Jack. I've been here before. The Beginning. Looking up at the light, at the world, from out of the darkness, out of nowhere. Black magic and the magician ain't me. The breathing is a struggle; I've got to concentrate. A Thread of breath, slender and miraculous. A wisp of a connection. In and out and in and out. The basics.

"Breathe," the man says. "That's it."

Kirkland's face appears out of nowhere, upside down and a few inches above mine. A laugh comes busting through his mouth, and then he's dripping tears onto my face. In and out and in and out. A Thread of Magic.

There are Sanchez and Jackson, Mookie Perry and Billy Davis and Willie Veal, and a million faces, all familiar. I'm lifted onto a stretcher, then floated through the crowd, through flashes of light and a thickness of voices, and in the ambulance I'm told to relax and shut my eyes. Damn, I thought they were *shut. In and out and in and out and then there are cold instruments at my throat, and The Thread stretches to the snapping point, pulls into a tightness at my throat, and I almost panic—in and out and in and out and God Damn, now, HANG ONTO THE THREAD!—until all at once there's air rushing into my lungs, a flood of Heaven, and I can breathe easy.*

"Just relax, Mr. Walker. You're going to be fine."

In and out and in and out and Pure Magic. A Sweet Connection. A Thread of Miracles. In and out and in and out and . . .

Beginnings and Endings

WHEN RHAPSODY WAS STILL A TEN-YEAR-OLD, AND A MID-YEAR NEW-comer in the fifth-grade class at Central Elementary School in Charlotte, North Carolina, he was skinny—though in a sinewy, wiry way—and of no more than average height. But he was quick and lithe, and moved with great confidence. Clearly, he was not the most impressive athlete in his class, and yet, during the daily recreation period, whether the game of the day was kickball, softball, dodgeball, soccer, or flag football, the captain with the first choice always selected Rhapsody to be on his or her team.

In sixth grade he became the star of the Central basketball team, for although he was not tall, and no better than a mediocre shooter, he possessed lightning hands and feet, could jump, dribble, and steal the ball far better than any of his team-mates and most of his opponents, and, perhaps of greater import, had an undeniably gutsy and inspiring presence—a superstar's presence—even in the sixth grade. He scored an average of nineteen points per game, the vast majority of those points coming on uncontested lay-ups off of steals, fast breaks, or quick drives past the defender trying to guard him.

And although his mother, Dr. Theresa Brown, approved of his athletic endeavors, her foremost concern was always his education.

"If you want to have an impact on the world you've got to be in a position of power," she explained to him. "And getting into a position of power starts with good grades. It's as simple as that."

But she needn't have worried, for academics came easily to Rhapsody. He found he could make good grades, rarely anything lower than a "B," with a minimum of studying. He read quickly and with excellent comprehension, and had almost the same talent for numbers that his father had once had. The only subject he disliked was geography, and yet he was the first in his class who could correctly and consistently name the capitals of all fifty states, including Salem (not Portland), Oregon and Jefferson City (not Saint Louis or Kansas City), Missouri.

Theresa Brown also felt strongly that the musical knowledge Rhapsody had already learned from his grandfather should not go to waste. At the same time, she knew he hated playing the piano, and so, instead of forcing him to take lessons (as Curtis had tried to do), for his thirteenth birthday she bought him a three-and-a-half octave electric synthesizer.

No more rock-hard piano bench or boring scales for Rhapsody. He could now lie in bed or sprawl on the floor, and with one finger call forth an orchestra of instruments. A simple touch of a button and he could drum out any one of a dozen rhythms, from standard four-four rock and roll to reggae, blues, or bossa nova. He could even use the synthesizer to record a note or phrase of his own creating, then instantly play it back, adding voicings and rhythms, layer upon layer, until, finally content, he was able to lie back, shut his eyes, and listen to, or even sing along with, a full band blasting his creation back at him.

Like good grades, composition came easily.

Rhapsody believed he had the finest, classiest, coolest mother in the world. (Even though he knew it was singularly *un*cool for a thirteen-year-old to believe such a thing.) He was proud of her status and wealth. Proud of her community standing. Proud of the way she looked and spoke and carried herself. And it felt perfectly right, perfectly natural, that he should be her son.

Unlike his grandparents, who, it seemed to him, were content to let the world gallop past them, his mother grabbed the world by the reins, rode it on its own terms, and tamed it with her skill and intelligence. And though he sometimes resented the fact that she'd left him on the orange grove to be raised by his grandparents, it was easy for him to admit that her gutsy decision had, in the end, worked out for the best.

Every Christmas Rhapsody returned to Florida to visit Curtis and April. He was happy enough to see them again, but always ready, after a day or two, to return to Charlotte, for there was never anything *happening* on the grove. It was all oranges and vegetables. Soil and heat. Breakfast, lunch and dinner. And, of course, the inevitable questions from April: How do you like school? What are you studying? What are your favorite subjects? Do you have any girlfriends? And on and on. Just a few hours with his grandmother and Rhapsody felt smothered by her presence, by her earthy odor, by her probing, persistent eyes, and by her endless, pointless questions. One-word answers never satisfied or discouraged her. Just drove her to asking more questions, her dark eyes patiently searching his face as if part of his answer might be there.

Curtis, on the other hand, seemed to do everything in his power to avoid talking with Rhapsody. At night he sat on his wooden porch swing, wailing away on his saxophone, barely pausing to catch his breath between songs. And during the day—because harvest time always coincided with Rhapsody's Christmas visits—he stayed busy supervising the picking of his grove.

Rhapsody found it easy to look down upon the itinerant orange pickers—mostly Haitians, Jamaicans, and indigent black Americans. Like April and Curtis, he thought, their inner rhythms were simply too slow to keep pace with the modern world. The real world. The world of money and machines, commerce and consumption. And worse, they were too gutless and submissive, too passive and accepting, to grab for their rightful share of the Great White Pie.

Three days before Christmas of 1985, when he was fifteen and a half, a high school sophomore, Rhapsody was walking through the grove to bring Curtis a ham sandwich, when he came upon a young woman squatting beside a basket full of oranges, and gnawing on a hunk of white cheese. She wore a black and yellow scarf, a knee-length white cotton dress which clung to her shoulders and chest where she was sweating, and brown sandals. Her skin was as dark as creamless coffee—three or four shades darker, he supposed, than his—and when he nodded at her, poker-faced and intimidated, she flashed a toothy half-grin that froze him in his tracks.

She was not beautiful—her chin was too strong and her face too thin—but there was a look of recklessness about her, a bawdy, inviting openness that he found daunting yet irresistible.

"You doing some picking?"

"Some," she said. "What are *you* doing?"

What he was doing was squeezing Curtis's ham sandwich with such nervous desperation that the mustard was running out the sides and through the foil. "I live here," he said. "I mean, I'm visiting. For Christmas. My grandparents live here."

"They the owners? The Walkers?"

"That's right." He was sure she was at least eighteen. Maybe older. Too old. But he squatted beside her anyway, casually as he could, and stared down the row of trees. "You go to school.?"

"Not no more," she said. "You?"

"Yeah. High school. Up in Charlotte, North Carolina. I live in the city now."

"Well well," she said. "The city. And what do you do in the city besides go to school?"

"Anything I want," he said with a phony cockiness. "I used to live right here in this sorry old town, but I hated it. Wasn't *nothing* to do. Up in Charlotte I do what I want. But here, I never did nothing."

"Too bad," she said, flashing her half-grin again. "Always seem to me like there is *plenty* to do here." She wet her lips with her tongue, then raised her eyebrows. "You understand what I'm saying?"

"Yeah," Rhapsody said, swallowing with some difficulty, his throat suddenly gone dry. "Well, I was lots younger back then. A punk kid."

"And now you older?"

He nodded. "That's right."

"Old enough so you know what there is to do, even if you ain't in the big city?"

"Listen," Rhapsody said, tossing Curtis's leaking sandwich into her basket of oranges. "I got a tree I want to show you."

Six rows over they found a tree with branches so fruit-laden the leaves almost touched the ground. They scrambled underneath the natural canopy, and though he thought he had a pretty good idea what to do, she mostly had to show him. Of course, excited and inexperienced as he was, he lasted no longer than three or four seconds. And when it was over she laughed, leaving him panting under the tree, his pants at his ankles.

A few minutes later he found her back beside her basket, finishing her cheese. Eagerly, he told her he was ready to try again.

"Hah! Mr. Big City Hot Shot. No wonder you can't find nothing to do here. You don't even know *how* to do it."

"Let's go," he said, grabbing her elbow.

"Shit," she said, quickly jerking free and coming to her feet. "You got the hips and ass of a white boy and a dick to match."

He slapped her cheek, and she instantly knocked him flat with a right cross, her cheese still in her fist. "Don't even *try* messing with me," she growled, pointing at him with a lethal-looking finger. "Or I'll hit you so hard you'll hurt all the way back to North Carolina."

It was to be an eventful year for Rhapsody all the way around. Not only did he lose his virginity—though barely and shamefully—and begin to pad his sides with an undershirt in order to hide his "white boy hips," he became the youngest member of Dry Ice, a well-established rock and roll band, which, the year before, had won the prestigious Battle of the Bands at the state fair in Raleigh. And though Rhapsody only sang back-up vocals, and played his synthesizer while sitting on a piano stool to one side of the stage, he was thrilled for the opportunity to practice, learn from, and perform with older, already reputable musicians.

But, while it was an exciting time for Rhapsody, it was, at best, a stressful time for his mother, the obstetrician.

It terrified Theresa Brown to see her son growing up so fast. Too fast, she believed, for his own good. Certainly too fast for her good. By the time he was a junior—not yet seventeen years old—he was spending hours every day, after school, then after dinner, making music with young men who were three or four years his senior, or older; young men who'd already graduated from—or dropped out of—high school; young men who wore black sunglasses, spoke in a hip, city jargon, drove cars, and, no doubt, chased women, drank alcohol, and smoked dope. She could only guess at the kind of influence they were having upon her son. She worried about AIDS and unplanned pregnancy. She worried about car crashes and drug overdoses. She worried about his grades and his self-important attitude.

And it was doubly distressing for her to contemplate the fact, which she frequently did, that sixteen and a half years earlier, when Rhapsody was born to her, *she* had been a sixteen-year-old. The same age he now was.

Nor was life at her medical office any less of a challenge. For the past six years she'd enjoyed taking on maternity patients whom other doctors ran from: women, most of them black, who for reasons of age, income, health habits, or medical histories were considered high risks. And because of her willingness to work with such patients, her insurance rates had, as of late, skyrocketed, and she was beginning to have doubts that she could continue helping precisely the women who were most desperately in need of her services.

Only recently, she'd agreed to take on a big-boned and big-jawed, unmarried, uneducated, and uninsured twenty-year-old white woman who couldn't even find a partner to help her through her birth.

The young woman's name was Clara Fry, and she claimed to want nothing to do with her baby's father, who, in any case, was now serving four years in the state prison for armed robbery. Clara's parents and her one sibling, a younger brother, were fundamentalist Christians, and had refused to speak with her (though they prayed for her daily and with great zeal) since she'd confessed to her out-of-wedlock pregnancy. And her one close girlfriend might have agreed to act as her birthing coach, but she regularly fainted at the sight of blood and the sound of pain.

"Just knock me out," Clara Fry instructed her doctor, Theresa Brown. "Knock me out and, if you have to, cut me open. I just don't want a lot of pain."

"It's not that easy," Theresa Brown tried to explain. "I can't do a section without a legitimate medical reason. And if I give you enough medication to knock you out, you and your baby will be at greater risk."

"Christ, it can't be all that bad," Clara Fry insisted. "My mother is a goddamn mouse, and she survived two babies. I mean, practically every woman in the world survives it. Right?"

As a woman who, sixteen and a half years earlier, had gone through a lonely, gruelling, and terrifying twenty-nine hour labor without benefit of natural childbirth classes or a husband-coach, Theresa Brown was particularly sensitive to the issue of solo deliveries, and always insisted that her maternity patients find a willing partner. "You must know someone!" she told Clara.

But if Clara Fry knew of a potential birthing coach, she was not naming names.

Moments after Clara Fry's six month check-up, while Theresa Brown was still sitting at her desk and writing notes in Clara's chart, she received an urgent phone call from the principal of Central Charlotte High School.

"I'm afraid your son has been suspended for three days," he told her. "For his fighting and belligerence."

God Almighty, Theresa Brown thought. Trouble wherever I turn.

The fight had erupted during Rhapsody's physical education class, while he and seven of his classmates were playing a half-court basketball game. Though Rhapsody was out of shape (perhaps because he had lately been spending all his free time practicing with the band instead of running the basketball court) he was still a flashy dribbler with quick moves and a nose for the basket. But Jimmy Latham, an acne-plagued young white man, who had been the only junior on the Central Charlotte wrestling team to make it to the conference finals, was guarding Rhapsody. And Jimmy Latham took his sports seriously, for he considered every athletic event an opportunity to prepare himself for the real battles he one day hoped to fight.

His father, a marine colonel, had been killed by a bouncing betty land mine in the Vietnam War, and it was Jimmy Latham's single-minded goal to surpass his father's rank while fighting in his own war, most likely, it seemed to him, a guerrilla jungle war in Central America, where he could prove himself in hand-to-hand combat.

As it happened, basketball was Latham's worst and least favorite sport, and for good reason. He was an atrocious shooter, a foul-prone defender, and, owing to his size, a poor rebounder and shot blocker. And yet, when he was given the task of guarding the hot shot, Rhapsody, he took it as a supreme challenge and a sacred mission.

Though he was two or three inches shorter than Rhapsody, and not nearly as quick, he was thicker and wider, and in superior condition. What's more, he was fierce, bullish, and grimly intense, and he approached his mission with zeal and abandon.

To Rhapsody, basketball was more a dance than a battle. He played for the art of it more than the sport of it, to express himself rather than to win. He played, above all, to look good and feel good.

But it was hard to look good or feel good—hard to express himself—with Jimmy Latham, a guerrilla in tennis shoes, hounding him all over the court. Whenever Rhapsody had the ball, he couldn't take a step or a dribble without being grabbed, pushed, poked at, or taunted by Latham. Every time he tried to drive around him, he was blocked by Latham's knees, bumped by his chest, or jabbed by his elbow.

"Quit foulin' me, man," he finally complained.

"You do what you've got to do, and I'll do what I've got to do," Latham replied, not backing off an inch.

If Rhapsody had been in better shape he could have easily avoided Latham's pointy knees and elbows, and his sweaty chest. But after twenty minutes of Latham's brutish defense, he was exhausted, and finally, in frustration, whipped the basketball into Latham's face.

There had been no fight, because the ball had broken Latham's nose, and his eyes had teared up so quickly he couldn't see Rhapsody to hit him. And Rhapsody, wanting nothing to do with Latham, had simply walked away. The problem was that he'd refused to apologize for throwing the ball at Latham's face and breaking his nose, even when, as he stood before the principal, he was given a choice between an apology and a three-day suspension.

"He brought it on himself, Mr. Summers," Rhapsody told the principal. "No way I'm apologizing; I've got my principles to consider."

But later, sitting across the kitchen table from his mother, he had a more candid and disturbing explanation.

"That pock-faced fool is nothing but trash," he said of Latham. "Redneck white garbage. And I don't apologize to garbage for no one."

Theresa Brown pursed her lips, took a slow, deep breath, then drummed the table with each of her fingers, one after the other. "Of course, I wasn't there," she admitted to her son. "I don't know the Latham boy, and I didn't see what happened. It sounds to me like maybe he *is* a fool. Maybe he *was* at fault. Maybe you don't owe him an apology. But that's not what concerns me. I'm not even concerned anymore about the three-day suspension." She folded her arms on the table and, raising her eyebrows, leaned close to her son. "What I am concerned about, now, are your comments and your attitude. I've always assumed you understood that racial prejudice is ugly and intolerable, no matter whose heart it springs from. Now I don't give a damn if you like this boy or not, or even if you apologize or not. But I want you to assure me that you will not base your judgment of him on the color of his skin."

"Hah!" Rhapsody said, but he was not laughing. "You're gonna tell me he would be acting that way if he was black? It's only white garbage acts that way, and you know it as well as I do."

Theresa Brown understood precisely how her son felt. In fact, if push came to shove, she might even have admitted there was some truth to what he said. And yet, bottom line, she believed he was fundamentally wrong, and she was determined to press her point.

"Until you can assure me that you do not base your judgments of people on the color of their skin," she said calmly, "I'm going to take away your synthesizer."

"Go on and take it, then," Rhapsody snapped, pushing back his chair and turning away. " 'Cause I'm not assuring you of nothing!"

It was later that night, while she lay awake in bed contemplating her most recent troubles at home and at work that the perfect solution came to her, a lovely stone for her two most difficult birds.

First thing the next morning, as Rhapsody was eating his cereal, she told him, "I know a way you can earn back your synthesizer. And you won't even need to assure me that you've given up your bigotry."

"I'm *not* a bigot," said Rhapsody, who, since the previous night's encounter with his mother, had been having second thoughts about postponing or giving up his musical career. "I'm just not afraid to face the facts. Now what you want me to do to earn back my synthesizer?"

"I have a maternity patient who needs a coach," she explained. "If you go to childbirth classes with her and coach her through her labor, you can have back your synthesizer."

Rhapsody wiped milk from his chin with the back of his hand. "When?" he said.

"She'll be starting her classes in May—another two or three weeks."

"What I meant," Rhapsody said, "is when can I take back the synthesizer?"

"After the baby is born. July."

"July! Man, I'm gonna be needing it before then; we've got most of our gigs in May and June. Prom time." Frowning, he set down his spoon. The last thing he wanted was for his friends in the band to find out that his mother had the power to take away his synthesizer and that he was incapable of standing up to her. "How about if I agree to do the coaching, but I take back my synthesizer *now?*"

Theresa Brown considered his offer for only a moment before agreeing to it. "Okay. You can take it back as soon as you start the classes with her. But don't even *think* about backing out. Because if you do I'm going to keep that synthesizer for good."

Clara Fry was not at all thrilled with the idea of having a black teenager for a birthing coach. "Jesus Christ! Sixteen years old!" Clara Fry moaned.

"He'll be seventeen by the time your baby is born," said Theresa Brown. "That's just three years younger than you are. And he's a trustworthy young man. Hardheaded, sometimes, but always trustworthy."

"He's a kid!" Clara Fry protested. "How the hell trustworthy can a kid be?"

But, according to Dr. Brown, Clara had limited options: she could use Rhapsody as a coach, find another coach by the end of the week, or find another doctor.

"Hell," Clara Fry. said. "If he's your kid I guess he can't be all bad."

When Rhapsody Walker met Clara Fry at his mother's office he almost reneged on the deal. And if the consequences—not just losing his synthesizer, but explaining to his friends in the band *why* he was losing his synthesizer—hadn't been so onerous, he surely would have reneged.

"She's white," he hissed, as soon as he had a chance to corner his mother alone. "You set me up. You just want me to do a good deed for some white garbage to make up for what I said."

"You're wrong," Theresa Brown said truthfully. "But it's up to you. You can go ahead and coach this young lady like you agreed, or you can admit to me that *your* bigotry is no better than a white man's bigotry, and that you are in serious need of a change of heart. Or, if you don't like those options, you can always tell your musician friends that they had better start looking for a new piano player."

Rhapsody left his mother's office, shaking his head. "A set-up," he muttered. "A set-up and nothing else."

Normally, Theresa Brown refused to recommend one natural childbirth method over another, for each, in its own way, seemed effective to her. But in the case of Clara Fry she decided to recommend the Heisler method because the breathing techniques were so simple; and she was certain that simplicity would be of great benefit to Clara Fry and her dubious young coach.

Beginning in May, the Heisler classes met once a week on Tuesday nights for eight weeks. In all, seven couples had signed up for the class, two of them black, and all of them, except for Clara and Rhapsody, husband and wife. And so it was predictably awkward for Clara and Rhapsody, when, during the first class, the couples took turns introducing themselves.

"He's a friend," Clara explained. "A friend of a friend, actually. Just helping out."

"It's a long story," added Rhapsody, looking to the black couples as if to assure them that this wasn't his idea. But they returned his look with friendly smiles, and he breathed easier.

The teacher was a skinny young red-headed woman with four children, one of them a toddling seventeen-month-old who, shortly after the introductions, interrupted the class with a demand for his mother's breast. "Milk," he whined, wrinkling his brow, then poking a stubby finger at her right breast. "Jeffrey milk now!"

"Use your polite speaking voice, Jeffrey," she instructed him, then swept him off his feet and expertly held him to her breast while the women watched with awe and envy, and the men kept their eyes moving, none of them quite certain if a direct look would be considered proper.

Halfway into the class, Rhapsody finally began to loosen up. He found it fascinating to be sitting among these big-bellied, big-breasted women, who were all, he soon noticed, unusually easy with their bodies, each of them flopping onto the floor to attempt their birth preparation exercises without a hint of self-consciousness. Tailor sitting, squatting, and pelvic rocking. They just hiked up their dresses and went at it; to hell with crossed legs and patted-down dress fronts. And Rhapsody enjoyed all this immensely. Not because he had any great desire to look up the dresses of pregnant women, but because they seemed to trust that he *wouldn't* look up their dresses, or not to care if he did. It was as if the rules were different here. The possibilities wide open. And all due, it seemed to him, to the bulging presences of those hidden babies.

The first four classes the couples spent most of their time practicing their exercises and learning the physiology of pregnancy, labor, and birth. They learned that labor pains were nothing more threatening or mysterious than muscular contractions: the cervix flattening out, dilating, and pulling itself over the baby's head like a turtleneck shirt. They learned how the diligent practice of their exercises could help them avoid vaginal rips and episiotomies. They learned the three stages of labor and the myths of circumcision.

And at the end of each class they sat on the floor in a circle, drank Perrier or apple juice, and ate whole-wheat crackers with cheddar cheese.

The classes, Rhapsody quickly decided, were really not so bad. A painless way, in any case, to have won back his synthesizer. And, better than painless, they were fun. In fact, Rhapsody actually began looking forward to the classes. He no longer felt embarrassed to be thought of as Clara Fry's coach. It was true that when she drove him to and from class in her old red Plymouth Valiant, they didn't have much to say to each other. But, although Rhapsody hated the country-western music that Clara kept her radio tuned to, the volume always cranked way up, he enjoyed listening to her sing along, because her voice was strident and sassy, if not always on key. And, more than listening, he enjoyed *watching*. The way her big jaw dropped and quivered with each lyric as she drove through the night, her fabulously round and ripened belly pressed nearly to the wheel, and the streetlights and shadows strobing across her homely, pale face.

The fifth week of class Clara was singled out by the teacher for her proficiency at squatting and pelvic rocking, and Rhapsody patted her shoulder proudly. Later, as they sat knee to knee on the floor, eating crackers and drinking apple juice, Clara leaned close and whispered to Rhapsody that her baby wasn't just kicking, but leaping and tumbling, performing fetal acrobatics. She took his hand, then, and for the first time pressed it to her stomach so that he could feel the movements.

"Whoa," he said, as he felt her stomach bulge from one side to the other. "Man, it's doing cartwheels and somersaults.!"

"Another Mary Lou Retton," Clara agreed.

During the final classes they learned the all-important relaxation techniques and abdominal breathing, and Rhapsody finally began to feel like a real coach. "Relax all the muscles in your face," he read out loud from his cue card, as they rehearsed on the floor with their classmates, Clara lying on her side in runner's position, her eyes shut gently. "Relax your forehead and temples, and all those tiny muscles around your eyes . . . your mouth and your jaw. That's it. Good. Now let your head sink into your pillow. Breathe steady, and take your breath all the way to the bottom of your stomach. Let your stomach sag into the mattress and float away. Let your stomach relax completely so all the muscles in your uterus can do their job and squeeze out the baby."

He learned how to time contractions, and how to rub her back in the right places with the heel of his palm. He learned how to help her sit at the proper angle during the pushing stage, and how to coach her to hold her breath for as long as she comfortably could while she was bearing down, pushing out her baby.

On the way home, after their final class, Clara told Rhapsody he had a perfect voice for a coach. "All I gotta do now is hear your voice, and I relax," she said. "It's automatic. Better than a tranquilizer."

"Bring on the baby," he told her. "You're gonna do great."

"*We're* gonna do great," she corrected him, then turned up the radio and sang along while Rhapsody watched her jaw drop and quiver, and her face strobe through the light and shadow.

There were still almost three weeks to go until her due date, so they agreed to keep meeting every week to practice their breathing and relaxation routines. And whenever he left home he called Clara to give her a phone number where she could reach him.

Four days after the due date, at 3:17 in the morning, the phone rang and Rhapsody leaped from his sleep to answer it.

"My water just broke," Clara cried. "And the contractions have started."

"Okay," Rhapsody said, rubbing his eyes. "No problem. Just stay calm."

"Stay calm!" she shrieked. "I'm all alone, I've got a goddamned flood in my bed, I'm cramping like crazy, and you want me to stay calm!"

"Right," Rhapsody said. "Let me think now. Why don't you just tell me how far apart the contractions are."

"Jesus Christ! How the hell am *I* supposed to know how far apart they are?"

"Listen, did you call a cab yet?"

"No way," she said. "I don't need a cab, I need a coach. I need *you*!"

"We'll be there in fifteen minutes," Rhapsody assured her. "Just remember your breathing. And try to relax."

"Shit," she moaned. "How can I relax when it hurts like a sonofabitch?"

Good doctor that she was, Theresa Brown was ready to go in seconds. She hadn't planned on chauffeuring Clara and Rhapsody to the hospital, but she didn't mind. She wanted everything to go perfectly. A typically arduous and onerous—but successful—delivery.

Once they were signed in at the hospital and set up in the birthing room, Theresa Brown found an empty office and slept, while Clara Fry labored, and Rhapsody coached.

"Listen to your breath," he told her as soon as a contraction began. "Take it all the way down to the bottom of your stomach."

And, as she lay on her side, concentrating, his voice was all that she heard.

"Picture your uterus pulling back your cervix. Pulling it over the baby's head like a turtleneck shirt."

His voice blended into her uterus and smoothed the contracting muscles like a thick oil.

"Let your stomach sag into the mattress and float away."

And she felt her stomach sagging and the pain floating out from her, almost detaching itself. In between the contractions, she did not open her eyes. She imagined she was in a dark movie theater watching slow-motion replays of a turtleneck shirt pulling over a small head.

Boring, she thought, but, preferring the boredom to the pain, kept her eyes shut and continued to watch the cervical replays.

At noon, almost eight hours after Clara Fry's contractions had begun, Theresa Brown came in for a quick examination and announced that Clara was dilated five centimeters. "You're doing fine." she said.

"Doing *great*!" Rhapsody whispered to Clara, and she nodded, her eyes never opening.

"Keep up the good work," Theresa Brown said. "I'll be back to check again in a few hours."

A few hours! thought Rhapsody, who was already starving, stiff-limbed, and brain weary. "*She's* got the easy job," he told Clara.

It was shortly after Dr. Brown left that Clara's back began to ache, and she ordered Rhapsody to push hard a few inches above her buttocks and just to the right of her spine.

"Harder!" she barked, while Rhapsody pressed at her back with the heel of his hand. "Down! Lower! I said *lower*, not higher! There. Jesus! Now harder!"

He pressed harder. "Try to relax," he advised her. "Let your stomach sink into the mattress and float away."

"I can't even *feel* my goddamn stomach," she said. "Just push my back! God, it hurts!"

"Breathe," he suggested.

"Hey!" she cried. "Harder! You're letting up!"

After ninety minutes of pressing against her back with all of his might, he gasped, "Try another position. Try the sitting position."

"Harder!" she commanded. "To the right! Now move! There! Don't let up!"

"Where's my mother?" Rhapsody, the coach, groaned. "Where's the fucking doctor when you need her?"

"Harder!"

Never in his life, not even on the basketball court in that triple-overtime game, had he felt so exhausted. The contractions seemed to be running right into one another, now, almost overlapping, so that the restful interludes between back-pushing lasted only seconds, barely enough time for him to shake his hands and arms, and stretch his back. It was clear to him that he could not go on.

"Push, damn it! Harder! Move!"

"Man, this is torture," he muttered. "Cruel and unusual." But he continued to push.

When the nurse stepped in to check Clara's blood pressure, Rhapsody gasped, "I need some help here. I need a rest."

"Of course you do." The nurse smiled sympathetically. "But think about *her*. Think about what *she's* going through."

"Right," Rhapsody said. "Tell Dr. Brown I need to see her."

"You're letting up!" Clara Fry shrieked, as if he were betraying her. "Harder goddamn it! I can't take this!"

"The baby," Rhapsody encouraged her. "Just keep thinking about the baby."

"Fuck the baby! Push harder!"

Rhapsody pushed so hard he was afraid he might put a dent in the baby, afraid—and partly hopeful—that he would push Clara off the bed.

"Harder!" she cried. "Don't let up."

When Theresa Brown finally showed up she helped Clara roll to her back for a quick exam, then explained that the baby was in the posterior position. "Nothing to worry about." She smiled. "It just means you're going to have some back pain to deal with."

"Shit," Rhapsody muttered. "No fooling?"

"The good news," Theresa went on, "is that you're right at about ten centimeters, so you should be feeling the urge to push any time now."

"The urge to push," Rhapsody repeated. "I'm glad *she's* finally gonna feel the urge to push. Because I'm just about *done* pushing."

Theresa Brown helped Clara to a sitting position.

"Better," Clara panted. "The back pain is better."

"Sometimes a change in position helps."

"Man, that's just what I tried to tell her," Rhapsody complained.

Theresa Brown laughed and squeezed his hand. "You're terrific, kiddo," she said. "And I mean it. The best."

A half-hour later, just before 3:30 P.M., she was completely disrobed and pushing hard, her elbows hooked under her thighs and pulling them open and back, Rhapsody at her shoulder, urging her on, and Dr. Brown at the end of the birthing bed, monitoring her progress.

"Two deep breaths," Rhapsody reminded her. "Good. Okay, hold it, hold it, hold it—now push!" It was a joy for him to be saying the word instead of doing it. "Push hard!"

As she pushed, two or three or even four times with each contraction, her face turned red and seemed to be stretching and flattening out, her lips and nose and cheeks all straining against one another in a great tug of features.

Rhapsody had never, he thought, seen such a wildly contorted and distorted face. It was almost shocking, a nightmare face, and yet, at the same time, more astonishingly beautiful, more angelic, than any face he'd ever seen. And it was the same with her body. Huge breasts that drooped and spread against her ribs, partially flattened by their own weight. A giant belly ready to pop like an overblown balloon. A dark line running from her navel to her black pubic hair. And a cunt that looked capable of anything. Capable of singing, spitting fire, sprouting wings, or swallowing a doctor, whole. A body hopelessly out of proportion. Bulging, straining, and ugly. And yet divinely gorgeous. A body to worship. A body to pray over.

Between pushes he gave her sips of water, mopped her forehead, cheeks, eyelids, and lips with a wet washcloth, and told her she was doing great. "The baby," he kept whispering. "Just a few more pushes."

The nurse slipped a cuff over Clara's arm to take her blood pressure. "Her systolic is 158," she announced.

"No problem," Theresa Brown said. "We've got a head showing, now. A dime's worth."

"You're doing great!" Rhapsody said, though in truth he couldn't imagine that Clara Fry could keep holding her breath and pushing. Her face was red, her veins stood out, and her body was trembling and slick with sweat.

"Blood pressure's over 160," the nurse said.

"Forget Michael Jordan," Rhapsody told Clara. "Forget Michael

Jackson. My new hero is *you.*"

Another half-hour of pushing and Theresa Brown announced that the head was crowning and full of hair.

"Oooh-wooh," Clara Fry gasped. Then after three quick breaths bore down again.

"The baby," Rhapsody whispered.

"Here it comes," called Theresa Brown. "Just a few more pushes."

And then the baby's head slipped out while Clara squealed and Theresa Brown instructed her *not* to push.

"Man, there it is!" Rhapsody cried. "The head! Can you see it!"

But Clara just laughed and grimaced, her legs spread wide, while Theresa Brown and the nurse suctioned out the baby's nose and mouth.

"Jesus," Rhapsody said, astonished to see the head just hanging there, alive, halfway between worlds, turning in the doctor's hands.

"Okay," Theresa Brown said. "When you feel the urge, go ahead and push."

Two more pushes and the baby slipped out, and into the hands of Dr. Brown, who immediately lifted it onto Clara's stomach, its head at Clara's breast, the umbilical cord a deep purplish blue, and intact. "You've got yourself a daughter," Theresa Brown said.

"A little girl," Clara cried. "A beautiful little girl." She turned to Rhapsody and kissed him on the lips, while he stared at the wrinkled, bloodied, vernix-caked little being as it rooted its way to Clara's big nipple, then tentatively latched on and began to suck.

Even hours later, when he was at home and resting on the couch with his mother, unable to sleep in spite of his exhaustion, he kept shaking his head. Occasionally he laughed out loud, or gasped and touched his cheeks.

And his mother smiled. "So what do you think you learned?" she finally said.

"Learned?" The word seemed hopelessly mundane to Rhapsody. Blackboards and textbooks. *That* was learning. This, he was sure, had been something else. Something different. Something bigger. Something which required no explanation.

"Well," Theresa Brown nevertheless went on to explain, "I hoped you might learn something like what I learned when I started delivering babies. I hoped you might learn that it doesn't matter *what* color a baby is. They all come into the world the same way."

A set-up, Rhapsody thought, astonished. A set-up right from the start. And yet, when he pictured Clara on her back, her face straining and contorted, her thighs pulled wide, and her cunt turning inside out, ready to split apart from the ineluctable pressure, he had to agree with her. Color wouldn't have mattered in the least. "Yeah," he said. "I can see that. It wouldn't have made any difference what color the baby was."

"No difference at all," Theresa Brown said. "Because coming into the world is beyond our control. Out of our hands. The only thing *we* control is what comes after. And if color makes a difference *after* we come into the world, that's *our* doing. Human doing. And we're the ones who have to take responsibility for that. Every one of us. Including you. You see my point?"

Rhapsody only shrugged, but Theresa Brown nodded, satisfied, then leaned over to hug him. "Enjoy your synthesizer," she said,. "I believe you earned it."

It was, to the day, six years after the birth of Clara Fry's daughter and two months after Rhapsody's graduation from the University of North Carolina (but two months before he and his new band finished recording their debut album) that Dr. Theresa Brown, forgetting to check her rear view mirror as she switched lanes while zipping along in her air-conditioned white Rabbit on her way back to the office after a successful midday delivery at the hospital, found out—in a swift crunching of metal and shattering of glass—that human ends (the same ends that now caused Rhapsody, fatherless and motherless, to hold his breath every time his jet swooped in for a landing) were as far beyond her control—as entirely out of her hands—as the human beginnings with which she'd grown so happily familiar.

The Real Rhapsody

♪

LATER THAT NIGHT, AS RHAPSODY LAY IN THE HOSPITAL BED, ALREADY surrounded by flower and balloon bouquets from well-wishers, Dr. Jimmy Brock, the plump little man who'd saved his life, explained it all to him. "When your throat hit the rim of the drum your larynx broke."

Rhapsody couldn't yet speak—his throat still housed a plastic tube and ached as though someone had taken a hatchet to it—so he nodded.

Brock went on: "When the larynx breaks, the vocal cords immediately swell together, closing off the flow of oxygen to the lungs. Like elevator doors shutting together." He illustrated the effect with his hands. "Which is why doctors seldom have the opportunity to talk to patients with broken larynxes. We generally just ship their bodies on to the coroner. Case closed. But you're the exception, Mr. Walker. A very lucky young man." He squinted at Rhapsody's throat. "A nail file and a Bic pen. Otherwise I'm in my office right now, writing up the final papers."

Pointing to his throat, Rhapsody attempted to ask a question, but his voice seemed to be stuck in his lungs.

"Whoa now, don't try to talk," Jimmy Brock cautioned him. "Give it at least another day." He pulled open a drawer beside Rhapsody's bed, and whisked out a small pad and pen. "Here you go."

"My voice," Rhapsody wrote. "Will I still be able to sing?"

"Of course you will," Brock assured him. "And I meant to tell you that first thing. Now, I'm going to guess that the swelling will go down by tomorrow morning. Tomorrow night at the latest." He again held up his hands to demonstrate the opening of the elevator doors. "And as soon as you can breathe normally we'll see about removing the tube and getting you out of here. I'm afraid your throat's going to be sore for a week or so, and you'll need to give your vocal cords plenty of rest. But, really, there's nothing to worry about. A little rest and antibiotics, and I can almost guarantee that your voice will return to normal in a matter of days."

Rhapsody smiled. He wanted to explain to Brock that his voice didn't matter. Not really. It was *the In and the Out* he cared about. His connection to that Thread of Breath, slender and miraculous.

"One more thing," Brock went on. "Now that I've got you with a pen and paper, how would you feel about signing a few autographs? One for me and one for my daughter, Cathy. I'm afraid she'd hate me forever if I didn't ask."

Rhapsody nodded, lifting his pen.

"Now me, I'm a country-western fan, and so the first time I really paid attention to your music was when I heard your tribute to Hank Williams—very funny stuff. But Cathy's a real fan: has every one of your albums and likes to wear her shirts double, same as you. In fact, if she hadn't begged Dolores—that's my wife—and me to take her, I doubt I'd have been at the Kingdome tonight."

"And then *I* wouldn't be here now," Rhapsody scribbled. "Why don't you bring her by for a visit tomorrow, and I can sign her albums."

"Really?" Brock looked from the pad to the superstar. "She'd be thrilled!"

Rhapsody shrugged, grinning, then folded back the top sheet of paper and wrote, "To my friend, Dr. Brock. If I ever write another country-western song I'll dedicate it to *you!* For saving my butt! Thanks for the extra time. Another fifty years, I hope." He tore the autograph from the pad, handed it to Brock, and mouthed the words, "Thank you."

As he tried to sleep that night with the tube in his throat, he felt like a snorkeler with his head underwater, intensely aware of every breath—In and Out and In and Out. He dreamed fitfully of black skies and torrential rains. Streets turned to turgid rivers clogged with debris. Floating tree limbs and furniture. Dogs struggling to keep their noses above water.

First thing the next morning, Brock dropped by with his excited, prepubescent daughter, and Rhapsody signed her albums and kissed her cheek. Then, after breakfast and a brief exam by an ear, nose and throat specialist, he carefully slid from the bed and hobbled past his jungle of flowers to the window, pushing aside an arrangement of yellow roses on the sill.

Outside, it was both gray and blue, sunny and showery, sunlight glinting off puddles and wet glass. A flock of birds cut across the sky, dipping, hopping, and wheeling in perfect synchronization; and, as he watched, it thrilled him to think that within each of those swooping feathery forms was a miniature set of lungs plugged directly into that slender Thread of Miracles—that holy Thread of Breath—*same as he was.* And that was all it took: he stepped back from the window, astounded at himself, wiping his eyes with the front of his hospital gown, his throat aching.

Man, I'm like a pile of mush, he thought. A loaded sponge.

And it was true: he felt full to the bursting point, as if his skin could no longer contain him, the emotional detritus of a quarter-century pressing at every seam, thumping at every exit point.

When he'd finished wiping his eyes, he smiled at the yellow roses on the windowsill. *Even the flowers,* he thought. Cut off at the stems yet still connected. Still hanging on. Not by lungs, but by some other Magic. He bent over to sniff them, quickly realized he couldn't—not yet, not with those laryngeal doors still shut tight—and, laughing to himself, gently fondled the delicate yellow petals in lieu of smelling them. The funny thing was that he suddenly couldn't stop wondering where the scent and color came from—questions he had never before been troubled by. From the flower, sure. But from which point? Where and how did The Thread connect and the transfer take place? A pair of rabbits out of the Black Hat, out of nowhere, and with no sleight of hand. No hidden pockets or trap doors.

It was when he glanced back out the window to find the birds that he saw it: *more* Magic—abracadabra—a full rainbow, curving over the skyscrapers, fading at both ends then re-solidifying, sharpening into spectacular focus against the patchwork of gray and blue, a great, arching Miracle, right there for all to behold, spanning the entire city, bright as neon.

Who needs rock and roll superstars? he thought. Who needs Rhapsody Walker? There's *the real rhapsody,* Jack!

Emotionally supersaturated as he felt, Rhapsody refused to visit with anyone that morning. He slept through his lunch; woke up hungry, with a tray of cold turkey tetrazini beside his bed. But as soon as he pushed himself to a sitting position he found that his swollen vocal cords had parted enough to enable him to breathe through his nose and mouth, tentatively at first, and then deeply, in great, sweet gulps.

His first full breath was an epiphany; there was a palpability to fragrance he had never before been so intensely aware of. And mixed in with the scents of his cold turkey lunch and all the flower bouquets was an olfactive stew of memories. Pre-city memories. Orange grove memories. A heaven of blossoms, thick but delicate, and a time and place when all the world was alive and full of possibility. When a sweet bite of orange or a perch on a tree limb was all he needed, and the mountaintop—*the real mountaintop*—was everywhere, never farther away than a look or a listen, a touch or a taste, or a great gulping sniff.

And it was suddenly quite clear to him where he would be going to convalesce when he left the hospital.

As the small jet roared, accelerating, across the wet Seattle runway, Rhapsody pressed his face to the window, his nose going flat. The front wheels lifted, the jet angling upward then lifting off the ground while Rhapsody willed it higher, his breath fogging the window.

It was odd. Like everyone else, he'd heard the stories, not at all uncommon, of people who, declared dead medically, had confounded the experts and, Lazarus-like, come back to life. While they were dead many had had "out of body experiences" and metaphysical revelations. They'd heard indescribably beautiful music, been touched with and filled by an ineffably lovely light. And having experienced such feelings of peace, love, and at-one-ment, they were no longer afraid of death.

But with Rhapsody (though he hadn't actually been declared dead) it was just the opposite. He suddenly couldn't get enough of life, and the thought, now, of dying in a plane crash—of diving through the sky encased in steel, hurtling to his doom just after his eyes have popped back open to *the real rhapsody*—was enough to send great waves of anxiety washing through him and throbbing into a tightness at his chest. *Not now, Jack! No way!* He had to, once again, smell the orange blossoms, pick the oranges as they dangled from the branches, taste the sweet sections that grew facing the sun. And, of course, he wanted to listen to Curtis play the saxophone, and help April milk the cow and feed the chickens; dig with her in her flower and vegetable garden.

Quite a pair, they were, Curtis and April. Senior citizens, he thought. Sixty-eight and sixty-seven. They'd lived in the grove, now, for over forty years. Nearly half a century of the same rhythm, the same action. In and Out, sow and reap, sniff the blossoms and eat the oranges.

Until the phone call from the hospital, the last time he'd spoken to his grandparents was eight months ago, two weeks after the release of the album *Rhapsody in Black and Blue* and five months before the start of the Black and Blue Tour.

"I love the funny songs," April had proudly told him. "Where did you get such a sense of humor?"

"*Rhapsody in Black and Blue.* Clever title," Curtis had said a few moments later. "And the songs just as clever."

"Thanks," Rhapsody said, though he wasn't quite sure what to make of Curtis's tone, or of the word "clever."

"But . . ."

Ah, here it came.

"If you'd have stuck with the piano instead of the synthesizer, you'd know where a *real* song comes from."

"It's a keyboard," Rhapsody said defensively. "Same difference."

"No way," Curtis said. "It's a machine, not a instrument. And a machine ain't got nothing to take from inside itself but white."

"Oh yeah? What about Stevie Wonder?" Rhapsody cried. "What about Herbie Hancock, Quincy Jones, and Lionel Ritchie?" He squeezed the phone, hard. "Shit, I don't need this." Not, he thought, from some crazy, half-assed saxophonist who couldn't even make a living at it.

But now, his small jet soaring over the tops of the snow-capped Cascades, it was clear to Rhapsody that Curtis had been right in questioning his talent; his stardom was mostly a matter of clever words, a good beat, and some talented musicians backing him up. The rest was all theater. A song and a dance. Slick production and manufactured hysteria; and with the willing complicity of his worldwide audience and the international media. (A hunger for superstars. A hunger for thrills of any kind.) In an honest duel of musicianship his grandfather could take him to the woodshed any time.

And yet, upsetting as these insights should have been, Rhapsody felt nearly manic with ecstasy as he stared out his small window at the mountain peaks below, poking like jagged islands through the floor of clouds. How could he be upset at anything when he had *everything,* all there was, the In and the Out.

Just keep those engines humming, he thought. The rest is icing. A Thread of Miracles.

Kirkland, of course, had been appalled to learn that Rhapsody was returning to the grove.

"What do you mean you going back to the orange grove? You hate the fucking orange grove."

"Blossom time," Rhapsody explained. "A feast for the nose. The air so thick you can hardly take it in."

"Sure," Kirkland said. "Right. And after three days of smelling the blossoms you gonna be so bored and sorry, that you gonna be *begging* for the city. Begging to smell the smog."

"Come on down any time," Rhapsody invited him. "The smell of blossoms would do you some good."

Kirkland smiled. "See you in a few days, Rhap Man. Just as soon as you tired of using your nose. Soon as you ready for action."

"In and out," Rhapsody told him. "That's all the action there is."

At the West Coconut Beach Airport, the black limousine pulled right up to the jet and whisked away Rhapsody and his luggage. It had been a smooth escape, all the way around. Only Kirkland—and now the limousine driver—knew where he was staying. Maybe in a few months, after all the hoopla and speculation had died down, he could call a press conference and explain that he had bigger and better things to tend to now—all those rabbits out of his lost black hat: April and Curtis, soil and saxophone music, blossoms and oranges.

Riding through town, and west toward the grove, Rhapsody was astonished by the changes of the past six years. Housing developments had sprouted up like mushrooms after a heavy rain; townhouses and condominiums sprawled across what used to be farmland; shopping centers and malls had seemingly dropped from the sky, flattening huge stands of Australian pine trees or covering over swamps and glades; the quiet old road running adjacent to his grandparents' orange grove was now a heavily trafficked, four-lane divided highway lined with fast-food restaurants, banks, and gas stations; and creeping right up to the grove's northern border, a huge construction site crawled and rumbled with bulldozers and backhoes, steamrollers and steam shovels.

Soon as the chauffeur turned into the dirt driveway, Rhapsody asked him to stop, then kicked open the door and took a deep gulp. He could smell the blossoms immediately, sweet and luscious, almost dizzying, even through the cloud of dirt and exhaust raised by the limousine.

He thanked the driver—a tall black man with short-cropped hair, a layer of black velvet—tipped him well, then insisted on hoisting his own bags from the trunk. Just around the driveway bend he spotted them on the porch swing. April sprang to her feet and raced down the steps into the dusty driveway to meet him halfway with a running hug. Her odor—the smell of cow's milk and cowhide; citrus, sweat, and soil—was as familiar to him as the orange blossoms.

"Let me look at you," she said, backing away, fussing with his shirt collar. "You're going to tell me that's all they put on your neck? One little band-aid?"

"That's it," he admitted. "Not too impressive, I know. And the doctor says there might be a small scar after it's healed up, but nothing else."

"It doesn't hurt you?"

There was still some soreness every time he swallowed, but Rhapsody shook his head. "I'm good as new. Better than new."

"And even more handsome than all those magazine and newspaper pictures." She hugged him again. "We're so proud, I can't tell you."

"You're looking good too," he said, though in truth he was surprised by how much she'd aged in six years. She seemed shorter than he remembered and slightly stooped. Her arms were thinner, and that gap between her front teeth looked even wider, he was sure, than it used to: like a pair of gaping boards on an aging fence.

They hugged a final time, then turned and strolled down the driveway, arm in arm, April telling him how worried they'd been when they first heard the news report about his accident. As they approached the front porch, Curtis was standing, waiting at the top of the steps, hands in the pockets of his old bib overalls.

Sixty-eight years old, Rhapsody thought, grinning up at his gray-haired grandfather. Medicare and Social Security. Ten percent discounts.

"Get on up here, boy," Curtis growled down to him. "I got a bear hug for a lost lemming."

Fruit and Music

♪

CURTIS WALKER WAS BORN IN THE EARLY FALL OF 1927— JUST OVER a year after his sister, Feyla—in the sleepy, pre–air-conditioned town of West Coconut Beach, Florida.

His father, Lincoln Walker, was a huge, obsessive man capable of intimidating anyone, even the local Klansmen, with his dark-eyed glare. But Lincoln's prodigious potential for violence was held in check by his love of the piano and by the six-day-a-week job he had playing it.

Curtis's mother, Eudele, was a seamstress and laundress who, as a diffident seventeen-year-old, had been afraid to say "no" the first time Lincoln asked her to go out with him, afraid to say "no" later that night when he wanted to make love to her, then afraid to say "no" four months later, in the winter of 1926, when he proposed, or rather demanded, that she marry him because she was carrying his child. It was not a storybook romance, though Lincoln claimed to love her deeply. At least when he was sober.

But more than being addicted to alcohol, it was Lincoln's great misfortune to be addicted to piano playing. As a brooding, burly high school dropout with hands thick and meaty as steaks, Lincoln played the piano for silent movies shown at Fitch's Theater. A self-taught musician, he had developed a unique, though problematic, style: that is, he played by ear, strictly improvisation, for he couldn't read a note and knew nothing of music theory. It would have astonished him (particularly with all the black keys he hit) to learn that all of his improvising—and thus, all of his playing—occurred in the same key: the key of D-flat. Up and down the keyboard he worked his fingers, often at tremendous speeds and with remarkable precision. Some theatergoers found the sound unique and mesmerizing. Others thought it monotonous, at best, and obtrusive and obnoxious, at worst. But to Lincoln it was trance-inducing. He could go on for hours, scarcely aware of the movie flickering above and behind his beefy right shoulder. He might pound out somber chords during the film's most lighthearted moments, or run off a sequence of joyful arpeggios during the scenes of high drama or quiet intimacy. Often, he played right through the end of one show and continued, without pause, into and through the following show, entering and exiting various stages of depression and euphoria.

Roy Kincaid, the manager of Fitch's Theater, might have fired his intense young bear of a piano player, but the idea was too terrifying to seriously contemplate. Whenever an unhappy customer complained that the piano music was boring or inappropriate, Kincaid always flashed an agreeable smile and said, "Well now, it's an unfortunate thing that I, myself, know nothing about music. But if you have got a good suggestion, go on and tell it to the piano player. I'm sure he'll be interested to hear it from you." Another glance at Lincoln and the customers invariably decided that his piano playing was acceptable, after all. And so he received no suggestions; just leaned into the piano and worked over the keys—which, when he pounded them, seemed to cry out for mercy—changing volume, rhythm, and speed, but ever trapped, unaware, in his D-flat rut.

He hit the whiskey bottle once or twice a month, but piano music was his drug of choice. Many times Eudele's father, Cody Swain, a small, gentle man, urged his son-in-law to give up his piano playing and join him and his two sons in the roofing business. But Lincoln refused to quit his job at Fitch's, even after Cody Swain and his two sons helped him build a small house, a block to the west of the railroad tracks, on two and a half acres of decent West Coconut Beach land, which in twenty-five years would turn out to be a two and a half acre gold mine.

And then it happened: in 1927 Al Jolson starred in the first commercially successful feature-length talking movie, *The Jazz Singer.* Soon, the studio heads were all waxing effusive over their lucrative new technology, while silent movies tottered toward extinction, Lincoln and his beloved job tottering with them.

He became obsessed in his hatred of Al Jolson: the phony black face, the exaggerated, wide white eyes—a racist caricature which the white audiences flocked to theaters to see and howl at. Within two years Lincoln was out of a job, and it was the phony black face of Jolson that he blamed.

Without his theater job Lincoln had no place to play. Roy Kincaid had wasted little time in shipping off the old movie house piano, and Lincoln couldn't afford his own piano. And his peculiar single-key improvising coupled with his unfortunate lack of even the most rudimentary knowledge of music theory prevented him from playing with or joining any of the local bands.

And yet he was hooked: a piano junkie with a habit he couldn't kick. So two or three nights a week, whenever he needed a fix, he would steal into the First Baptist Church, feel his way through the dark until he found the bench and keyboard, then indulge himself for as long as necessary, sometimes straight through to twilight.

The surreptitious playing continued regularly for almost a year, until he bought an old upright piano—with half of the ivory keys badly nicked or chipped—for thirty dollars at the Elks Club Annual Rummage Sale.

And though he at last had his own piano, he still missed playing for pay, playing for a living, and the old piano shoved against the wall—and covering half a window—by the front door merely served as an ever-present reminder of his dream that was doomed to go unfulfilled.

It didn't take long for Lincoln to grow bitter and taciturn. He hated his new work: hated harvesting the stinking sugarcane and serving as a "gofer" for construction crews. Yet, stubbornly, he continued to refuse to join his father-in-law's roofing business.

Work and depression sapped his energy. He gained weight and spent most of his free time lying in bed or drinking. Whiskey (the drinking of which, unlike his music-making, required little effort) replaced piano playing as his favored addiction.

And when he did play the piano it only depressed him further, for he was out of practice and his fingers, like the rest of his body, felt slow and clumsy, incapable of hitting the right notes at the desired speed. More and more frequently he played for only a few minutes before giving up and turning, frustrated, to the bed, or to his bottle.

In spite of his intimidating physical presence, Lincoln had never been a particularly violent man, though perhaps this was because, owing to his size and wild dark eyes, no one had ever seriously challenged or crossed him. (It was true that since leaving his job at Fitch's Theater he had, hundreds of times, ripped Al Jolson's painted black clown face off its stubby white neck. But this was only in his mind. A bit of pleasurable fantasy. No damage done.) Now, however, tormented by the knowledge that he might never again earn a living doing what he loved—might never even experience the ecstasy of another self-induced piano trance—Lincoln began, during drunken bursts of high energy, to lash out at Eudele. He could never have been considered an especially sensitive sexual partner, and now, after a serious bout of drunkenness, he was more nearly a rapist than a lover.

"Easy," Eudele would quietly beg him, ignoring his bloated belly and stinking breath, trying, without success, to turn his heaving violence into love.

Occasionally, when he was drunk enough, he even began to beat his two children: Feyla, who was six years old, and Curtis, who had just turned five. Without warning or purpose he might suddenly charge into their bedroom, like a tornado out of nowhere, and slap them about until they lay whimpering on the floor, afraid to show their faces. Then, ashamed of himself, he would haul them onto his lap and make them hug him as tightly as they could while he kissed the tops of their heads over and over, sobbing as he told them how much he loved them, a behavior which bewildered and frightened Feyla and Curtis almost as much as the beatings.

Every time Lincoln Walker beat his children, Eudele thought about moving back home with her parents. But there were risks involved, not the least of which was the possibility that Lincoln would, in a drunken fit of rage, kill them—all of them: her, her children, her father, and her brothers—would beat them to death with his monster hands before he came to his senses and apologized to their corpses, sobbing sweetly while professing his love.

In any case, the risk factor notwithstanding, it was easy for Eudele to convince herself that Lincoln never really wanted to hurt her or her children. Rather, it seemed to her that through the mouth of the bottle the devil sometimes entered Lincoln's soul and took charge. And, no matter his physical stature, how could she fairly expect him to do battle with the great and terrible Satan, particularly when he was intoxicated and weakened by alcohol. Thus, she passed the buck down to the devil—to a realm where she and Lincoln had no power or influence, and therefore no responsibility—and focused her efforts on enduring and surviving, and seeing to it that her children endured and survived.

And, though Feyla and Curtis indeed seemed to be enduring and surviving, their occasional beatings were enough to permanently alter their emotions and personalities. Terrified of their father they would sneak about the house in hopes of avoiding him, leery of every encounter. Of course he would sense their skittishness and, wanting to reassure them, to gain their love and trust, often acted in an unnaturally sweet manner, which made them even more skittish. Who was he, they wondered. And why was he theirs and their mother's.

Thus, survivable and endurable though the beatings may have been, they were enough to keep the children off balance, ever-cautious, and on the defensive, constantly wondering when and why he would next choose to lash out.

By the time they were eight and nine Curtis and Feyla had established a regular post-beating routine: a method of dealing with and easing their mutual trauma.

"Ready?" Feyla would whisper from her bed, ten or fifteen minutes after they'd been thrashed about the room, then hugged, apologized to, and tucked in.

"Let's get," Curtis would hiss from under the sheets, across the room.

And in a minute they'd slipped into their homemade denim overalls, and climbed through their bedroom window, never looking back as they raced toward the west, across the small field behind their house and into the grove of mango trees, where they would stop to catch their breaths and, if the season was right, gorge themselves on the sticky sweet fruit, not even worrying about the juice as it streamed down their chins and stained the bibs of their overalls.

Beyond the grove of mangoes was a clearing bounded by ferns, clematis, and melaleuca trees, and there they would quietly settle, lying back and holding hands, sometimes chewing on grass stalks as they listened to the crickets and watched the stars wheel slowly across the sky.

Simple though it might have seemed, their secret ritual came to be a powerful emotional elixir for Feyla and Curtis. The cricket songs, the trees and the stars were always there for them, predictable and dependable, providing them with a sense of rootedness and belonging.

They began sneaking out to their haven under the stars whenever they felt bad about their father, whether he'd been abusive to them or not; and then whenever they felt bad about anything. By the time Feyla was twelve (and already on her way to becoming an accomplished pianist, Bertha Hall's star pupil at Carver Grammar School) and Curtis was eleven (and already the third-best saxophonist in the Carver Grammar School band), they were sneaking out regularly, at least once a week, unhappy or not.

Sometimes they had nothing to say to one another: just held hands, watched the stars, and listened to the crickets. But at other times they fantasized about running away together, finding a spot just the same as this one, and living in a tepee like the Indians.

Curtis was a great admirer of the Indians, who, he knew, rode horses, paddled canoes, hunted deer, grew their own corn, and scalped every white head that they could.

"Why you suppose colored people don't do like the Indians?" he asked Feyla one night as they lay in the grass, faces to the stars. "Fight to the finish. With tomahawks and arrows."

"Fight white people?"

"That's right," Curtis said. He had just turned ten. "There's more of us than there is of Indians. And *they* ain't scared to fight."

"That's why there's more of us," Feyla said, "than there is of Indians."

They often discussed white people. Feyla believed white people, other than their colorlessness, were not so different from black people, and that such differences as there were were attributable to circumstance: to money, power, and schooling.

But Curtis was certain she was wrong. "They evil," he told her. "Ain't got no souls."

"You crazy," Feyla said. "Maybe they *learn* how to be evil. But when they young they the same inside as *you* are."

Curtis shook his head. "They ain't got no souls. You can hear it when they sing; ain't nothing inside but white. They evil from the start."

"What about Daddy?" Feyla wanted to know. "He just as colored as you and me. Ain't *he* evil?"

"He mean," Curtis said. "But he ain't evil. If he was evil you could hear it when he play his piano."

And, fortunately, Feyla and Curtis did hear their father playing his piano more and more often. Thanks to Eudele's father, Lincoln had, in the fall of 1938, been given a job at the famous Whitehall Hotel in Coconut Beach, an easy thirty-minute stroll from the Walkers' home—across the railroad tracks, a mile to the west bank of Manatee Lake, half a mile across the bridge, then a block to the south—but a world away: a world of movie stars, royalty, and mega-opulence. And while the hours of Lincoln's job were regular, and the pay was excellent, the job itself was relatively simple, requiring a minimum of exertion on his part. All he had to do was pedal the wealthy white hotel guests to and from the beach in a sort of rickshaw tricycle—a white whicker carriage the width of a love seat, with two small wheels beneath it, and a larger wheel with pedals, a bicycle seat, and handlebars behind it.

The only difficulties Lincoln had were with his appearance and demeanor. Obviously, he was not, and would never be, anybody's obsequious, happy-go-lucky, shit-grinning shoe shine boy; would never be the wide-eyed and carefree Al Jolson nigger that many of the Whitehall's lordly white guests had at least tacitly come to expect of their rickshaw chauffeurs.

Fortunately, Herb Fowler, the veteran captain of the Whitehall's all-colored taxi-carriage squad, knew approximately what he was up against even before Lincoln arrived for his pro forma interview and pre-job training, for he'd been duly cautioned by Lincoln's father-in-law,

Cody Swain, who had practically begged Fowler to hire his depressed, often-unemployed son-in-law.

"He something to look at all right," Cody Swain had warned Fowler, raising his hands high above his head, then spreading them far apart. "He big enough for two people. And his arms come out of his shoulders thick as a man's thighs."

"He ain't been in no trouble?" Fowler wanted to know.

"Hell no, he never hurt nobody. He be happier to play the piano than to arm wrestle, and that's the God's truth. But see, the problem he got is that he don't have the knack of cozying up to people—white or colored—the way my boys do. Seem like he more of a lone wolf, which work against him because of how big and mean he look."

"Don't you worry about that, I'll take care of him," said Herb Fowler, who owed Cody Swain twenty dollars and two—maybe even three—favors, and felt obliged to reciprocate with a favor of his own. As it happened, he was also in desperate need of young blood, for his dozen current employees were all over fifty, three of them over seventy, and it seemed at least one of them was always sick or otherwise ailing. "You just tell him to come talk to me tomorrow, and I'll see about hiring him."

Early the next morning Herb Fowler got his first good look at Lincoln Walker and couldn't keep from shuddering as he greeted him. Lincoln's hand seemed to swallow his when they shook. His body, even with the burgeoning liquor-and-torpor gut, was awesome. But those dark, implacable eyes, Fowler thought, would be the real problem. Worse, even, than uppity, they were defiant, unyielding and inscrutable, with more than a hint of danger about them.

"You sure you gonna want this job?" Fowler asked, after giving him the standard pre-employment orientation and a careful explanation of the daily routine.

Lincoln, who, unlike his father-in-law, was not the sort to beg, shrugged, then gave a scarcely perceptible nod.

"All right, three rules!" Fowler suddenly barked, pushing three fingers perilously close to Lincoln's face. "You got to come to work sober and on time, that's number one. You got to smile at your riders and talk to them real nice, whether you like them or not, that's number two. And . . ." He looked Lincoln up and down. "You got to wear what I tell you to wear, and that's number three."

Although Lincoln didn't at all care for those three stubby fingers waving in his face, and although it seemed to him that Fowler's rules ranged, in order, from obvious to onerous to absurd, he nevertheless agreed, with another poker-faced nod, to abide by them.

"Good, then I'll see you Monday. Seven o'clock sharp. Give you time for more job training."

But Herb Fowler knew that training the young giant would be the least of his concerns. He knew he was going to somehow have to transform Lincoln Walker so that he appeared friendlier.

Or at least less lethal.

And so when, the following Monday, Lincoln reported to work, Fowler was ready with an oversized tropical shirt and a floppy straw hat with seashells and miniature coconuts glued to the brim.

Lincoln cocked his head skeptically when his new boss handed him the ludicrous attire, but Herb Fowler snapped, "Go on, now. You got to wear what I say. That's one of the rules."

Lincoln slowly put on the shirt and hat while Fowler inspected him. The sleeves of the shirt hung loosely, nearly to Lincoln's elbows, and hid the most intimidating of his muscles, while the straw hat softened his fierce eyes and gave him a carefree and clownishly tropical look.

"All right." Herb Fowler nodded his approval. "Just remember. That hat stay on your head at all times."

Lincoln shrugged. He was unimpressed by Fowler's vaudeville spunkiness, but was too intrigued by the job and its benefits to let the old man's personality stand in his way.

And, amazingly enough, the job worked out. Lincoln was more neutral in demeanor than friendly, but as long as he wore his baggy shirt sleeves and floppy-brimmed hat, the guests didn't seem to mind. In fact, because all of the carriage pedalers were at least two decades Lincoln's senior (and at least twenty or thirty pounds of leg muscle his junior) he soon developed a reputation as a speedster, the young Turk of the Coconut Beach roads. (Rumor had it that with a strong tail wind he could get you to the beach as fast as any motorized taxi.) And because speed was an important consideration for all those guests following a tight schedule, Lincoln often earned heftier tips than even the friendliest, grinningest, most eager-to-please of his co-workers.

Of course, pedaling rich and overweening white people to and from the beach could never have given Lincoln the smallest fraction of the pleasure he'd once experienced as the piano player at Fitch's Theater. But he knew that Fitch's was just a chapter in history, irretrievably sealed by his enemy-for-all-time, Al Jolson; and so he was clearheaded enough to understand that the carriage pedaling at least beat the hell out of the lifting and bending, the wear and tear, the pennies-a-day sweat of sugar cane harvesting and construction work. And, best of all, at the end of each day, now, he had plenty of energy left for piano playing.

Whether he was behaving well or abusively—and since he'd begun his new job he was, for the most part, behaving tolerably well—the one and only thing Feyla and Curtis understood about their father (the one and only thing they genuinely admired him for) was his love of piano playing. They even understood why—those times he had come home exhausted from a day of sugar cane harvesting or construction work—he had chosen, instead of playing the piano, to curl up in bed with a bottle of whiskey. They had, after all, seen him play the piano and, young though they may have been, could clearly observe the quiet zeal and feverish abandon and intensity he compulsively brought to his music, the total and single-minded commitment the piano seemed to demand of him. Thus, it was easy for Feyla and Curtis to appreciate the fact that, whatever his faults, their father could never be expected to approach the piano in a frivolous or half-assed manner. Rather, he could be counted on to come to his instrument as one comes to an altar: with a sort of trembling reverence, a hushed and holy veneration.

He might have been trapped in one key—a fact that Feyla had discovered after less than two years of Bertha Hall's piano instruction—but that never kept the deep secrets of his agonies and ecstasies from penetrating and permeating almost every note he struck.

It was on a humid summer night in 1940, almost two years after Lincoln began his Coconut Beach carriage pedaling, that fourteen-year-old Feyla and thirteen-year-old Curtis lay in their bedroom, stirring the heat with their hand-folded paper fans, and listening to one of their father's long, impassioned improvisations.

"You ain't going to make nothing sound like *that* if you evil," Curtis said to Feyla.

"Music got nothing to do with evil," she said. It was an old argument, and Feyla was no more persuaded by her brother's theory than ever. "They say Adolf Hitler can sing tenor fine as any man. Now, you gonna tell me *he* ain't evil?" In truth, Feyla knew nothing of Hitler's singing talents. But she did know that her brother considered Hitler the most evil man in the world, and thus thought her point to be singularly illustrative, whether it happened to be factual or not.

"He evil all right, " Curtis argued. He despised Hitler not so much because he was a warmongering killer (an occupation which was not, it seemed to Curtis, particularly unusual for a white person in a position of power), but because he'd openly and demonstratively snubbed Curtis's idol, the track star, Jesse Owens; had refused, while thousands watched and millions listened, to shake Owens's heroic black hand when he won four gold medals in the 1936 Olympics at Berlin. "He evil because he white and soulless. And it don't matter what you say about how fine he sing; if he sing for me I could hear how all he got inside is more white. Nothing but evil. No room for even a ounce of soul."

But though Feyla and Curtis continued to squabble over the nature of evil and skin color, they agreed, with more certainty than ever, that the one quality of their father's worthy of emulating was his profound capacity to utterly and lovingly give himself over to his music.

And young Curtis was already beginning to learn that he'd inherited this same capacity. He didn't have the patience or theoretical detail that Feyla had, and would never become the technical master, the virtuoso, of his instrument that she would become. But when Curtis blew his saxophone the air that shimmered through it came from some place deep inside, so that even when he hit a wrong note it seemed shaped and textured with the perfect emotion—filled with an incandescence that was, itself, of more import than the mistake.

"You got to practice," Feyla would tell him on those now occasional nights when they snuck from the house to relax in their secret, starlit clearing. "Jazz is becoming big time now, and you got a chance to be great; got a chance to make something of yourself."

"*You* gonna be the star," Curtis insisted. "Ain't *nobody* can play "Rhapsody in Blue" the way you can, and you just fourteen."

"I'm good," she admitted. "But never a star. Not like you. I'm good because I practice."

"Shit," he said. "You was playing "Rhapsody in Blue" by the time you was ten. I'm thirteen and I *still* can't play it."

"But if you could!" she said. "If you would just practice like I tell you."

Of course, in spite of all his feeble denials, Curtis understood precisely what his sister was talking about, and knew she was right. He had clearly inherited his father's musical soul, but it was a legacy he wasn't quite sure how to deal with.

One of the ways he dealt with it was by putting much of his considerable thirteen-year-old energy into running the 100-yard dash for the Carver Rattlers track and field team.

"I'm gonna be a star all right," he would tell his sister. "A track star. Like Jesse Owens. And if Hitler refuse to shake *my* hand I'm gonna rip his ugly moustache from his face and make him eat it."

"You still gonna have to pay food and rent." Feyla always reminded him. "They ain't gonna be giving you money for running round a track, don't matter how fast you are."

"I can build me a tepee," he would say, just to infuriate her. "Eat mangoes and go fishing. Play my sax whenever I *feel* like playing it."

"Then you nothing but a fool," she told him. "You got the talent to play in a big band someday—maybe stand up on stage next to Count Basie—but you just gonna waste it all away with some fool excuse about running."

Though Lincoln was peripherally aware that his children were becoming first-rate musicians, he never heard them play, not only because they were still so reflexively skittish in his presence that they were afraid to play for him, but because *he* was afraid that if his children believed he was at all interested, they might ask his musical advice and find out how little he really knew.

Eudele, who understood nothing of these complicated dynamics, was constantly attempting to build a musical bridge between her husband and children, hopeful that if she could just get them together for one session of music they might end up passing tunes around like peace pipes.

It frustrated her no end that her children—though they hadn't been beaten by their father in over two years—were still so reluctant to cross paths with him, even if the point of crossing was a musical one—a point they could share so easily and profoundly.

And it appalled her that her husband would be anything but enthused by the idea of sharing a musical experience with his children. It seemed, she thought, the perfect way for him to make amends and, at last, win back their love and trust.

But whenever she happily told him what talented musicians his children were becoming he simply nodded, poker-faced, not a hint of pride or delight. He responded to her suggestions of family music-making the same way he responded to most suggestions: with a shrug. And the one time she continued to push her idea, he glared at her, his dark eyes pushing back hard, a warning she quickly and wisely heeded.

The day before Thanksgiving, in 1940, Lincoln Walker was excused from work early—a one-hour pre-holiday bonus from Herb Fowler. He had just crossed the railroad tracks, and was less than a block from home, when he heard the first strains of saxophone music wafting through the humid, heavy air. Within thirty paces he was able to discern the piano chords beneath the melody and knew beyond a doubt from where and whom the music was coming. He hustled the rest of the way, ducking and skulking the last twenty yards, before squatting beside an orange-flowering hibiscus at the front of the house.

The music, George Gershwin's "Summertime," floated to Lincoln through the opened front window, and fell upon him with such a lilting sweet bitterness, such plaintive, dreamy perfection, that he felt half suffocated by it. In the notes, chords, and phrases of the piano and saxophone, he felt as though he could touch and feel his childrens' minds and souls; as though he could divine their very essences. He was meeting them, it seemed, for the first time, and he wanted to grab every elusive note and squeeze it tightly to his chest before it dimmed and finally dissipated. Sweet Jesus, he thought, nearly choking, overwhelmed by the musky perfume of sound. *Sweet fucking Jesus, and I can't even hold onto it. My own children, and they already gone from me.*

It was soon after this that Eudele began to notice the change in Lincoln. He returned from work each day languid and taciturn, hulking and gliding slowly about the house like a great shadow, darkening whatever area he moved through or settled into.

He stopped playing the piano.

His appetite dwindled.

Eudele waited for his drinking to increase, but instead it decreased. She braced herself for a new round of abuse, but his violent tendencies, like everything else, seemed to be turned inward, as if far below his surface there were battles and blitzkriegs raging; as if the great war in Europe had found a way into the linings of his spirit.

"It's like he all collapsed in on himself," Eudele confided to Feyla the day after her school Christmas vacation began. "Like he disappeared except for the shell."

"He always hate Christmas," Feyla reminded her.

But Eudele knew Christmas had nothing to do with it, and, indeed, as they headed into 1941 his condition only deteriorated. At work his reputation for speed turned into a reputation for pokiness. Half a dozen times Herb Fowler pulled him into a private corner to ask if he was okay, or if there was anything he could do to help.

But each time Lincoln responded predictably: with a shrug.

By the middle of February he had lost forty-five pounds. His tropical shirt, oversized to begin with, now hung from his shoulders like a great tent, which caught the wind, billowing and flapping, as he pedaled. He knew—as well as his wife and boss knew—he couldn't go downhill forever; the depth to which he could sink was not infinite. But no one, least of all Lincoln, had even a clue how to stop or slow his plunge.

And then Al Jolson came to town.

It was early in the morning on the day of Al Jolson's arrival that Lincoln had fortuitously spotted Jolson's photograph on the front page of a day-old *Coconut Beach Gazette* which had been left on the floorboard of Lincoln's rickshaw carriage. In a rage—the first emotion of any kind he'd felt in months—he snatched up the paper to glance at the picture, which was predictably insulting and demeaning: the wide pathetic eyes and the smiling, white circus clown lips.

It was when he read the caption and learned that Jolson would be arriving at the Whitehall *tonight* that his rage turned into elation. He double-checked the date, then tore the picture from the paper, folded it, and slipped it into his pocket.

The rest of the afternoon he spent planning and plotting as he pedaled his riders. And when he returned home early that night, he hopped through the doorway with a spryly gait, swept Eudele off her feet, and, laughing almost maniacally, kissed her hard on the mouth.

"Lincoln!" she gasped, gawking at him after he'd set her down.

"That's right," he said. "And feeling fine." He could clearly picture his hands closing around Jolson's neck from behind and squeezing the life from the source of all his pain. Squeezing until his palms met. "Yes ma'am. Feeling like a million dollars. Pure gold."

Eudele, who had never in her life seen her husband so openly enthused about anything, cautiously stroked his back. "What happened?" she said. "I ain't seen you smiling like this since I don't know when."

"I couldn't exactly say," he told her. "And it don't matter, anyway."

It's a miracle, was all Eudele could think. He'd been touched, she felt almost certain, by the holy spirit, and she could see the light in his eyes, strong and clear.

After a huge dinner of fried chicken and yams, black-eyed peas and collards, Lincoln sat at the piano and played past midnight without a break, the image of Al Jolson's scrawny white neck inspiring every note.

"He finally gone completely crazy," Feyla said to Curtis from under her sheet, over an hour after they'd gone to bed. "I'm afraid when he finish playing he gonna kill somebody."

"Let's get," Curtis whispered.

And they snuck through their window and scampered to their clearing to sit huddled in the cool, clear January night, watching the ever-reliable stars wheel overhead, and puzzling over what had happened to their father.

"He cheated on Mama," Feyla guessed.

"A woman with pure black blood," Curtis added. "An African Queen. I swear I could smell the black rising off the piano like a hot black steam."

"You crazy," Feyla snorted. "And I'm crazy, too. Ain't no woman could make him *that* happy. Ain't *nothing* could make him that happy."

After a four-egg, sausage, toast, and grits breakfast the next morning, Lincoln hiked to the hotel at double speed, squinting into the winter sun as it rose above the palm trees. He pictured how easy it would be: halfway to the beach he would simply stop pedaling the carriage, throw down his tropical hat, and wait for Jolson to turn and face him.

"Where is that fool nigger grin, now?" Lincoln would ask as his fingers closed around Jolson's neck. "Where's your fucking 'Mammy' when you need her, boy?"

Never had he felt so alive.

"I want to be the one to drive the movie star," he excitedly announced to Herb Fowler the moment he saw him. "I hear he a big tipper, and I need the money bad."

"You in some kind of trouble?" Fowler demanded. There was something worrisome, he thought, about Lincoln's instant reversal. In twenty-four hours he'd gone from half-dead to wholly effervescent—full of sparkle and purpose, spirit and spunk.

"Nothing wrong," Lincoln grinned, exposing teeth Fowler had never before seen: teeth no one but his dentist had ever seen.

"Like I say, I just need the money."

"Oh, and don't nobody else need the money? What I'm gonna tell the other pedalers? You more important than they are?"

Lincoln hesitated, then looked over both shoulders before whispering, "All right, it ain't really the money. It's Eudele. See, it just so happen that her birthday is January 30. Next Wednesday. Now I don't recall I ever told you, but she been collecting autographs of movie stars since before I met her. Gets 'em through those movie magazines."

"Autographs?" Fowler looked skeptical.

"Oh yeah. Mostly autographed pictures. She keeps 'em all in a big black book and won't even let me touch it unless she right there with me to turn the pages. She got dozens of autographs—maybe thirty or forty—but she don't have Al Jolson, and he one of her favorites."

"So you want his autograph for Eudele?" Fowler said.

"That's right," Lincoln said. "For her birthday."

"And you got a picture for him to autograph?"

"Sure I got a picture," Lincoln said, pulling out and unfolding the photograph he'd torn from the newspaper.

This was all beginning to make some sense to Herb Fowler. The about-face in Lincoln's demeanor did coincide, after all, with the news of Jolson's visit. Perhaps Lincoln and Eudele had been having serious problems with their marriage. Bedroom problems, no doubt. The same thing had happened to Fowler, himself, twenty or twenty-five years ago. Lasted three or four months and nearly paralyzed him with shame. No wonder Lincoln hadn't wanted to discuss his troubles, and had even lied, just now, about wanting to chauffeur Jolson for the tip money. And no wonder he was so excited about something as foolish as an autograph. It was a way to Eudele's heart. A way to re-connect.

"I believe I can help," Fowler said. "Just give me a chance to do some talking; and when Jolson come down, he gonna be all yours."

"Yes sir," Lincoln said, his heart giving an adrenaline leap. "All mine."

The first thing Fowler did was pull each of his crew aside, one at a time, as they arrived—all by foot—and told them the embarrassing truth about Lincoln. "We got to help him out," Fowler pleaded. "When Jolson come down for a ride I want you to disappear."

Next, with Lincoln standing beside him, Fowler called the bell captain to let him know he needed Jolson's beaching itinerary as soon as possible so that he could arrange to have his best pedaler available at the appropriate time.

For nearly an hour, then, Lincoln worked in the garage with Fowler, oiling spare chains, until the bell captain called back to relay the news that Jolson had left for Miami early that morning.

"He already left?" Lincoln held open his hands, stunned.

"Listen." Fowler was pulling at the bottom of Lincoln's tropical shirt. "Don't you worry. Just give me the picture."

"He's gone?" Lincoln said. "Not even a *look* at the beach?"

"I'll have Mr. Eddie to sign it," Fowler assured him with a wink. " 'To Eudele. Happy Birthday. Al Jolson.' And she never gonna know the difference."

But Lincoln was already pulling away.

And when, fifteen minutes later, he dropped an elderly couple off at the beach, he didn't even wait long enough for the old man to dig a nickel tip from his pocket; just pedaled away slowly, the muscles throughout his big body gone slack.

He turned his carriage right, onto Bridge Street, while palm fronds whispered in the wind, the Atlantic roared, and mockingbirds reeled off one brilliant medley after another, an unending skein of sound which Lincoln suddenly realized was remarkably similar to his piano playing: the notes all unlearned, programmed in the blood.

A pang of sweet sorrow washed over him. God, how he would miss his piano. Although, thanks to Jolson and his singing minstrel success, Lincoln had already missed the piano; had already missed Eudele and the children. Gone, they were. Nothing but ghosts and shadows. Fragments of a dream he'd long ago awakened from and would never again be able to return to. Not even if he *had* strangled Jolson.

As he pedaled, the sounds of the ocean, palm fronds, and bird songs all blended together and filled his head with a great, ringing cacophony—maddening, yet not unpleasant—as he rolled along the street, the wicker carriage leading the way—pulling him on, it seemed—like an empty white love seat.

Instead of turning left onto Lake Road, toward the hotel, he let the empty carriage draw him straight ahead. The breeze chilled him, now, as he pedaled slowly up the Manatee Lake Bridge, his carriage wheels barely fitting on the walkway, so that half a dozen fishermen had to hop from the curb, swearing, to let him pass, their poles held high so that he could duck under their lines.

At the apex of the bridge he abruptly stopped pedaling, slid from his carriage seat, then swung one leg, followed by the other, over the bridge railing. He pulled off his wide-brimmed straw hat and tossed it onto the seat of the carriage, then, turning his face to the sun, shut his eyes and smiled. All he could feel, suddenly, were the heat at his forehead and the pounding of his heart, as if those were the only things left of him.

He let go of the railing and fell backward.

The impact knocked the wind out of him, and his first breath, half a minute and two fathoms later, was all water.

The night after their father's funeral Curtis and Feyla snuck out the bedroom window (though there was no need to sneak, or use the window) and holding hands, dashed across the field behind their house. By the time they'd panted through the dark grove of mangoes and into their secret clearing, Feyla was crying.

"God damn it," she said, gasping for breath between sobs as Curtis hugged her. "I don't even know why I'm crying. I hated him, and I hate him still."

"He was crazy," Curtis said.

"He was *evil,*" Feyla corrected him. "A big evil bully and nothing else."

"Easy." Curtis stroked the back of her head to calm her. "Don't try talking till you catch your wind."

"Shit," she said, but allowed him to pull her down to sitting position on the ground. The night was balmy but cloudy, stars fading in and out of view, while behind them the leaves of the mango trees rustled in the breeze, barely a whisper, half the volume of the cricket songs. When she'd finished with her crying and caught her breath, she said, "It ain't just me. You hated him, too."

This sounded to Curtis like an accusation, but he nodded. "Sure I hated him. He used to beat us for no reason. And he beat Mama, too. Big as he was he had to pick on two kids and a woman."

Feyla ripped up a handful of grass and flung it to the side. "The way Mama been carrying on the past three days you'd think he was the greatest husband ever lived! It make me sick to my stomach to see her." She pressed the heels of her palms to her eyes, then choked back another sob.

Curtis believed that, in truth, his mother *had* loved their father—that perhaps she'd known the part of him his music came from—and that her mourning was genuine and understandable. But rather than explaining any of this to Feyla—who he knew would not appreciate it anyway—he decided to make a confession. "You know, I used to all the time wish he would die. I even told that to Mama once, and she whipped me good. But it didn't stop me from wishing it."

Later, he admitted to Feyla that the one thing he would miss about their father was, of course, his piano playing.

"The only thing in the world he cared about," Feyla snapped. She'd been expecting this from her brother. "Music and nothing else. But you think he bothered to listen to his own son and daughter? Never. Not once.

Didn't make no difference to him *how* good we were."

"You right," Curtis said quickly. "But I'm still gonna miss the way he play. Bent over the keys like a crazy old hunchback, squeezing everything out. Sweetness and meanness, all squeezed out together."

"One key, " Feyla almost hissed at Curtis. "That's all that old fool knew. And I won't miss a note of it. Not him or his music. He can take it to hell with him."

After her father died, Feyla had to force herself to sit at the piano. When she looked at her hands gliding over the keyboard she saw her father's hands. When she played with any sort of feeling—with anything beyond the purely technical act of striking the notes—she grew instantly aware of her father's malignant presence, and her fingers curled into a fisted, musical dead end.

As it became more and more traumatic for her to sit at the piano and attempt to play, she played less and less. But the less she played the more miserable she grew, and the more obsessed, in her misery, with her father. "I'm just like *him,*" she thought. *"The piano's the only thing that matters to me."*

Of course, it was clear to Curtis that there was something profoundly wrong with his sister. When she played the piano now he heard in her music a terrible sickness. Whiteness and sterility. Music as singularly off-center and out of balance as his father's, but at the opposite end of the spectrum.

And yet she wouldn't discuss her anguish with him; refused, even, to accompany him to their nighttime sanctuary. It almost seemed to Curtis that she was afraid to be healed.

"You got to try to *feel* it when you play," he told her. "That's all."

"I *can't* try to feel it when I play," she attempted to explain. "Because the only thing I feel when I *try* to feel anything is *him!*"

Early one morning in the middle of April, two months after her father jumped from the bridge, Feyla's crushed and broken body was found on the railroad tracks, a block from home, an unbroken but nearly empty bottle of her father's corn whiskey beside her. There was no way to determine if her death had been an accident or a suicide. And to Curtis it didn't much matter.

For almost a week after her funeral he kept vigil beneath the mango trees, playing Gershwin on his saxophone and eating only the fallen mangoes. And every time he tasted the sweet fruit, he could swear it was *her* sweetness he was tasting.

Mangoes and Gershwin, he thought, staring up into the leaves as he hugged his saxophone. *Fruit and music, and I can keep her alive forever.*

In and Out at Sixty-Eight and Sixty-Seven

♪

SINCE HIS LAST VISIT TO THE ORANGE GROVE SIX YEARS AGO, NOTHING much, aside from the nearby roar of traffic and construction, had changed. In fact it seemed to Rhapsody that nothing much had changed on the grove since the days of his early childhood. The old house, as far as he could tell, looked the same as always: same old appliances, furniture, carpet, and draperies; same old checkered table cloths on the same old knotty pine tables; same old piano and rock-hard walnut piano bench; and, outside, the same old pick-up truck parked in the same old spot in the driveway, the brown dirt gone black with decades of oil drips, which, like the furniture and appliances, were older than Rhapsody.

Curtis finally had broken down, however, and purchased a small color TV and a decent new stereo.

"I *made* him buy that stereo the day your first album came out," April confided to Rhapsody. "And even then it was a struggle."

His first morning back on the orange grove Rhapsody was awake and out of bed before the sun was up; even before his early-rising grandparents were up. He sat on the porch swing in a t-shirt, gym shorts, and bare feet, picking at the band-aid on his neck while he listened to the last songs of the crickets and the first songs of the mourning doves and mockingbirds, watched the sky and landscape develop out of the twilight like a photograph, and, of course, breathed in the orange blossoms.

It made him giddy to think that such a succulent aroma could originate within a tiny seed, buried in the soil; could rise, then, from beneath the ground, Threading its way up the roots and into the trunk, gathering force as it spread like a current through the limbs and branches, and finally exploded from the flowers, into the air. The entire process seemed not just unlikely, but impossible. The ultimate magic trick.

After a breakfast of freshly gathered eggs and April's homemade biscuits with her home-jarred orange marmalade, Rhapsody rode double with Curtis, on horseback, into the grove. While Curtis inspected the blossoms and sprayed the leaves with his special foliar brew—taking care not to stir up the clusters of nectar-frenzied bees—he complained to Rhapsody that the orange grove was, except for the golf course on the southern border, now surrounded by the concrete and metal, the noise and the stench, of the city, his well water already becoming measurably toxic so that he was forced to poison his trees (as well as the future consumers of his oranges) every time he fed them.

"The White Machine," he grumbled, shaking his head. "Always hungry for more."

But later that afternoon, as Rhapsody and April squatted together in the garden, staking the tomato plants and guiding the melon vines up their trellises, he learned that in spite of all Curtis's complaining he flatly refused to consider selling the grove—which is what April wanted to do—and moving to the Willamette Valley in Oregon, where, so they'd been told, they would have no trouble establishing a "U-pick" fruit or berry grove, and where the lush Northwest landscape was dominated not by buildings but by giant Douglas fir trees—trees that April had long ago vowed to one day live beneath.

"He says he can't stand the thought of all the poison and pavement coming closer and closer. But try talking to him about selling and he doesn't want to listen. He's turned down half a dozen offers already, and that's no exaggeration. He just shakes his head and says, 'If they hungry for more trees they better look somewhere else.' "

"Well, damn," Rhapsody said. "Why don't you just go on and buy a place in Oregon, and *keep* the grove? Maybe rent it out to some friends?"

"We could never afford it," April said. "If we're going to buy land in Oregon we *have* to sell the grove."

"Not if I give you the money, you won't have to sell it."

April reached over to touch his shoulder. "You're sweet to offer. But you know the man as well as I do."

"All right, then, I'll *lend* him the money. And if it makes him feel better we can go on and draw up a contract."

"He's even worse about borrowing," April said, "than he is about taking."

"That's craziness," Rhapsody said, scowling, though in truth it thrilled him (especially now, euphoric as he felt every time he took a deep breath of blossoms) to think of his grandfather holding out against the battalions of developers and their bulldozers, a lone, stubborn Black man standing guard over the trees, unfazed by the great white weapons of money and technology.

Later that night, after dinner and the evening news (which was typically grave—and, for Rhapsody, typically irrelevant: continued escalating tension in the Middle East with more bloodshed, accusations, ultimatums, and superpower maneuvering), Rhapsody followed Curtis out to the porch to watch the stars fading in and out behind the rolling cumulus and listen to nearly ninety minutes of his grandfather's saxophone music. Music with substance, Rhapsody thought as he glided with his grandfather on the porch swing in a state of dreamy serenity, not even the mosquitoes or nighttime mugginess bothering him. Music every bit as thick and filling as the smell of the blossoms. Music, he thought, from *the real rhapsody*.

Long after Curtis's final sweet notes had faded into the darkness, and he'd gone to bed with April, Rhapsody stayed up taking deep breaths, watching the stars duck in and out of the clouds, and wondering how he could ever have been so desperately eager to leave the orange grove and his grandparents. In fact it suddenly seemed to him that the past decade and a half—his school years in Charlotte and Chapel Hill, then his superstar years in L.A.—had been nothing more than a brief exhalation, a rush of breath, right up to the moment, six days ago, that the golden nail file punctured his throat.

And now he was breathing normally again—*In and Out*—for the first time since he was seven or eight and romping happily among these same blossoming trees, scampering up their limbs to snatch an orange, peel away the skin, and bite into the fruit, delighting in the explosion of sweet juice that filled his mouth and dripped down his chin: juice from a seed in the soil; juice, like magic, from the bottom of the Black Hat.

The world had come alive for him again.

And he could not imagine ever needing anything more.

He became convinced, as he sat there watching the half moon rising, humpside down, that he would be content to spend the rest of his life on the grove learning the rhythms of the orange trees, tending to their needs, admiring their beauty, gulping in their bloom-time aroma, and savoring their sweet healthful nectar. He would learn gardening and cooking from April, oranges and music—real music—from Curtis. What more could there be? (Well, a bit more, of course . . . but surely once his superstar image had faded sufficiently—once his instantly recognizable face had been out of the planetary spotlight long enough for the people to forget—surely then he would be able to find himself a woman to have and to hold, to touch and to love; a woman he could talk with, laugh with, cry with, and share his newly blossomed life with.)

Some time after midnight, he finally, reluctantly, bid good night to the heaven-scented trees, and headed for bed. It wasn't until he'd stripped off his t-shirt and gym shorts, and lain quietly atop his sheets, that he heard, barely audible above the din of the crickets, the garbled moans and squeaking bed springs at the other end of the house.

Un-unh, he thought, halting in mid-breath and straining to listen. No way.

Slowly, carefully, he pushed himself from the mattress and tiptoed through the living room and on down the hallway through the dark, his fingertips following the wall for guidance, the squeaking and moaning growing louder with every few steps. *No fucking way, Jack. Sixty-eight and sixty-seven. Medicare and Social Security.*

Their bedroom door was slightly ajar so that if he wanted he could peek through the crack at the hinges. Nothing but a Peeping Tom, he thought, feeling both juvenile and obscene, but nevertheless edging up close—unwilling to believe his ears—and incredulously pressing an eye to the opening.

And there on the bed, tastefully silhouetted in the moonlight, was his grandmother, April, bouncing and twisting atop his grandfather, Curtis, like a young cowgirl riding a bucking bronco, her head tilted back, her breasts merging in the dark with Curtis's hands.

Rhapsody looked quickly away, then almost laughing out loud in his befuddlement—sixty-eight and sixty-seven!—pressed a hand to his mouth and, not even breathing, slipped back down the hallway to climb into his bed and listen—disbelieving still—until the bedsprings at last stopped squeaking, and the moans diminished, fading beneath the cricket songs.

In and Out, Rhapsody told himself hours later as he continued to try without success to fall asleep. A Thread of breath or a Thread of love.

He felt tireless, almost immortal, as he lay there in the darkness, the nighttime alive with blossoms and Black Magic. Limitless Possibility. The basics, he kept thinking as he listened and sniffed. Scent and soil. Breath and body. Just stick with the basics, Jack, and *the real rhapsody* won't even fade.

White Poison

♪

THE FIRST TIME CURTIS WALKER LAID EYES ON APRIL WILKINS WAS THE week before Christmas of 1945, the week after he'd returned from a humiliatingly brief attempt to crack the Fifty-second Street jazz scene in New York City.

For three years, Curtis, who had just turned eighteen and barely avoided the war, had been playing in a popular local quintet, and was considered by the West Coconut Beach jazz aficionados to be a bright light among the local musicians. "You better get your ass on up to New York," many of his musician friends and fans advised him. "Fifty-second Street. That's where you want to be."

But Curtis was hesitant to leave his mother, who had, since the deaths of her husband and daughter, become something of a recluse. And he knew he could never leave for long his grove of mangoes, where he and Feyla had shared so many secret nights holding hands, listening to the trees and crickets, and watching the stars.

However, in all the photographs of the Hiroshima and Nagasaki ruins—which seemed to be thrilling, rather than chilling, many Americans—Curtis believed he was seeing previews of the world's end; a White

Hell come to earth; White power and evil gone utterly out of control.

And so he went to New York City. To see for himself. To take an accurate measure of his musical talent before the entire planet went up in a mushroom of White Heat.

But although Curtis Walker could coax from the bell of his saxophone as brassy and ballsy a sweetness as anyone, he was, when he went to New York, in no way prepared for his encounter with the Fifty-second Street be-boppers, whose stratospheric talents were soon to become legendary.

Standing by the bar in Monroe's Uptown House—cram-packed with some of the finest young jazz artists in the country, nearly all of them black, and all of them hoping for a chance to jam with the likes of Dizzy Gillespie, Charlie Parker, Kenny Clark, Thelonius Monk, and Oscar Pettiford—all Curtis could do was stare on in awe and bedazzlement while the great Dizzy Gillespie (with his trumpet angled up like a spectacular golden hard-on, and his famous bullfrog cheeks swollen, as he blew, into massive black hemispheres) played augmented eleventh chords, flattened fifths, thirteenths, and minor ninths—chords that Curtis had never heard of, much less attempted.

He was even a befuddled witness to Dizzy playing an A-flat with one finger, when everyone in the club knew that an A-flat had to be played with two fingers. Two valves. No other way. And yet, there it was. An A-flat on the trumpet with one finger.

It didn't take Curtis long to realize that he was way out of his league here. If he attempted to jam with these cats (which was what they called each other) he'd be blown off the stage. He wondered, as he pressed past all the bodies and smoke, and out into the frigid December New York night, if his sister Feyla would have been ashamed of him. "You just got to practice like I tell you," she surely would have scolded him. But to Curtis, New York City wasn't worth the effort. He'd hated the two days he'd spent there among the mountains of concrete and crowds of fast-talking strangers.

And if he was stunned by the discovery of his relative inadequacy as a saxophonist, he was nevertheless pleased to be spending a quiet Christmas at home with his mother, Eudele, beside the mango grove in the familiar tropical warmth of West Coconut Beach.

His third day home he was selected, as he had been for the past two years, to play a two-week stint in a Christmas all-star band organized and paid for by the West Coconut Beach chapter of the NABOBs (National Organization of the Brethren of Benevolence). It was a gig he'd found to be easy if not particularly inspiring. Maybe Dizzy Gillespie or Charlie Parker had the talent to turn "Jingle Bells" into a hot tune, but Curtis did not.

The band was scheduled to play for three hours in the afternoon and three hours in the evening, every day, from the Saturday before Christmas through New Year's Eve. The musicians—eight of them—would play Christmas medleys, one after another, while sitting in folding wooden chairs on a small stage in the parking lot of the A & P grocery store, beneath a red- and green-striped canopy, set up—just as it was every Christmas—beside a giant Christmas tree.

Raising the money to buy the largest Christmas tree available—almost always a Douglas fir tree from a forest in western Oregon—had become an annual civic project for the West Coconut Beach NABOBs. Each year the tree was located and cut by an Oregon contractor, then shipped cross-country by rail to the West Coconut Beach train station and loaded by two cranes onto a double flatbed truck. The next Saturday morning, the tree was slowly driven—accompanied by a festive parade of West Coconut Beach school children—to the A & P parking lot, where it was hoisted into place and dressed with a spectacular array of multi-colored flashing lights and decorations (including fabulous contest chains of popcorn and cranberries strung with fishing line, some of the chains long enough, when unraveled, to stretch across a football field) contributed by every school within thirty miles, and some as far away as Orlando, Daytona, or even Jacksonville.

Curtis and his sister, Feyla, had, each year, paraded with the rest of the town's school children, and had always been awed by the great trees that towered over the A & P every Christmas—trees that were, incredibly, two and three times the height of the huge mango trees they had so often climbed and hidden beneath in their secret, sacred grove.

This year's Douglas fir was taller, by over twenty feet, than any that had ever stood in the A & P parking lot. (Taller, no doubt, than any tree that had ever stood in *any* Florida parking lot.) The bright yellow star crowning the tree at 118 feet could be seen at night from anywhere in West Coconut Beach, and even miles beyond the city limits.

After all the New York skyscrapers, Curtis found it comforting, as he approached the parking lot stage that first Saturday afternoon, to be gazing up at a tree, a living thing, that dwarfed the surrounding man and machine-made structures. However, by the time he'd sat on stage and begun to warm up with the all-star band—his eyes still on the tree—his thoughts had turned naturally and longingly to his dead sister, Feyla, and he was scarcely able to muster the energy to make it through his first three-hour stint of Christmas jingles. And when the rest of the musicians hurried off for a dinner break before their nighttime set, Curtis stayed right where he was: slumped in his chair, his legs stretched almost straight out and his sax strapped to his neck, the instrument cold, hard, and heavy against his chest and stomach.

God damn, he thought. Four and a half years, and it still feels like yesterday.

He sat while the sun set and the pink drained from the sky. He sat while the tree lights flickered to life, and the people around the tree—mostly white—gasped and squealed. And then, still sitting, he slid his chair to the edge of the stage, swiveled it until he was facing the great Douglas fir and, his eyes fixed on the treetop star, lifted his saxophone to play "Summertime," in honor of Feyla.

Never, not even after her funeral, in the privacy of the mango grove, had he played the song—or any song—with such anguish and passion. And he played not only for his sister, but for his dead father. For his unhappy mother. For the great black jazz musicians in New York, whose brilliance was truly understood and appreciated only by one another. For every black soul to ever suffer, he played. Including his own. He felt himself turning inside out through the saxophone, his rawness and pain flowing through his instrument and into the South Florida night like a river of aching sound.

When, finally, he stopped playing, a voice immediately said, "It *is* lovely."

"Thank you," he said, letting his sax drop into his lap as he looked down from the star, wondering who would ever think to use a word like "lovely." "It's 'Summertime,' by Gershwin."

The girl looking up at him hesitated, then said, "I meant the tree, not the music."

"Oh, right," Curtis said. "The tree." It was too dark for Curtis to clearly see the girl's face, but not dark enough for the parking lot street lights or the flashing tree lights to help much. All he could tell for certain was that she wore her hair in two braids.

"Of course, I *did* enjoy your music," the girl admitted. "I mean, it was wonderful! But I assumed it was inspired by the tree. I don't think I have ever in all my life seen a tree so big. Or so lovely."

There was that word again. *Lovely*. Not to mention *assumed* and *inspired*. "It was inspired by the tree," Curtis said. "And by my sister." Then he guessed, "You're not from around here."

"I'm visiting my cousins," she explained as he hopped from the stage, the saxophone bouncing from his neck. "I live in Virginia. But I read in the newspaper that this tree is from Oregon; and if they have trees like this in Oregon, then that's where I'd like to live."

Standing close to her now, Curtis decided that the girl was at least a year or two younger than he. When she spoke he noticed a slight gap between her front teeth. But there was a sureness in her voice that he liked, and a liveliness about her eyes, even in the dark. Her twin braids emphasized her high forehead, and from the tip of each braid hung a marigold. Orange or yellow. It was hard to tell with all the shadows and flashing lights.

"If you like trees so much you ought to think about living in Florida," Curtis suggested. "We got trees all over. Some of 'em big, too. And with good sweet fruit you can eat. What's your name?"

"April Wilkins."

"April. That's *lovely*," Curtis said, grinning. "I'm Curtis Walker."

When they shook hands he was surprised by the strength of her grip, which didn't quite seem to him to match the way she spoke, much less the small size of her hand.

"Curtis Walker," she said. "Interesting. You've got the same last name as one of my heroes. David Walker. The Negro abolitionist."

"Abolitionist! Frederick Douglass is the only colored abolitionist I ever heard of."

She shook her head. "There were lots of them. More than we'll ever know about. But I do know about David Walker because of what he wrote. I've read his *Appeal to the Coloured Citizens of the World* three times, maybe even four. God, what a courageous, brilliant man he was."

Courageous, Curtis thought. *Brilliant*.

"My mother is a teacher, and every year she has all the students in her class read the *Appeal,* then memorize and recite their two favorite passages. I had my two passages memorized in the fifth grade, three years before I took her class—before I even read the book all the way through or understood what I was memorizing. And I'll bet you I still know every word by heart." She cleared her throat and squared her shoulders. " 'I speak Americans for your good. We must and shall be free I say, in spite of you. You may do your best to keep us in wretchedness and misery, to enrich you and your children, but God will deliver us from under you. And woe, woe, will be to you if we have to obtain our freedom by fighting. Get the blacks started, and if you do not have a gang of tigers and lions to deal with, I am a deceiver of the blacks and of the whites. The whites shall have enough of the blacks, yet, as true as God sits—' "

"Shhh!" Curtis shushed her sharply, glancing past her to make sure the white people milling about the parking lot and gawking up at the tree had not overheard her. "Shit, girl," he whispered, shaking his head. "You trying to work up a lynch mob?" But by the time he'd finished shaking his head, a thrill had risen up his spine and tickled the nape of his neck. "Damn," he said, then clenched his fist and whooped like an Indian with a raised tomahawk. "Hey." He took her gently by the elbow. "Can you come back tonight after I'm done?"

"Why?" she said.

"Why? Because I want to hear more about this abolitionist."

She hesitated. "I don't know. When do you want me to come back?"

"I ought to be finished here at ten o'clock."

"Too late," she said.

"Then tomorrow."

"I'm leaving tomorrow."

"Leaving!" Curtis said. "You can't. Not tomorrow!"

"I'm sorry," she said. "I'd like to talk to you, but I've already got my train ticket."

"Damn." Not only did he like the way this young woman used words, he liked the surprising strength of her grip; he liked the gap between her front teeth and the marigolds in her hair; and, above all, he liked her infatuation with the great Douglas fir tree and her admiration for the great black abolitionist. He hesitated for only a moment before turning to snatch his saxophone from the stage and take her by the hand.

"What are you doing?" she said, not resisting.

"You're a tree lover. Right? Well I'm a tree lover, too, so I'm gonna show you my mango trees. And you're gonna tell me about David Walker."

"What about your music? Your job?"

" 'Jingle Bells'! " he growled, still inspired by her David Walker speech. "Nothing but White. They ain't even gonna *miss* a black saxophone."

Curtis brought April Wilkins to the clearing beyond the mango grove where he and Feyla had spent so many secret hours watching the stars wheel across the sky and listening to the mango leaves whispering in the tropical breezes.

He told her the story of his father and his sister: of their astonishing musical abilities and their unnatural and premature deaths. He told her of his father's abusiveness, and of all the nights he and Feyla had escaped through their bedroom window and dashed across the field to eat mangoes and lie on their backs, here in this clearing, holding hands and whispering in the starlight. He told her—as she took his hand the way Feyla once had—of his recent musical failure in New York City: of the envy and pride he'd felt for all the black artists with all their black talent and intelligence, yet how, at the same time, he'd hated the city with all of its evil white concrete and pavement—no soil or trees, not even any stars.

And he told her of his plans to earn a living playing music and selling fruit; told her how he'd sold his past two mango harvests to the local grocery stores, and how, next, he wanted to plant orange trees right here where they were sitting, and grow fruit from the source of his sweetest and most precious memories.

And then April told Curtis of her life in Virginia: of her father, a skilled carpenter, who'd built for his children a fabulous three-level tree house (with windows and doors, shelves and cabinets) in a giant catalpa tree behind their house, and who had always reminded them that trees provided them with shelter, warmth, and sustenance. "Any time you walk past a tree," he'd often told her, "you better remember to look up, smile, and say 'thank you.' "

She told him of her schoolteacher mother who'd been born and raised in Montreal, who spoke French as perfectly as she spoke English, and who'd forced her and her two older brothers to study Negro literature and Negro history. And she told him all she knew of her hero, the abolitionist, David Walker: how he'd been born to a free woman on a North Carolina tobacco plantation nine years after the signing of the Declaration of Independence, and how, when he was barely a teenager, lanky and already long-legged, he'd left his mother and friends on the plantation to slowly make his way north, working at odd jobs and witnessing, daily, the injustices and atrocities that were perpetrated against his people. She told him how, after nearly a decade, Walker had at last settled on the Boston waterfront, where he loved to watch the great ships sailing in and out of the harbor, and was impressed by the number of black seamen who crewed those ships.

It was these same black seamen, who, years later, surreptitiously distributed at all the Southern harbors David Walker's two thousand pamphlets, entitled *Walker's Appeal to the Coloured Citizens of the World, but in Particular, and Very Expressly, to Those of the United States of America.*

" 'I pray,' " David Walker wrote in his *Appeal,* and April Wilkins now recited for Curtis by memory, " 'that the Lord may undeceive my ignorant brethren, and permit them to throw away pretensions, and seek after the substance of learning. Do you suppose one man of good learning would submit himself, his father, mother, wife and children, to be slaves to a wretched man like himself, who, instead of compensating him for his labors, hand-cuffs and beats him and his family almost to death, leaving life enough in them, however, to work for, and call him master? No! no! he would cut his devilish throat from ear to ear, and well do slave holders know it. The bare name of educating the coloured people scares our cruel oppressors almost to death.' "

After reciting, April explained to Curtis how, as Walker's *Appeal* began to circulate about the South—from the harbors and docks, inland—slaveholders shocked and outraged, alerted their public officials, who acted swiftly to outlaw the circulation of seditious literature and to scrupulously enforce the existing laws forbidding blacks to read and write. Throughout the South, she told him, rewards of up to ten thousand dollars were posted for Walker's capture or death. The mayor of Savannah wrote a letter to the mayor of Boston demanding Walker's immediate arrest and extradition. And one morning, less than a year after the printing of his *Appeal,* David Walker, born on a North Carolina slave plantation eight years before George Washington became the first president of the United States, was found murdered in a Boston harbor alleyway.

"A courageous and brilliant man," April whispered.

"I love you," Curtis whispered back, squeezing her hand. "Don't go."

"I love you, too. But I have to."

They kissed. Tentatively at first, awkwardly, and then deeply, while the mango leaves whispered and the stars glittered through the darkness.

"I'll be back next Christmas," she promised. "I know where to find you."

"Write me letters," he said. "I bet you write just as good as you talk."

She kissed both his eyebrows. "Send me some mangoes. And plant your orange trees. Right here." She pointed to the spot between them. "I'll stay," she said, "when you've sold your first crop."

♪♪♪

Curtis and April were married by a West Coconut Beach justice of the peace on Christmas Eve morning in 1948, three years after they'd met, and the day after he'd sold the last of his first crop of Sweet Hamlin oranges. They didn't even have a chance, that year, to buy each other Christmas presents.

"You're my present," Curtis told her when he woke up beside her Christmas morning. "Best I ever had."

"And you are mine," she whispered, spooning up against him, enjoying the feel and fit of his body, and pressing so close that it seemed to her she could discern the black heat of their souls penetrating and blurring the boundaries of their flesh. Those times they'd had a chance to make love she'd felt so filled and fulfilled that when they'd finished she was reluctant to unwrap her legs and let him pull away, for it seemed she was losing a part of herself—a lung or a kidney, or a chunk out of some other vital organ. She could hardly believe, as her hand slid over his shoulder and down his arm, that she would be waking up beside him every morning, now; that she would be there to feel this same flesh years from now, even as it aged and wrinkled, ever dark and warm and familiar.

Curtis turned to face her, his knee lifting then settling on her hip, and his heel cozying into the bend behind her knee. "Now that I got you," he said, "I got everything I need. Fruit and music. And you."

"No children?" April teased.

"Sure we'll have children," he said. "And maybe more land to grow more orange trees. But if I died with what I got now," he squeezed her with his leg, "I'd die content."

Curtis's mother, Eudele, had died almost two years earlier of unknown causes (though Curtis was sure *he* knew the causes: depression and starvation. She'd never really recovered from the deaths of her husband and daughter, and the last years of her life she rarely ate unless she was reminded.) When she died, Curtis inherited her house and her two and a half acres of land with its old grove of mango trees and, where the clearing used to be, the new grove of orange trees. But Curtis believed that if he hoped to support a family with his music and fruit he would need more property. Perhaps five or ten acres. The problem was that he didn't have the money to buy such a large parcel of land, yet was unwilling to sell the land he now owned, which was, to him, sacred with his family memories, particularly and most importantly with his memories of Feyla.

However, Curtis believed that if he could just persuade a few of his friends to pool their money with him, they could, together, purchase a nice chunk of land and divide it among themselves.

"It's a perfect plan," he told Vincent Lewis, the piano player in his jazz quintet. "We'll have a good life. A healthy life. Friends and family, fruit and music. What else you gonna need?"

But Lewis and his wife and two small children were already planning a move to Detroit to live with his sister, who had guaranteed him a job in the auto factory where her husband had found work.

"What about your music?" Curtis wanted to know. "What about us?"

"I'll always have my music," Lewis pointed out. "And I'll always have friends. But I got to do right by Debra and the kids. When opportunity knocks you got to answer the door."

"Listen," Curtis warned him. "If Detroit anything like New York, you better forget about answering the knock; you better lock the door and run."

"In Detroit," Lewis said, "my children ain't gonna grow up sitting in the back of the bus."

And it wasn't just Vincent Lewis. All of Curtis's friends seemed to be planning a move to some northern or western metropolitan area—Chicago or Boston, Los Angeles or San Francisco—or at least keeping that option open. In any case, they were unwilling to have their savings tied up in land that would be jointly owned and difficult to liquidate.

"We'll manage fine without more land," April assured him. "We've got plenty of land. More land than most people would ever wish for!"

"Maybe you right," Curtis admitted. "Maybe I can squeeze some more trees onto the land I already got." And by the week's end he'd bought five young Sweet Hamlin saplings from the local nursery and transplanted them into his small grove.

Within a year they had their first child, a boy whom Curtis named Porgy. Porgy was a relatively easy baby (nothing like George Gershwin Walker—or, much later, Rhapsody—would be), and Curtis could always keep him from fussing or crying by playing his saxophone. In fact, the only time he couldn't keep him from fussing or crying was when he *stopped* playing. (And stopping was rarely an issue for Curtis, who was usually delighted to play, for hours at a time if necessary, until his tiny son drifted off to sleep.)

Generally, Curtis played with his quintet five nights every week. During the day, when he wasn't practicing with the group, or fishing for catfish from the Manatee Lake Bridge for a family meal, or tending his orange and mango trees, he was spending time with his wife and son.

By the time Porgy was eighteen months old and toddling about with some proficiency, he would follow his parents into the mango grove and squeal with delight while the three of them played a combination of hide-and-seek and peek-a-boo. Sometimes Curtis would bring his saxophone and, in the shade of the old mango trees, play his son to sleep. And while Porgy napped, and Curtis played more and more softly, April would unbutton, then pull off, her husband's shirt and gently stroke his back, from the top of his neck and shoulders down to the base of his spine, and around to his chest and stomach, until his music turned to a whimper and a gasp, and he finally had to set down his saxophone and take her in his arms. And then, while the leaves whispered all about them, they would make love gently and quietly, so as not to wake their napping baby boy.

When Curtis was away, April spent her days shopping for groceries, washing dishes and clothes, cleaning the house, preparing meals, weeding and watering their small orange grove and the flower and vegetable garden, and, during all of those activities, entertaining Porgy. At night, while Curtis was playing with his quintet and Porgy was sleeping, she either relaxed with the radio or phonograph, or did her reading—the Negro literature that her mother had once demanded that she study: mostly, the poetry of Langston Hughes, Countee Cullen, James Weldon Johnson, Paul Laurence Dunbar, Claude McKay, and the young Gwendolyn Brooks; but also the novels of Zora Neale Hurston and the writings of and about Richard Wright, W.E.B. DuBois, Frederick Douglass, Marcus Garvey, Booker T. Washington, and, of course, David Walker.

Whenever Curtis came home and found her still awake and reading, he would proudly ask her to read a few lines out loud. And after she'd found her favorite passage of the evening he would, while she gave her reading, stare at her mouth—at the small gap between her front teeth—and fall in love all over again.

When April was pregnant with their second child (which, by her vivid and recurrent dreams, she reckoned was a girl), Curtis planted a dozen more orange trees in his small and already overcrowded half-acre grove in an effort to earn more money for his growing family. Perhaps it was the overcrowding, or perhaps it was Curtis's lack of knowledge regarding soil improvements. Whatever the reason, the leaves of the newly transplanted trees began to wither and turn a mottled yellow, and when Curtis described the problem to a local nurser he was sold a fungicide called bordeaux lead arsenate, which he wasted no time in applying to the diseased trees.

But the initial spraying seemed to have little or no effect on the yellowed leaves, and the next Saturday, while Curtis was out of town playing a lucrative weekend gig in Miami Beach, April thought she would help out by re-spraying the sickly trees.

It was a windy day, difficult for accurate spraying, but with Porgy toddling behind her, April drenched the small trees with the lead arsenate, which filled the air with a bitter and pungent smell. Little Porgy, who was almost two now, had a ball romping through the drifting mist, which felt pleasingly cool as it settled on his skin and refreshed his small lungs in the Sep-tember heat. This might not have been a problem if April had known that she was supposed to dilute the fungicide. But she did not know, and an hour after the two of them returned to the house for lunch, Porgy suddenly began to wretch and heave, his eyes going wide with shock.

April, who didn't own a telephone, ran, carrying Porgy three blocks to the home of Curtis's grandfather—Porgy's great-grandfather—Cody Swain.

"We have to get him to the hospital," she gasped, too winded to cry.

"Get on in the truck," said Cody Swain, who, though now in his late sixties, was still a vital and active man. "I'll run you out to Saint Anne's."

"Too far," April huffed. "They'll help us at Good Samaritan."

"Not when they see he's a colored baby they won't help us."

"My baby might be dying," April said. "They're going to *have* to help him, colored or not."

Cody Swain, not bothering to heed the speed limit or stop for the red lights, sped, in less than five minutes, to the emergency entrance of Good Samaritan Hospital. With her baby clutched to her breast, April kicked open the truck door, then rushed into the emergency room and directly to the admissions counter with Cody Swain right behind her.

But before she could begin to explain, the woman behind the counter stood and shook her head, pointing back to the entrance. "I'm sorry, Miss, but you'll have to go on to Saint Anne's."

"Look at my baby!" April cried, turning her small boy around for the woman to see. "He won't *make* it to Saint Anne's!"

"God forgive me," the woman said. "I don't make hospital policy. And even if I let you in—"

"Then you're a murderer!" April screamed. "A fucking baby killer!" She spat over Porgy's head at the glass divider.

But Cody Swain was already pulling at her elbow. "Come on," he hissed in her ear. "Ain't no time for this."

He was right, and when, almost ten minutes later, they roared up to the emergency entrance at Saint Anne's, Porgy had already begun to convulse, his eyes rolling up under his lids. He was dead before the doctors could decide how to treat him.

Cody Swain was able to reach Curtis in Miami late that night to stun him with the news that his son had died, and that his wife was at Saint Anne's Hospital, miscarrying.

"They say it was the tree spray," Cody Swain told his grandson.

"How is she?" Curtis whispered into the phone.

"Well, she breathed the poison, same as the baby, but the doctors think she big enough that it ain't gonna hurt her except for the miscarriage. Only thing is she ain't yet stopped cramping and bleeding, and the nurse say they probably gonna need to scrape her clean inside."

"Scrape her clean?"

"A D-and-C she called it. Because they want to make sure they got out all of that baby she was carrying."

"God damn." Curtis couldn't even swallow. "Tell her I'm gonna catch the first bus back. Tell her I'm gonna be there quick as I can."

Sitting in a corner seat at the bus station, his saxophone case at his feet, Curtis wept into both hands, pressing hard at his eyes to keep away images of Porgy's lifeless little dark body, and the even tinier body, now in scrapes of pieces, of the baby that was to have been: the little girl April had so vividly dreamed of.

As he rode the bus through the South Florida darkness, he tried to remind himself that fruit, music, and April were all he needed; that if he died with what he had right now he would die content. But the reminder didn't keep the images from haunting him, and didn't seem to affect the deep aching at the center of his chest.

Poison, he kept telling himself as he pressed harder and harder at his eyes. I killed them with *White fucking poison.*

Serendipity?

♪

THE MORNING AFTER HE PEEPED AT CURTIS AND APRIL THROUGH THEIR cracked-open bedroom door, Rhapsody—who had, following his shocking glimpse of their convergent, moonlit silhouettes, lain awake for hours considering the possibilities, the endless Thread of the In and Out, the fadelessness of *the real rhapsody*—woke up stiff-necked, drenched in sweat, and slapping at a mosquito that was biting him just below the band-aid on his throat. According to his bedroom clock, it was past ten thirty; Curtis and April had, no doubt, already been up for hours.

He stumbled from bed, slipped on his gym shorts, and, bleary-eyed, hurried to the front porch to gulp in the orange blossoms.

But something had happened.

It seemed he had somehow, overnight, grown immune to the holy aroma. It was there, all right, fragrant as ever, yet without the same effect, the magic all but gone. So he sat on the porch swing, the chains squeaking as he drifted back and forth, and tried to focus on his breath. In and Out, he thought. Here we go. But in less than a minute he was sweating profusely and slapping at mosquitoes (same mosquitoes whose bites, last night, he'd easily overlooked), far too irritated and distracted to concentrate.

"Where's the Magic," he whispered, taking a deep breath—In and Out—then rubbing at his band-aid as if it were a genie's bottle. "Come back, Jack."

He stood, the bottoms of his sweating thighs peeling from the wooden slats of the porch swing, and started down the steps to find April, who was, he knew, most likely at work in the garden. But the thought of joining her—sweating on his bare knees in the dirt and donating his flesh and blood to the mosquitoes—did not much appeal.

So he hustled inside to eat an orange; to let the sweetness explode in his mouth like a juicy epiphany straight from The Thread. But the orange was bitter as hell. Probably from California. He tossed it in the sink, half-eaten.

For lack of anything else to do he sat at the piano to pound out the simple chords to his reggae version of "Over the Rainbow." But halfway through the song he'd hit half a dozen wrong notes and his back and bottom were already aching.

Finally, he returned to his bed, thinking he might simply be in need of more sleep. But after an hour of *pretending* to be sleepy—turning, fidgeting, and sweating—he sat bolt upright, feeling hopelessly caged in and having difficulty breathing. For a minute it even occurred to him that his vocal chords might be swelling shut in the heat, and he nearly grew faint gulping the air, trying not to panic.

"The hell with In and Out," he finally cried, jumping from his bed and heading for the door. "I'm getting *out,* and now."

Coming upon April, who was bent over, hoeing in her garden, Rhapsody said, "I got to get to town."

April stood up straight, shading her eyes and squinting. "What's wrong? What do you need?"

"What I need is to get to town. But I'm not going anywhere unless I can find me a decent disguise."

"I could go for you," April offered. "Really, it's no problem."

"No," Rhapsody said. "That's all right. Just help me with a disguise."

She thought for a moment, a hand resting on her hoe handle, then smiled. "Santa Claus."

"Santa Claus?"

"Every Christmas, now, Curtis dresses up in a Santa suit and we invite the pickers to bring their children so he can give them toys from his sack. The outfit's in a box at the top of the hall closet. I made it myself. Everything except the boots, the belt, and the beard."

"It's still October," Rhapsody said. "Too early for Santa Claus."

April smiled. "If anybody complains, just tell him you're early this year. Who's going to get mad about an early Santa Claus?"

An early Santa Claus, Rhapsody thought. Why not?

So he dressed in the suit—too baggy for him even with a third pillow stuffed under his shirt—parted his white beard and moustache to kiss April on the cheek, and, accepting the keys from her, hopped into the driver's seat of his grandfather's old pick-up. But before he made it halfway down the driveway, he was sweating in his suit, the red felt clinging to his skin; so he backed up, switched off the ignition, and hurried inside to call for an air-conditioned limousine. "Sometimes," he told April, "it pays to be rich."

Near the center of town, Rhapsody instructed the driver to pull over. Then, stepping from the limousine air-conditioning into the heat, he hustled past the storefronts without purpose or destination, smiling nervously at the grins and pointing fingers of nearly everyone he passed. Children, especially, could not keep themselves from staring at him—almost the same hungry and expectant stares that he saw on the faces of his starstruck fans; not at all the effect he'd intended. It was as if he'd simply traded one superstar guise for another.

He ducked into Floyd's Bar and Grill to escape the heat and the children, sat at a table in the corner and decided to order the lunch special, a beer-steamed hot dog with onions and sauerkraut. (If his un–Santa-like skin color and unseasonable appearance didn't discourage the kiddies, maybe his breath would.)

A wide-screen TV was set in a corner high above the bar, and, though the sound was too low for Rhapsody to hear, he watched a pair of bantamweights jabbing, feinting, and clenching until the waitress, a young black woman—nineteen or twenty, he guessed—came to take his order.

"Ho ho ho," she said, whipping out her pad and pen. She wore blue jeans with a maroon "Newport Jazz" t-shirt; her hair was plaited and small silver birds dangled from her ear lobes. "Look like you a little bit early this year."

"It's been a cold fall," Rhapsody said, noticing that she had a singularly graceful neck and an easy, loose-limbed way of moving. "I came down for the sun, but what I need now is to cool off with a beer. And one of those lunch specials with extra onions."

"A beer?" she said. "If you want a beer you gonna have to show me some ID."

"ID!" Rhapsody didn't even flinch. "Now why I got to show you any ID when you know Santa Claus is 100 years older than your great-great-granddaddy?"

The waitress set her hands on her hips and leaned back, grinning. "All I know, Mr. Black Santa Claus, is that you got a nasty white beard covering enough of your face that I can't even guess how old you are. So if you really thirsty for a cold beer you better quick show me a driver's license."

"I got a sleigh and reindeer," Rhapsody said. "Why I need a driver's license?"

"Ho ho ho, " she said, then leaned close to him and whispered slyly, "If you ain't gonna show me your driver's license, then you gonna have to show me what you got behind your beard."

"Well," Rhapsody pulled at his beard. "The only way to show you what's behind it is to shave it off, and I ain't about to do that." He leaned close to her, now, so that their faces were just inches apart. "Not unless I get to know you better."

"But you ain't gonna get to know me better," she said, not retreating an inch, "unless I see who's behind the beard. And you ain't gonna get a beer, either."

"Okay, then," Rhapsody surrendered, suddenly afraid that, spunky as she was, she just might take it upon herself to rip off his beard. "An orangeade with extra ice."

"We got lemonade," she said, backing away. "No orangeade."

"All right, lemonade with extra ice."

She started to write his order on her pad, then stopped and held her pen to her lips, studying his eyes. "So what kind of beer does Santa Claus drink?"

"Heineken Dark."

"All right, but don't even *think* about asking for a second one. Not unless you can find some ID or a can of shaving cream, one."

As she put up his order, then attended to the other tables, he stared after her the same way the kids outside had been staring after him and his red suit. With hope and yearning, fear and awe.

He'd known plenty of women with prettier, more perfect, features. But she exuded a breeziness and an unforced, unpretentious sensuality that made him lightheaded. (It may have been that he was simply more attuned to necks since his near-tragic accident. But he had to believe that, his newfound appreciation for necks notwithstanding, hers was the softest, most dizzyingly graceful neck he'd ever seen.)

What's more, she wore no wedding ring. And their impromptu banter had been so remarkably easy, their mutual feistiness so perfectly balanced, that he suspected their meeting was not simply a chance encounter, but a rare and wondrous moment of serendipity—*so this was why he'd rushed downtown in a panic and ducked into Floyd's*—presided over by a special gathering of the Black Gods.

But within minutes he could see that it wasn't just him she was easy with. In fact to watch her—throwing her head back to laugh, winking, flapping her elbows—he'd have thought she was old friends with each of her customers, no matter their age or sex, or even their color. She was easy with them all, an ability he was at once impressed with and dismayed by.

When she brought back his Heineken, he told her he'd just checked his list twice, and found that she'd been extra nice this year. "So what do you want me to leave under your tree?" he asked her.

"A car." She shut one eye as she tilted his glass and poured. "Don't matter what kind. Long as it's small and red. Bright as your suit."

He frowned, concentrating to keep from staring at her neck. "Too dangerous," he said. "Especially the small ones. How about an instrument? A piano or a saxophone?" He motioned to her t-shirt. "Looks like you're into jazz."

"Sure," she said. "All kinds of music if it's good. But I don't play nothing."

"Free piano lessons!" Rhapsody cried with genuine excitement. "It'll come with the piano, a package deal. I'll teach you myself!"

"I'll tell you what," she said, winking, "You get the piano under my tree and maybe show me what's under that old phony beard, and we'll talk about lessons."

As she turned to head back to the kitchen, he had an overwhelming urge to jump from his chair, rip off his beard, and let her gawk at his famous face. The superstar. In the flesh. She could leave with him now, lucky lady. Throw down her ordering pad and never look back. They'd return to the orange grove and live happily ever after. She was his missing link, his sure connection to *the real rhapsody*; with her at his side the smell of the blossoms would never fade.

But even as his fantasy was blossoming, his hopes were dimming. He *couldn't* show her who he was. Same old story. He'd be winning her with his fame, and whether he looked at her, talked to her, touched her, kissed her, or loved her, she'd be thinking of his superstar persona, his money and worldwide renown; thinking how it would be to tell her friends. And, knowing what she must be thinking, knowing that those wide, excited eyes were not for him—not really—he would grow cool and hostile, bitter and frustrated, the relationship ending almost before it began. It was the nature of superstardom. Not her fault. There was nothing to be done.

As the waitress disappeared, arms swinging, into the kitchen, Rhapsody felt a great emptiness spreading from the center of his stomach, consuming him from the inside out. And, suddenly eager to escape this latest disappointment, he borrowed a pen from a man at an adjacent table, scribbled "Merry Xmas" on a fifty-dollar bill, signed it "Old Black Santa," then hoisted his beer glass, drained it halfway with three quick gulps, and, setting it on the face of the bill, hurried from the bar and grill, into the heat.

He sped along the sidewalk toward Manatee Lake at a half-jog, not even bothering to acknowledge or return the smiles coming at him from every direction. By the time he reached the lake wall, sweat was dripping over his eyebrows, into his eyes, and down his cheeks—a steady, salty stream—his white moustache and beard absorbing the overflow.

First thing, he pulled off his floppy hat, then his boots and socks. But the sidewalk was too hot for his bare feet, so he stuffed the socks into his back pocket and, stepping into his boots, barefoot, tore open his red felt shirt and hastily removed his three-pillow stuffing. Then, hat and pillows tucked under an arm, his Santa shirt flapped open at the front, he used his free arm to catapult himself from the walkway to the top of the retaining wall.

Serendipity, he thought, staring eight feet down into the choppy lake water as it lapped and splatted against the concrete. Maybe this is what I came to town for. *A small step, a quick drop, and it's all cool water, Jack. The sun blotted out and the emptiness filled forever. Two birds with one stone. An easy solution.*

He flexed his knees and swung back his arms, ready to spring. But it was all theater. A bad act. Even if he jumped, or if someone snuck up from behind to mercifully push him over, he knew he would simply kick off his heavy black boots and swim to the surface. Anything, even the heat and emptiness, was preferable to The End—The Final Landing.

Shit, he thought, then dropped his pillows on the wall for cushioning and sat facing the lake, trying to figure out why he was there and what he would do next.

But after a minute of the sun beating on his head and shoulders, he could sit no longer, so stood and walked carefully along the wall top toward a small dock twenty yards ahead. A ladder—steel rungs in the concrete—led from the top of the wall to the wooden deck below. Rhapsody scaled down the ladder, then stripped off his shirt and set it on the creaking wooden deck, along with his boots, socks, hat, and pillows. There was nobody nearby, so he even pulled off his white beard, and, wearing only his red felt pants, took a wild running leap and crashed into the water with his knees pulled to his chest.

Though he was underwater for only a few seconds, when he gulped in that first breath he felt an exhilarating sense of *déjà vu*. But it faded quickly as he kicked his way back to the landing and hoisted himself, somewhat refreshed, onto the dock, a half-naked, dripping black Santa Claus.

He felt better—cooler at least—and able to think more clearly. And as soon as he'd strapped his beard to his face it occurred to him that he was feeling, above all, terribly lonely and in need of a friend to talk to. Excited by his idea, he dipped his hat, socks, and shirt in the lake, then slipped them back on, wringing wet—temporary protection against the heat—and slogged his way to the nearest phone booth. He dialed Russell Kirkland's New York condo, instructing the operator to charge the call to his L.A. number. And though he smiled in anticipation with every ring of the phone, as soon as he heard Kirkland's voice he slammed down the receiver. What the hell could he tell him? That he'd grown immune to the smell of the blossoms? That he'd just found the woman of his dreams, then lost her because he was dressed up in a Santa suit—in October? in South Florida?—and couldn't bring himself to take off his beard?

Before he could decide whether to call back, there was a sharp tug at his shirt sleeve. He whirled around, startled to see a tiny white girl, no older than six of seven, grinning up at him, breathless with excitement.

"Hi!" she chirped, still hanging onto his sleeve. "I already know what I want."

"Sheila!" It was the little girl's mother, not far behind. "Come back here this instant!" She'd apparently been caught by surprise when Santa, whirling around from the telephone, turned out to be a dripping and desperate-looking young black man with an unbuttoned shirt, three ratty pillows tucked under an arm, and pants so waterlogged they appeared to be in imminent danger of slipping below his waist.

Before the little girl had a chance to tell Santa what it was she wanted for Christmas, her frantic mother had whisked her to safety.

"Ho ho ho," Rhapsody bellowed after them, then hiked up his pants and turned back to dial for a limousine.

Across the street from the phone booth and halfway up the block toward Floyd's Bar and Grill was a white bench. And it was on this bench that Rhapsody—still dripping wet in his Santa suit—was sitting, waiting for his limousine, when a heavy-set black woman came walking toward him, a small boy in her arms.

She stopped a few feet from the bench, the top of the boy's head tilted into her cheek, two fingers in his mouth. "Look there," she pointed. "Who you see? Is that the Easter Bunny sitting on the bench?"

The little boy shook his head, then cupped a hand to whisper in her ear.

"Santa Claus?" the woman said, pulling back to stare at the boy, her eyes wide. "From the North Pole? The man who come down all the chimneys every Christmas with a bag of toys?"

"Ho ho ho," Rhapsody said. "What's your name?"

Instead of answering, the boy nuzzled into the woman's shoulder, his face hidden.

"You gonna tell Santa Claus your name?" the woman asked.

The boy shook his head without lifting it.

"Is your name Sam?" the woman asked.

Again, the boy shook his head.

"Gus?"

Another shake.

"Willie?"

This time a nod.

"Willie?" Rhapsody said. "Is that right? You know, I have a friend—an elf—with the name Willie."

The boy now swiveled his head slightly, his cheek resting on the woman's shoulder, his two fingers sneaking back into his mouth. He looked at Rhapsody through one eye.

"Yeah, the Willie *I* know is an elf just about the same size you are. Only I think he's older than you. Now how old did you say you were?"

Willie blinked his eye, but his mouth didn't move.

"Are you two and a half," the woman asked him. "Gonna be three in February?"

He lifted his head to nod ponderously, still too shy to speak.

"I swear," the woman shook her head. "When you ready for some quiet he like to talk your ear right off your head. But when you want him to talk he act like he don't know how."

Rhapsody pushed a few white moustache hairs up from his lip. "All right tell me this, Willie. What do you want Santa Claus to bring you for Christmas?"

Willie chewed on his fingers for a few seconds, then lowered his head back to the woman's shoulder.

"Well," Rhapsody said. "If you won't tell Santa Claus what you want, maybe you could tell your mama, and she'll tell it to me."

The woman put a hand to her mouth and fluttered her eyes. "Listen up, Willie," she hissed. "Santa Claus think I'm your mama."

And right away Willie raised his head to giggle, his eyes squinted almost shut. "Mee-maw," he said, patting the woman on the shoulder with both his hands.

"I'm his grandma!" the woman beamed. "His mama work over to the

Bar and Grill."

"Floyd's Bar and Grill?" Rhapsody tried to hide his surprise. "A waitress?"

"That's right. She working there right now, and we on our way to visit. You know her?"

"No!" Rhapsody said. "I mean, I know who she is, but she doesn't . . . it's just . . ." He thought of her achingly graceful neck and ringless finger. "It doesn't matter, but I didn't know she was married."

"She ain't married," the woman said. "And never was. Because that fool up and left her just as soon as he found out what he done to her. And now, with a two-year-old to take care of, the only ones been interested in marrying my Daphne are twice her age, and she ain't been interested in marrying none of them. And it ain't even her I'm worried about. It's him." She kissed the boy, her grandson, on the top of his head. "Because it ain't right for a little boy to have to grow up without a daddy."

"You got that right," Rhapsody said. "A little boy *should* have a daddy." It was an idea he imagined he could easily and happily get used to: the sly little rascal of a boy in his arms and the sweet-necked waitress at his side. But, tempting as it was to consider, he knew it would never work—not a chance—and felt nothing but relief when the limousine pulled up to the curb, and the chauffeur hopped out and hustled around to open the back door.

"Listen," he tried to reassure the woman, while the chauffeur waited for him, blinking askance at those wet, droopy pants. "Don't you worry about Willie. I never knew my daddy, either, and look at me now." With his head he gestured to the limo and chauffeur, but without much conviction. Then shrugging, he ducked into the back seat, not even bothering to bellow a final "Ho ho ho."

The White Machine

♪

BY THE TIME RHAPSODY'S DADDY, GEORGE GERSHWIN WALKER, WAS born early in 1953, Curtis and April had decided to sell their property—property Curtis had wanted to keep sacred for as long as he lived; property he would never even have *considered* selling had it not been for the advent and spread of air conditioning. For the once sleepy town of West Coconut Beach had, of late, begun to awaken and develop, and air conditioning was its growth hormone. As air conditioned homes and businesses became more and more commonplace, developers discovered that South Florida was not only a tolerable area for people to live year round, but a highly desirable one.

Ever since he was a boy, the land Curtis lived on had, itself, been surrounded by wooded areas containing small houses sparsely situated in the shade of great banyan and mango trees, and large stands of Australian pines. But when air conditioning turned what had been a trickle of South Florida newcomers into a stream, and then a torrent, the developers leveled the woods in order to create new neighborhoods, then connect them to one another with newly paved streets. Not only could Curtis see the encroaching "whiteness," he could hear it and smell it every day, and feel it in his bones as he lay in bed with April every night. The evil—with all its noise and poisons, speed and energy, steel and concrete—had surrounded them and begun to close in. The heat, it seemed, was hotter. The air and water were less sweet and less clear. Even the sky had lost some of the luster off its blue, had gone flatter, as if the color were slowly retreating behind a sheen of whiteness.

When, early in 1952—a year after Porgy's death—a developer offered to buy Curtis's two and a half acres, he refused flat out. But by the time—less than a year later—he'd received his fourth offer he was ready to start negotiating. He dickered and bargained for months, for as long as he dared, until he got the price he wanted, which was a good one for him *and* the developer, who immediately leveled the house and the grove of mangoes and small orange trees, and built a shopping center, anchored by a Sears and a Winn-Dixie, which soon became one of the busiest shopping areas in the city—though to Curtis it would always be a giant and obscene tomb for his mango grove and nighttime sanctuary; an ugly and shameful graveyard for his sacred memories.

When Curtis bought the twelve-acre grove he figured he would have to hire pickers at harvest time, for he owned far too many trees, now, to handle all the picking himself. He hoped, however, that he could manage the rest of his business without assistance. After all, the grove was already set up with a simple drip irrigation system, and, since the fatal poisonings of Porgy and the baby in utero, he'd already concocted a harmless, organic, foliar spray (not a drop of White Poison) and had learned that he could improve his soil by planting the grove in clover and annual rye following each harvest, and spreading rock phosphate over the sandy soil.

By now, every member of Curtis's quintet had moved to the North or the West, to the jazz scenes or factory jobs of the big cities, and so his music had become his hobby at the same time his fruit was becoming his livelihood.

April, meanwhile (who, when Curtis bought the twelve-acre grove, was more disappointed than she let on that they didn't escape the South—escape Jim Crow, as many of their friends already had—and move to Oregon, where they could live among the great Douglas fir trees and go to any hospital they wanted—or needed—to go to), was busy raising their second son, but only child, George Gershwin, whose lighter complexion and sharper features reminded her of her Canadian-born mother.

From the start, George Gershwin was a fussier, feistier, and more willful baby than Porgy. It almost seemed to Curtis and April that their little boy's spirit had somehow been deposited into a body that was not really his, and that the fit was clearly an awkward and improper one. Even his eyes, an unusual amber-brown, appeared slightly out of place, as if staring from behind a mask.

When he was fifteen months old and toddling about with only a modicum of competence, April left him sitting in the garden for what she was certain would be only a moment, while she ran inside to grab some twine in order to re-secure her burgeoning tomato plants to their stakes. It was a mild morning in late January, the cumulus clouds piled thick and high, and Curtis was deep in the grove sowing crimson-clover seeds among the roots of his orange trees.

The moment his mother entered the house through the back door, George Gershwin pushed himself up from the ground, turned from the tomato plants, and waddled off toward the hibiscus bushes that bounded the west side of the garden. He sniffed at two pink flowers, and then, while working his way toward the next bush, nearly stepped on a sleeping armadillo, which scrambled to its feet with a startled snort before lum-bering off, sticking to the line of small trees and shrubs that curved toward the south, away from the house and garden.

George Gershwin had never seen such a creature, but was delighted to find one that could apparently move with even less grace, and at only a slightly faster speed, than he could. Laughing, his arms stretched before him, fingers waggling in anticipation, he followed the armadillo as fast and as closely as he could. Several times he heard his mother call his name from somewhere far behind, but the sound only registered as a familiar picture, hardly worth a thought. Certainly not worth slowing down for.

There was a narrow canal which separated the southern tip of Curtis's orange grove from the eighteenth hole of the Melaleuca Lakes Golf Course. The hole was a long par five which narrowed considerably the last eighty yards, while doglegging to the left and, at the same time, sloping to the right, toward the canal, so that if a golfer pushed or sliced his approach shot even slightly he was doomed to lose his ball in the water.

Just beyond the eighteenth green was the clubhouse, and outside the clubhouse, sitting on the south bank of the canal, the tall, whip-thin young assistant pro of Melaleuca Lakes was gobbling the last few bites of his sardine and boiled egg sandwich. It was his favorite sandwich, but every time he brought it in for lunch he was mercilessly harassed by the head pro, and anyone else in his vicinity, about the sardine and boiled egg odor, until he was forced to retreat outside and finish his beloved sandwich in solitude.

He had licked his fingers clean and rolled his lunch bag and napkin into a ball, when, across the canal, he was startled to see three white ducks quacking their way down the bank and into the canal, their wings lifted in anger, followed closely by a toddling, laughing brown baby in a dirt-smudged diaper.

When the baby tumbled, splashing, head first into the murky water, the assistant pro threw down his balled-up lunch bag and charged down the bank. Hustling into the canal, nearly waist deep, he quickly felt for, found, and scooped up the small boy.

Little George Gershwin gasped and coughed, then wailed loudly, his eyes stinging with the muddy water as his stork-like deliverer carried him to safety.

"Jesus," the skinny young man said to the baby he held in his arms. "You may not be baby Moses, but I just saved your little ass, and that's a fact!"

Thrilled by his extraordinary deed, he carried the baby to the clubhouse, pushed backward through the double glass doors, and sloshed his way, dripping, toward the counter.

"What the hell's going on, Pete?" the head pro asked, gawking from behind the counter at the wailing black baby.

"It's the damnedest thing," Pete said, awkwardly holding up the baby as a crowd of golfers gathered around. "I fished him from the canal."

"Too small," one of the golfers joked. "Better throw 'im back."

"I don't know," the pro said. "He sure as hell smells better than Pete's sardines."

" 'Gator bait," another golfer laughed, then hissed and snapped at the baby, who wailed even louder.

"Hey!" Pete quickly pulled the baby away. "He doesn't need to be scared any more than he already is."

"It must have been abandoned by its mother," someone suggested.

But the head pro, still standing behind the counter, shook his head. "You know, a colored family bought a few acres of the old Watkins grove across the canal. He must be theirs."

"Better call the sheriff," one of the golfers said.

"Never mind the sheriff," Pete said. "I'll run him on over there myself. I'm wet already, anyway."

George Gershwin's wailing had softened to a steady whimper by now, and Pete, the assistant pro, held him securely as he waded across the canal, a crowd of golfers cheering him on.

By the time Pete came upon April, not 100 yards from the canal, George Gershwin had stopped crying and was enjoying the view from high up on Pete's shoulders.

"Thank God," April cried, reaching up to take her baby. "Thank you, thank you, thank you."

Pete wasn't sure if the woman was thanking him or God, so he just nodded, while George Gershwin protested his mother's hugs and kisses, and squirmed to be put down, eager, it seemed, for another misadventure.

But, in spite of his propensity for recklessness, George Gershwin survived his year as a toddler and, almost before Curtis and April could catch their breaths, was talking, running, climbing, and singing, then entering kindergarten and grade school.

On December 25, 1962, George Gershwin's ninth Christmas, Curtis gave him a present unlike any he'd ever received. A present unlike any that *any* nine-year-old had ever received. The present was a fallout shelter beneath their home. A present, Curtis solemnly told his son, of life.

Two months earlier the high-stakes confrontation between the United States and the Soviet Union over the placement of missiles in Cuba had convinced Curtis that a nuclear holocaust was now both unavoidable and imminent. A question not of if, not even of when, but of how soon.

And so, early in November he'd hired his two uncles, Alfred and James, of the Swain Construction Company, formerly the Swain Roofing Company, to build an unfinished half-basement, fortified with a thick concrete ceiling and wall, and lined with wooden storage shelves. The basement was completed on December 22, but Curtis wouldn't allow his son to see it until Christmas morning.

"It ain't just a basement," Curtis told George Gershwin as they stood looking at the propane stove, the barrel of peanuts, the crates of oranges, the boxes of dried beef stick, the bottles of water, and the cans and jars of fruit, vegetables, tuna fish, and sardines. "It's a bomb shelter basement. When the bombs are dropped we go down to the shelter. You, me, your mama, and maybe Uncle Alfred and James. For a month we eat lots of oranges, tuna, beef jerky, and your mama's canned food. And when we come back up there's gonna be grass and wildflowers growing where the streets and buildings used to be."

It was Curtis's pastoral version of the Second Coming, his myth of natural retribution and justice, the powerful, avaricious, and evil White Civilization getting, in the end, exactly what it deserved, the dark earth finally returned to the meek, rid, at last, of its suffocating concrete shackles and all the White noise and stench.

But April was unimpressed with Curtis's bomb shelter, for she had a more realistic vision of the world after the bombs. A vision of poisoned food and water. A vision of dying children, tortured trees, and ubiquitous suffering. A vision that one tiny fallout shelter could do little to alter.

And young George Gershwin was too busy and full of life to take seriously such grave ideas; he and his friends played bomb shelter the way other children played house. And the shelter, as it turned out, was a splendid place for George Gershwin and his friends to retreat to during tropical thunderstorms and summer (or fall, winter, or spring) heat waves. They could crawl across the cool concrete floor, using only flashlights, while they played hide and seek, told ghost stories, or snitched peanuts and beef jerky.

"The best Christmas present you ever gave him," April kidded Curtis years later, long after he'd given up his benign and bucolic vision of Armageddon. "The only Christmas present you ever gave him that didn't end up in the garbage after a month!"

In 1965, when he was twelve years old, George Gershwin spent his early summer mornings raking the canal by the difficult eighteenth hole for lost balls, which he collected, then sold to golfers back on the seventeenth tee, out of sight of the clubhouse, for five, ten, or fifteen cents apiece, depending upon the ball's condition. It was not unusual for him to earn two or three dollars a day this way, seven days a week, a rather hefty income for a twelve-year-old in 1965.

He was raking balls from the canal early one morning, an hour before the golf course opened, when he was startled by a tall, gangly white man dressed like a golfer, who came striding down the opposite bank, his legs so long and skinny that George Gershwin half expected them to bend backwards at the knee as he walked, like the legs of a flamingo or a great blue heron.

"How about if from now on I give you two cents for your cut balls, and a dime for all the rest?" the man said from where he stood across the canal.

"No thanks," George Gershwin immediately said. "No deal."

"I could call the police," the man said, but without much threat or conviction in his voice.

George Gershwin thought for a few seconds, then said, "I'm on my own property. The police ain't gonna do nothing."

"Listen," the man said, startled by the belligerent response of this weed of a boy whose life he'd once saved. "You're not thinking like a good businessman."

George Gershwin said nothing, though the man's comment rankled, for in fact he did think of himself as having a good head for business, and considered his daily income from the golf balls to be proof of that.

"You're forgetting to figure your time," the rangy man across the canal now told George Gershwin. "Sell the balls to me and you don't have to waste your day sneaking around and trying to unload them a few at a time. Of course, with all your leftover time you could be finding more balls, and making more money."

George Gershwin considered this.

"It's a matter of volume," the man said.

"And I could hunt for balls any time?"

"Anytime and anywhere! Anybody gives you trouble, you just tell them to talk to Pete."

Again, George Gershwin pondered the offer, trying to calculate if, in the extra time he'd have to spend hunting for balls, he'd be able to find enough of them to offset the lower prices.

"I'll even throw in free golf lessons," Pete said.

"Golf lessons?" George Gershwin narrowed his eyes.

"Sure," Pete said. "I'm the pro here."

"And how I'm gonna take golf lessons without clubs?"

"No problem," Pete said. "I'll dig you up a set."

George Gershwin pictured himself standing at the tee-off area among the golfers with their fancy clothes and two-toned, spiked shoes; pictured himself stepping up to confidently and gracefully whack the ball down the fairway, fifty yards beyond all the white players.

"What about spiked shoes?" George Gershwin asked.

"Jesus Christ," Pete said. "Now you're thinking too much like a businessman."

"And I can play for free before the course open and after it close."

"Okay, okay," Pete said, figuring he'd better agree before George Gershwin threw in any more demands: a free golf cart, perhaps, or a lifetime supply of Izod shirts. "You got yourself a deal."

If George Gershwin had a natural aptitude for business, he had a supernatural aptitude for golf. Perhaps it was his huge hands—hands he'd inherited from his grandfather, Lincoln. But, for whatever reason, George Gershwin could swing his clubs at a phenomenally high speed without trying—smooth and fast as a whip, utterly unforced and efficient.

"If he keeps up," Pete Dugan told his friends, "he'll be better than me by the time he's sixteen."

Naturally, it pleased George Gershwin to know that he was capable, after just six months, of beating ninety percent of the grown white men who hacked their way around Melaleuca Lakes, and who had been hacking their way around Melaleuca Lakes for years, or in some cases, even decades.

But what satisfied him most of all was the thrill he got out of hitting a perfect shot: the clean crack of a drive, the tiny ball soaring into the blue, already seventy-five yards away and rising by the time he looked up.

Curtis, of course, thought his son must be crazy.

"Golf?" he said to April, shaking his head. "You got to be rich and white to play golf."

But when he watched from across the canal while his son sent ball after ball screaming across the sky, from one end of the driving range to the other, he was as proud as he was befuddled. And yet he couldn't keep from feeling uneasy about George Gershwin and his golfing fanaticism.

"Where it all gonna lead to?" he asked April. "All those hours chasing after white balls."

"It doesn't have to lead anywhere," April said. "As long as he keeps up his grades I can't think of anything to worry about. At least we know where he is after school."

By the time he was fifteen, George Gershwin's huge hands were so callused from all his hours of golfing that he could stick pins anywhere along the top ridge of each of his palms without feeling pain or drawing blood; stick them in deep enough so that they would stand by themselves, like toothpicks in a steak.

Unfortunately, George Gershwin had no real opportunity to showcase his astonishing talent, for Carver High School, with its all-black student body, had neither the funds nor the student interest necessary to start up a golf team. Which was disappointing to him, but not devastating. For it wasn't competition that ultimately mattered to him, but the moment of impact, the pure euphoria to be reaped from the sound and feel of the solidity of a perfect shot. Crack! And then the sight of the white dot climbing against the blue.

It was during the spring of George Gershwin's sophomore year at Carver High that Pete Dugan hired him to operate the old driving range tractor after school let out every afternoon.

The tractor, eighteen years old, had been recently painted white (same color—same paint, in fact—that had been used to re-coat the electric golf carts at Melaleuca Lakes), and was covered by a red- and white-striped vinyl canopy. A four-sided wire cage had been built around the seat to protect the driver from the balls that were hit from the driving range tee-off area. And the tractor towed behind it a ball-gathering mechanism, which, with its long row of rubber wheels and metal baskets, looked something like a plow. As the rubber wheels passed over the red-striped range balls, the balls were scooped up—wedged tightly between the rubber—then automatically deposited into the metal baskets behind wheels. And when the baskets were loaded with balls, George Gershwin would simply drive back to the clubhouse, park the tractor, and empty the baskets into large barrels, from which small wire buckets of balls could be refilled and sold to the Melaleuca Lakes customers, who would then hit the balls back onto the driving range.

The sturdy wire cage effectively protected George Gershwin from the balls that were hit as he drove the tractor through the golfers' lines of fire. But, protected though he knew he was, he often felt as if he were driving a tank across a mine field, and couldn't keep from flinching every time a rock-hard ball cracked against the tractor or the wire cage at high speed, inches from his body.

Curtis, already uneasy about his son's absorption with golf, grew even more wary when he learned of the tractor job. Not only was George Gershwin immersing himself in a white world, he was now being paid to operate a white machine.

"You don't even have a driver's license yet," he cautioned his son. "And here you are driving a tractor big enough to flatten a barn."

"I got my learner's permit four months ago," George Gershwin pointed out.

"Learner's permit? What you think the insurance company's gonna say when you have an accident with that tractor, then show them your *learner's* permit?"

"How am I gonna have an accident when I'm driving on a wide open field?" George Gershwin demanded. "Ain't nothing for me to run into."

But Curtis shook his head, unconvinced, and tried to ignore the prickling at his scalp every time he thought of the huge white tractor sweeping across the range with his son at the wheel.

The worst part of George Gershwin's job was that every weekday afternoon between 3:15 and 3:45, the white boys from the West Coconut Beach High School golf team would, with their daily warm-up buckets of range balls, use George Gershwin and his moving tractor for target practice. And whenever one of them hit the tractor or the protective cage they would all engage in a ritualistic war dance, whooping and slapping hands.

What bothered George Gershwin most about their behavior was that he was never—and could never be—certain if it was simply a matter of schoolboy immaturity, or ugly racism; a harmless game of hit the moving tractor, or a mock nigger-lynching.

It was a question that festered for months, gnawing away at him, slowly spreading from the particular to the general, until it finally became, in his mind, a great symbolic question that spoke directly to the plight of all black people, so that any time he interacted with the white world, now, The Great Question began to impinge upon and give shape to that interaction. When the lady at the grocery check-out counter failed to acknowledge his smile, was it simply because she didn't see his smile, or because he was black? When the cop pulled him over that night on his bicycle—the siren wailing and red light flashing—and ticketed him in front of all the gawking and hooting passers-by, was it really because he didn't have a proper head light, or because he was black? Every encounter became a brush with conspiracy. He could never quite be certain.

Soon, he found himself becoming too paranoid to leave the orange grove unless it was to go to school or the golf course. And even the golf course was difficult. Did Pete Dugan ask him to eat his lunch in the back of the clubhouse among the white rows of electric carts because it looked bad for him, an em-ployee, to be chowing down in front of customers, or because he was black?

At 3:15 every weekday he broke into a cold Pavlovian sweat in anticipation of the arrival of the white boy sharpshooters from the West Coconut Beach golf team. He tried not to let it bother him as they stepped up to their balls and took aim at the tractor (or was it at him?); but every time one of them rattled his cage then whooped and cele-brated with the others, he felt a great, helpless rage welling up inside.

And when the golf course closed every night, and George Gershwin slung his bag and clubs over his shoulder, headed for the first hole, and teed off into the darkening sky, he would dream of using his talent and superiority to bludgeon the white boys on the golf team—to bludgeon the entire White world—beating them at their own white game with all its silly white accouterments: the special shoes, hats, gloves, shirts, and slacks. He would join the professional tour. Wear blue jeans with an unbuckled belt, Stokely Carmichael shades, and black high-top tennis shoes. He'd grow his hair into a fine bushy afro with a long-handled black comb mounted to one side, and roll a toothpick around his mouth as he strode down the fairways or bent over to putt a ball. In tournament after tournament he'd collect the winner's check—twenty-five and fifty thousand dollars at a time—frustrating, yet again, Arnie's white army and Nicklaus's white navy, the great white heroes dethroned by the cool and superior black king.

In the fall of 1969, George Gershwin fell in love with Theresa Brown shortly after they became lab partners in their chemistry class. Theresa had been in two of George Gershwin's soph-omore classes, but was quiet, almost aloof, and he'd never paid her much attention. However, watching her as she hunched over the intense blue flame of their Bunsen burner, then recorded, with impeccable precision, her measurements and observations, he grew quickly infatuated. She had, he decided, the most fiercely, darkly intelligent eyes he'd ever seen. Eyes that missed not a trick or a turn. Eyes without a trace of self-doubt.

Like him, he thought, she was a conqueror. Together, they could take on the White world, attacking it at two of its greatest strongholds, two of its most eminent domains: science and golf.

And when Theresa Brown, after a third invitation, finally saw the way George Gershwin could hit a golf ball she began to believe in his dreams. (*Anyone* who saw the way George Gershwin could hit a golf ball would have believed in his dreams.) With all the money he would earn from his tournament victories he could, among other things, put Theresa through the best schools in the country, so that she could, as was *her* dream, become a famous research scientist, or a doctor—perhaps a great surgeon—and together they would surely become a force to be reckoned with, a force that could not be ignored, a force that would ultimately erode the very roots of The Great Question.

So smitten was he by Theresa Brown, so certain of their bright future together, that he was unwilling to even mention her to his parents, afraid they might somehow disapprove the fervid nature of their relationship, or even, if he confessed to them his dreams of early matrimony, forbid him from seeing her.

And so they met secretly. Usually at the golf course after he got off work. She would hike with him along the fairways, from shot to shot, from hole to hole, until it grew too dark for them to follow the flight of the ball. And then, on a soft bank beside the nearest putting green, they would undress and make love beneath the darkening sky, rolling naked and wild upon their dewy bed of grass.

For the four months that George Gershwin knew Theresa, even the white boys from the golf team could not upset him. In fact, he began to feel sorry for them with their white-scrubbed pimply faces and inferior talent. If his fortunes were on a secret rise, theirs were on the wane, and their outrageous—possibly racist—behavior was simply the final colorful sunset of The Great Question.

And then Theresa Brown told him she was pregnant.

George Gershwin Walker and Theresa Brown had both been virgins when they fell in love, but the first time they kissed it was clear to them that they would not remain virgins for long. Right and wrong, responsibility and irresponsibility, had little to do with it. It was a matter of soul and instinct taking precedence. A matter beyond the purview of reason or intellectual choice, beyond the constraints of age or maturity. And yet they were a responsible and rather mature young couple, and did take what they believed to be reasonable, even meticulous precautions. But, though the odds were heavily in their favor (at least according to the claims of their prophylactic manufacturer), they lost the gamble.

When Theresa Brown told George Gershwin of her pregnancy, he quickly denied the possibility.

"No way," he said. "I used a rubber every time. I spent half my paycheck on rubbers!"

"I just came from the doctor," Theresa Brown reminded him. "And he told me I *am* pregnant, and said if I come back in three weeks he will probably be able to hear the heartbeat."

"The heartbeat?" George Gershwin whispered, stunned. It somehow just didn't seem possible that he and Theresa, still juniors in high school, could by themselves have really been responsible for the creation of a heartbeat; didn't seem possible that they really had *that* kind of power. Hitting a golf ball 300 yards was one thing. But creating a heartbeat . . . "What are we gonna do?" he asked Theresa.

"I don't know." She shrugged. "Maybe an abortion."

"An abortion?"

"Listen," she said, annoyed at the shock in his voice. "I've seen what happens if you don't get an education. And I'm not going to end up like my mama. No way!"

"An abortion," George Gershwin repeated, cringing at the thought of some white doctor with his cold instruments scraping the awesome, tiny, black champion heartbeat into oblivion; cancelling that soft, sweet ticking for the sake of a diploma, a piece of paper. "Isn't there some other way?"

"You tell *me,*" Theresa suggested.

"I don't know," he said. "We could get help from our parents."

"Your parents don't even know who I am," she reminded him. "And even if they did agree to help, a baby would still change everything. All our plans. Your golf and my education."

"For a few years," George Gershwin said. "Then we could get back on track. Back to the plans. Golf and science."

"Maybe. And maybe not. What if we had another baby?"

"But we *wouldn't* have another baby."

"I'm sure you'd agree," Theresa Brown said, patting her belly, "that it's at least a possibility."

"Right," George Gershwin said, feeling suddenly young and foolish. "I suppose it could happen."

"Anyway, we've got to decide soon. Because the doctor says the sooner we decide, the easier it will be."

"The easier *what* will be?"

"The abortion," Theresa Brown said. "If that's what we decide."

They were still undecided the next afternoon when George Gershwin roared onto the driving range, enclosed in the cab of the old white tractor, to begin retrieving the scattered hundreds of red-striped balls.

It was distressingly clear to him that Theresa was leaning toward an abortion. The eternal silencing of that small pulse of life they had, together, created.

George Gershwin was sickened by the thought.

And yet he had to admit that the decision would ultimately have a much greater impact upon her than it would upon him. It was her schooling, not his golfing, that would be put on hold if they had the baby. And her womb, not his, from which the tiny beating heart would be scraped if they opted for an abortion. Logically, therefore, she should be the one to decide.

But what about him, then?

It was too difficult a decision, George Gershwin decided as he steered the tractor toward the 175-yard marker. Worse than difficult, in fact, it was unfair. They'd been so careful. And now, as a result of the joyful expression of their deep love, and in spite of all their care and caution, they'd been handed a multiple choice quiz with nothing but bad answers to choose from.

So intently was George Gershwin contemplating all this, that he scarcely noticed the arrival of the golf team. He was sweeping laterally across the range just beyond the 150-yard marker when a solidly hit ball caromed off the tractor's front axle and shot up through the bottom of the protective cage, ricochetting once before smashing into the side of his foot. Immediately, George Gershwin knew what had happened, and yet he was oddly disoriented by the scope and intensity of the pain. That is, although he knew he'd been hit by a golf ball, when he looked down he fully expected to see a sixteen-pound axe embedded in his foot. And the sight of his foot, still intact inside his black tennis shoe, simply did not jibe with the gruesome picture the pain had instantly painted in his mind. He howled, then looked up to see the boys on the golf team whooping and cheering, slapping hands to celebrate the direct hit.

The boys had no idea, of course, that George Gershwin had been hit. They believed, rather, that one of them had hit the tractor and scared a howl from the normally unflappable driver. In truth, an old man at the far end of the tee-off area had duck-hooked a three-wood shot into the tractor, but nobody—not the old man, not the boys from the golf team, and certainly not George Gershwin—was aware of this.

When George Gershwin saw the boys celebrating his agony—laughing over the great pain they had intentionally caused him—he finally believed he could seem them for what they were, and it was as though a lifetime's worth of uncertainty had been suddenly clarified, The Great Question finally answered unequivocally. Even the pregnancy, which he'd taken such scrupulous care to prevent, made sense, now. The Conspiracy extended to the heavens! *It was, ALL OF IT, because he was black.*

He turned the tractor toward the tee-off area, the pain in his foot so intensely excruciating that it seemed to him he could actually hear the throbbing over the roar of the tractor engine. With his good foot he pressed on the gas pedal until he could press no further. Never had George Gershwin needed to shift beyond second gear, but now he quickly shifted from second to third to fourth gear, grimacing as he worked the clutch and the tractor surged forward like a great white stallion going from a trot to a canter to a gallop. Within seconds he was beyond the 100-yard marker and closing in fast on his targets.

The boys on the golf team had little time to react. When they saw that the tractor seemed to be bearing down on them, they assumed George Gershwin must be bluffing; they'd given him a momentary and embarrassing scare, and now he was going to turn the tables. It wasn't until they could actually see his face—thirty yards away and closing fast—that they understood he was not bluffing.

Like chickens running from a dog, they scattered, two of them racing toward the far end of the tee-off area, and four of them stumbling toward the clubhouse.

With an implacable calm, George Gershwin turned toward the group of four, his machine gulping up the yards between them.

By the time the four boys reached the clubhouse he was right on their tails; and when they turned the corner sharply George Gershwin hit his brakes and tried to turn the corner with them. But instead of following the boys, the old white tractor followed the laws of gravity and motion, skidding sideways across the asphalt cart path, then halfway down the bank before tumbling into the canal.

When Pete Dugan, the Melaleuca Lakes head pro, heard the screeching of the tractor and the screams of the bystanders, he raced from behind the clubhouse counter, afraid that some drunk or maniac driver had plowed through the golf course parking lot and flattened some unlucky golfers. Before he could push through the front door, however, the four boys had pushed through from the other side and nearly knocked him over.

"Crazy fucking nigger," one of them said, bending over to catch his breath.

"Tried to kill us with the goddamned tractor," another one huffed.

Shoving his way past the four boys, Pete Dugan hustled through the front door. A small crowd had already gathered near the tractor, which was upside down, the caged-in cab almost submerged in the canal—the same canal Pete Dugan had fished George Gershwin from fifteen years earlier.

"He's stuck in there," a golfer screamed from beside the tractor. "And his head's underwater."

Pete Dugan raced down the bank, splashed into the waist-high murky water, and pulled hard at the cab door, which was bent out of shape and seemingly jammed and unopenable. All he could see of George Gershwin were his black tennis shoes and his ankles.

"Somebody call for help," he yelled, then ducked below the surface of the water and reached through the wire cage, feeling for George Gershwin's hand.

When he finally located the hand, floating limp, he pulled away, chilled, then exploded from the water to try the cab door again.

"God damn, give me some help, here," he finally gasped, punching at the wire cage in frustration.

Three of the boys from the golf team, plus five men and an elderly woman, hopped into the canal to try and help push the tractor over. But they didn't have the strength or leverage.

"Somebody get me a club," Pete Dugan shouted. "An iron."

A five iron was quickly passed to him and, until the rescue squad arrived several minutes later, he tried, in vain, to pry open the cab door.

In the end, all Pete Dugan could do was sit on the bank and watch, stunned and dripping, while the emergency crew cut away the wire cage, pulled George Gershwin from the water, and tried to bring him back to life.

When Theresa Brown had recovered from the initial shock of the news of George Gershwin's death, her thoughts turned quickly to the baby. It's all that's left of him, she thought, staring with wonder as she stroked her belly, tentatively, with the tips of her fingers, then caressed it with her hands, and finally hugged it with both arms as tightly as she could.

And seven months later the new life George Gershwin Walker had left behind was set carefully in an orange crate on Curtis and April's front porch.

Part Two

Top of the Line and Center Stage

♪

STILL DRESSED IN HIS WET SANTA SUIT AND BEGINNING TO SHIVER, now, in the air conditioned limousine as he rode back to the orange grove after his fruitless venture into town, Rhapsody, his beard in place, his shirt buttoned, and his pillows on the seat beside him, decided he had regrettably but obviously been badly mistaken. His brief vision of the Holy In and Out, his fabulous glimpse of *the real rhapsody,* had been nothing more than a thirsty man's mirage, a touch of post-accident trauma. It seemed he was destined, after all, to remain a superstar instead of becoming a musician; to make music that thrilled instead of music that filled. He would soon leave the grove to sniff exhaust rather than orange blossoms, admire the city lights rather than the stars, ride limousines instead of horses, and screw strange women instead of loving a familiar one. And if the emptiness at the pit of his stomach continued to persist, at least it would never again take him by surprise.

Slumped low in the back seat, Rhapsody was feeling somewhat content with his mature and courageous acceptance of his unhappy destiny when, not two miles from the grove, the driver, a stocky, balding white man, said, "Jesus Christ!" and abruptly hunched forward to turn up the radio.

A newscaster was reporting that unidentified sources in both the Administration and the Pentagon had confirmed that the United States armed forces were on a high level state of alert; our bombers were airborne, our land- and submarine-based missiles ready to be fired on command. The president remained unavailable for comment, and the White House press secretary would neither confirm nor deny the reports, but advised that the American people stay tuned to their televisions and radios.

Jesus, Rhapsody thought, feeling suddenly small and vulnerable, his eyes shifting to the sky. *No way. Un-unh. No fucking way, Jack. Not this. Not now.*

As the broadcast switched to the Pentagon for an on-the-scene report, horns began to blast, the traffic whipping into a frenzy, cars roaring past on the left and right, some drivers even climbing the sidewalks with two wheels and ignoring the red lights at the intersections, faces everywhere gone grim behind windows.

"Sorry Bud," the driver said, lurching to the right without warning, then fishtailing to a stop on the roadside shoulder. "I got a wife at home, kids at school."

"Man, it's just up the road," Rhapsody pleaded. "Maybe half a mile. Listen . . ." he pulled his beard down until it collared his neck. "I'm Rhapsody Walker. You get me home and I'll pay you plenty."

"Nothing personal," said the driver. "But if you're not outta here in three seconds then you're coming with me."

Quickly unbuckling his seat belt, Rhapsody glanced through the rear window to make sure he wouldn't be stepping into the path of any fear-frenzied drivers, then pushed open his door and, leaving behind his pillows, stepped into the sunshine.

To avoid the dangerous roadside, he cut through a gas station, a deserted fast food parking lot, and the quickly emptying parking lot of a mini-shopping center, shedding his shirt, hat, and beard as he ran, undisguised now, his world-famous visage mattering little. By the time he made it across the construction site adjacent to the orange grove, and scrambled over the concrete wall, his boots had become impossibly heavy. So he kicked them from his feet and jogged, barefoot, down a pathway between two long rows of blossoming orange trees, screaming for his grandfather—"Grampaaa!"—and huffing miserably, his eyes constantly shifting between the ground and the sky.

He kept thinking, as he ran and shouted, that he could sense a change in air pressure—the peculiar stillness and silence that would come, he could imagine, the moment before the sky lit up. *Any second, Jack. Maybe before my next breath. In and Out and . . .*

When he heard Curtis calling for him, now, he began to whimper as he stumbled forward, his new and only goal in life to avoid being alone at the unthinkable moment of the blast—the Final Crash Landing of the entire planet. He almost collided with Curtis's horse when it leaped from the trees. But in seconds Curtis was on the ground and looking him over to make sure he wasn't hurt.

"It's okay, boy," Curtis said, his hands at Rhapsody's shoulders. "Tell me what's wrong, now."

"Shit," Rhapsody gasped for breath. "Don't you hear the fucking horns?" His words came out in desperate blasts, only on the exhale. "It's on the radio. They getting ready to blow up the fucking planet."

"What you talking about? Who's getting ready?"

"Them," Rhapsody said, his eyes once again darting skyward. "Us. Who the fuck knows."

Curtis

"The White Machine," I whisper to him. "Top of the line and center stage." I been expecting this for almost fifty years—half a century—but it don't matter; there ain't no way you can be ready for how it comes so sudden. How one second everything is solid and familiar, same as ever, and the next second you understand it's almost all gone, like you about to wake up from a sweet sweet dream you can't ever go back to.

And the only thing I want, now, is to get to her fast. All we ever been through together is racing round and round in my head. But what finally does it is when I picture her teeth—that lovely *lovely* sweet gap I have felt a million times with my tongue and admired every day with my eyes. I kick old Dizzy hard, and when she bolts ahead I feel Rhapsody come close to slipping off behind me. And I'm glad he keeps a hold because it would be a hard thing for me to stop or even slow down, now.

Because I just got to see that gap one more time and got to hold her close and feel her head, her soft cheek, moving against mine the way it always does, so familiar, and make sure she knows how when it comes right down to it, she is the only thing that matters to me, the only part of the dream I don't ever want to wake from.

Before the horse is completely stopped, we both on the ground, then racing up the steps, and there she is, come to greet us at the door, and smiling so that for a few sweet seconds I can see the gap, so perfect I want to freeze it forever, before The Evil can get to it. But by the time we reach her she can tell by looking at us something is wrong, and the gap disappears behind her lips. Maybe for the last time.

April

When they tell me what's happening I don't want to believe it because Curtis is wrapped around me so dark and warm, so solid and alive, that I am, for a moment, absolutely certain this must all be a terrible mistake, a wild rumor gone out of control.

But after a minute he is still hanging on tightly—pressing even closer, like he wants to blend right into me—and I know I *have* to believe it, and am all at once too terrified to do anything but shut my eyes and hide deep in his arms. And when I open my eyes back up and peek past Curtis's ear to see Rhapsody hunched over and switching on the TV, he is already so skinny in those droopy red pants, and his face is already so deathly, that it doesn't take much for me to imagine him down on his bony knees, screaming, those dark eyes, once so lively, melting down his cheeks, the radiation eating right through him.

When Curtis finally pulls back from me, the three of us sit, huddled together on the couch, and listen to the TV, which Rhapsody has turned up nearly full volume so we don't miss a word.

The first thing that's clear is nobody really knows what's going to happen. You get the feeling that there are fingers poised over buttons, all right, but they haven't been pushed yet, and if we're lucky we still might be spared.

Of course, even watching the television and knowing we aren't alone in this, it is still hard for me to think beyond the three of us—beyond this tiny, familiar circle of warmth and life. And when I do think beyond us, it isn't other people that I think of, huddled together as we are, but of the great Douglas fir trees in Oregon—which I might never get to see, now—standing silently in place by the forestful, stretching to the sky, not even running or hiding or screaming their outrage to the heavens, *just standing in place and taking it,* dying in innocence for our sins, their limbs and branches flaming through the night like a million blazing crucifixes.

Curtis

We don't even think about going downstairs to the old bomb shelter . . . which shows how far we've come in thirty years. If the bombs are gonna drop, we don't anymore want to be *the last* to die, we want to be *the first* to die.

Rhapsody

We sit together for the next two hours and, man, none of us can get out more than a few words. I keep trying to follow what the TV people are talking about, but the only thing I can think is it's all too fucking crazy to be real. How the fuck did we get here, Jack? I can't even remember why we're supposed to hate the Russians, and can't imagine there's anybody, right now, crazy enough to think it was in any way worth it. Man, because what in all the world could possibly be worth *this?* Ain't *nothing* worth it unless you completely mad. Stark raving, motherfucking, head-up-your-ass mad.

Even so, I keep trying to listen, but it's impossible to follow what anyone is saying: Persian Gulf, the flow of oil, strategic interests, national security. It just doesn't matter or add up. Not to this! And then it hits me that my life was saved exactly one week ago; it's a fluke I'm even alive now.

"God *damn,*" I whisper, and April squeezes my hand and looks me sadly in the eye, and there is so much beauty, so much life, in that sadness that I feel a rush of love for her like I've never felt for anyone or anything. Here it is, the end of the world, and for the first time in my life I feel real love. And, man, it's crazy, I know, but I can't help it: I break into a smile that I can feel spreading right across my face—ear to ear, Jack—stretching to its limit and beyond. A smile! And, just as crazy, she is right there with me, smiling back, a smile just as big as mine. And when we hug I feel so much love, a flood of it—a flood of love for Everything, but all of it coming through her—that it almost hurts. But we keep right on hugging, squeezing tighter, flesh to flesh and cheek to cheek, until, craziest of all, I suddenly notice I got myself the first small stirrings of a hard-on. And, man, it doesn't even bother me, not for a second, because it feels like the most natural thing in the world. Because it's not a hard-on for April, my grandma, sixty-seven years old, or not *just* for her, but a hard-on for Everything. A hard-on for her and for Curtis; for the waitress with the sexy neck and for her shy little boy who kept hiding his face and wouldn't talk except to say "Mee-maw"; for the blossoms and oranges; for music and dancing; for rainbows and superstars; for everything I've ever seen, heard, smelled, tasted, or touched, pretty or ugly, good or bad; for the whole Thread of Miracles, Jack—In and Out, End to End—from the stars to the soil. A hard-on for *all* of it.

I don't even notice when or how the flood of love starts to recede, but it does, and quick, and by the time I pull away from her it's almost like it never happened. None of it. Just a tilting of mirrors and sleight of hand, same as any other magic: in and out, on and off, here and gone. And we're right back where we started: staring at the television and scared shitless.

After two hours of reporting and speculation, it was, at last, confirmed that the crisis had, indeed, been real—the armed forces *had* been placed on a high-level state of alert—but was now over.

The scenario had apparently gone something like this: In the midst of months of heightening tensions in the Middle East and increasingly hostile communications between Washington and Moscow, a major Soviet computer malfunction (due, it was later reported, to the failure of a fifty-seven-cent micro-chip) had resulted in a Soviet state of alert. The immediate U.S. alert in response to the unprovoked Soviet alert had been taken by the Soviets as incontrovertible evidence of the correctness of their computer warning, thus triggering an escalating Soviet response, which in turn triggered an escalating U.S. response, the escalating responses continuing, tit for tat, until both countries were on full-scale alert, each poised, ready and willing to annihilate the entire planet in order to defend its national interest.

The newscasters, of course, did not bother to speculate upon the meaning of all this; they spoke, instead, of the recent timely advances in communications technology, and the apparent unblinking coolness of the president, who, under the greatest pressure imaginable, was reportedly able to resolve the crisis without backing down or displaying even a moment of weakness or lack of will.

But none of this analysis mattered to Rhapsody, who, while his grandparents continued clinging to one another on the couch, was already on his feet, dancing off the energy of his accumulated terror. "Details," he said to the newscaster, then turned his back to the TV, happily jiving and boogeying his way across the living room and through the front screen door, his red pants still drooping, but his superstar feet flying.

After the screen door slammed shut, Curtis continued to cling to April, not even wanting to open his eyes. "I don't want to let you go," he finally whispered, his biceps beginning to ache and tremble from the embrace. "Never again. Because The Machine still out there." He opened his eyes and nodded toward the TV. "And it ain't a goddamn thing been changed."

"I love you," April said, brushing her lips across his collarbone, then burying her nose in his neck, "Let's go to Oregon and live beneath the fir trees."

Closing his eyes again, Curtis smiled like a ten-year-old, then hissed, "Let's get."

♪♪♪

The heat had never felt so good to Rhapsody. Stretching his arms, he turned his face directly to the sun, to its great throb of life, and romped his way past the horse, the chickens, and the cow—"Yo!" he greeted them. "My main animals."—then through April's lushly blooming raised-bed garden, and, reveling in every sweet breath, out into the grove. There, in the shade of the orange trees, he rubbed his face in the leaves and blossoms, ignoring the bees, then dropped to the ground to hug and hump the earth.

In and Out, he thought, the warmth from the soil radiating up through him. *The real rhapsody* is back, Jack. And this time I know it's no mirage.

Too excited to continue celebrating alone, he skipped his way back to the house and up the porch steps. Never had he felt lighter on his feet. Never had he felt freer or happier. He was even amused by the thought that all it took to snap him from his depression—to cheer him up and pop his eyes back open to the Thread of Miracles—was a simple threat of planetary annihilation. *Who needs pills?* He laughed out loud—"Ha!"—feeling giddily absurd. *Who needs therapy? Man, just show me the fucking apocalypse, and I'm ready to sing and dance.*

Inside, still too charged up to sit or stand still, Rhapsody bounced on his toes behind April and Curtis, who remained snuggled on the couch, their heads tilted together as they listened to an interview with an eloquent young spokesman from the State Department.

The spokesman, well dressed, bright, and upbeat, was denying that the day's crisis would have any significant bearing on the future of U.S. arms control policy.

"So what you're telling us, then," the newscaster said, "is that mutually assured destruction is not just a strategy or policy that is subject to debate, but a fact of life that we are, for better or worse, stuck with."

"Precisely," the spokesman congratulated him. "We quite simply have no other choice. Particularly now that the space-defense theories have been thoroughly discredited."

"Well, allow me, for a moment, to play devil's advocate with you," the interviewer said. "All right. So we made it safely through today's crisis. And we've made it safely through nearly half a nuclear century. But what happens if just one time—tomorrow, or next year, or even next century, let's say—the fact of mutually assured destruction does *not* keep the buttons from being pushed?"

The young man from the State Department answered without hesitating. "Let me just explain that we consider such a question to be inequationable."

"Inequationable?" Rhapsody said out loud, squeezing the back of the couch.

"That is to say," the spokesman went on, "we believe our greatest responsibility and most serious challenge is to maintain a foolproof system of checks and balances that will keep such a question from ever having to be factored into America's arms control equation."

"What the fuck did the man just say?" Rhapsody cried. "*Inequationable?*"

"He said The White Machine got the world in its teeth," Curtis explained, his head remaining warmly nestled against April's. "And that it ain't about to let go. Not now, and not ever."

"Right," Rhapsody said, then headed for the front door, leaving Curtis and April to snuggle and watch the rest of the interview.

Rhapsody

Inequationable? Shit. Only thing inequationable is that The End might have come today. The In and The Out permanently disconnected. And I'm not just talking about a blow to one fool's throat, but a blow to *every* throat. Extinction, Jack. The Thread of Miracles snapped clean at every point, and snapped for all time. Snapped for eternity. White Magic. Abracadabra. Blam! Poof! All gone. All of it!

Man, and the only thing inequationable is that it *still* could happen any time. Any second. The very next tick of the clock. *Even now*, while I'm hustling past these orange trees, sucking the sweetness from the blossoms, In and Out, and nothing but sweetness and magic, and more sweetness and magic, and In and Out and In and...Boom! Blam! There it is. *The last breath for all time* for every man, woman, child, and baby, *born or yet to be born,* our entire history and future burning up and floating away in a final fucking wisp of White Smoke. GONE FOREVER, Jack. And *that's* the only thing inequationable.

Man, and if The End really comes, then all my ancestors were born for nothing. Sweated, suffered, struggled, and slaved for nothing. Sang and cried for nothing. And the civil rights struggle was for nothing. The freedom rides and protests, the boycotts and speeches, were for nothing. The fucking abolition might just as well never have happened. Because if the plane crashes at The End, then it don't matter *what* went on during the flight. And so the only thing to do is to keep it from crashing; and the only questions are *Who* and *How.*

Curtis

When he comes dancing up the porch steps he's still too excited to sit. And the way his eyes gleaming you'd think the world just begun instead of almost ended. He pulls the rocking chair around so that when he sits he's gonna be facing us in our swing. And when he finally does sit it's right at the edge of the rocker so that it tilts forward and he tilts with it.

"Listen," he says. "I've got to leave right away. I've got to get back to L.A. and start writing and recording. Start another tour. Because if anyone can spread the word, it's me."

"Spread the word?" April says.

"Abolition," he says. "The *new* abolition. And *this* time around it ought to be easier to do the abolishing. Because *this* time around we're *all* the slaves."

"What you talking about?" I ask him.

And he explains it to us. "What I'm talking about is the banning of the bombs. The dis-as-sembling of The Machine. I'm gonna attack it with my music. Attack it with every bit of power I've got. Because who else is gonna have a *better* chance? Who else is gonna have a bigger stage or a louder microphone? Who else is gonna have crowds hungry to listen all over the world, and TV and newspapers to follow every step of the way?"

"Goddamn, boy," I tell him. "You make it sound like all you got to do is open your mouth and tap your toes, and The Machine just gonna roll over and die a peaceful death. You ought to know better than that."

"You're right," he admits. "It *won't* be easy. And that's why I need *you* to help me."

"Say what?"

"I need three saxophones," he says. "We're gonna get a new soprano man, and Willie Veal is still gonna be playing the alto. Which leaves *you* to play the tenor."

It makes no sense. I been waiting for him to ask me for three years, but now when he does, all I feel is mean and ugly. "Thank you, but no thank you," I tell him. "It's a very generous offer. And I do appreciate the thought. But I got business to tend to." I pull April closer to me, and she tilts her head way back to kiss my chin. "We planning to move to Oregon and live beneath the fir trees."

"Not if the bombs start dropping you won't be living beneath the fir trees," he says, making it sound like if it happen it will be *my* fault. "And anyway, if you move to Oregon, how are you gonna afford to keep the grove?"

"We won't," I tell him.

"But you'd like to," he says with a smile. "And you can! All you've got to do is come to L.A. to record with me—just play the first concert with us; see how you like it—and I'll pay you enough so you can keep the grove forever. Maybe rent it to some friends. Or, if you want, just let it sit here so the developers can drool and shake their heads. And in the meantime I'll be paying you enough so you can buy all the land you want. In Oregon or anywhere else."

"A U-pick orchard?" April asks, backing away and sitting straight up to look from me to Rhapsody while she squeezes my hand. "With a house tucked back in a grove of Douglas firs?"

"Anything," he assures her. "I'll advance you the money today if you say so."

"Goddamn, boy." I reach out to shake his hand while April hugs us both. "You just bought yourself a tenor." Of course, he's a fool if he really believes he's gonna stop The Machine, or even slow it down. But I can't be calling him a lemming no more, and that's a fact.

April Showers

♪

The articulate young spokesman for the State Department had been exactly right. The initial, expected outcry for disarmament was in the spotlight for a number of weeks. But the uproar soon began to wane. The media found other crises and disasters to focus upon. Beneath almost everyone's feet, the ground regained its solidity, and it was back to business as usual.

But not for Rhapsody, or for Curtis and April.

While Rhapsody was busy in L.A. composing and refining his new songs—songs for The Rainbow, he hoped (remembering that first mind-popping glimpse, from his Seattle hospital window, of *the real rhapsody*); weapons for the new abolition—Curtis and April were overseeing the harvesting of their final orange crop, then driving across the country and up through California into Western Oregon to search for the perfect U-pick grove. They found it in late January, just north of Chintimini in the lush Willamette Valley: eighteen acres bordered by a state forest that could not be developed, and a two-lane highway which led north into Portland and south into Chintimini and Eugene. Thus, although their property was nearly surrounded by forested hills, it was nevertheless conveniently accessible to large numbers of motorists, a circumstance which had enabled the former owners to build up and maintain a modest U-pick business.

There were, on the property, three acres of blueberries, three acres of peach trees, an acre of raspberries, and another acre that was used for a spring crop of snow peas and a fall crop of pumpkins. The rest of the land was mostly in pasture and Douglas fir trees, with several stands of white oak and black walnut, and a few clearings for annual vegetable crops. And though their shake-sided cabin was barely half the size of their old Florida house, it was perfectly adequate for their simple needs and cozy enough to be easily heated by wood.

The only drawback to living in the Willamette Valley was the rain, which Curtis and April soon discovered was nothing like the Florida downpours they were accustomed to: the great tropical bursts—inches of it by the hour—with massive drops that could soak you in seconds if you were caught in it without an umbrella. In Oregon the rain seemed to be a cross between a mist and a drizzle; it floated and hung for days and weeks on end, slowly saturating and penetrating everything it came in contact with. Curtis and April found that most days they could work in the rain, umbrellaless, for a good thirty minutes before they even felt wet. Though by the time they did feel wet they were often chilled to the bone.

"Maybe if we was younger," Curtis told April, while he was in bed and shivering with the flu just three weeks after they'd moved. "It might have been easier to leave the sunshine."

But, though he missed the Florida climate, Curtis endured his flu and sniffles and his cold toes and fingers with a minimum of complaining, and looked forward to the Oregon spring and summer, which he'd heard were glorious, and to their first crops of peas and blueberries, raspberries and peaches.

April, unlike Curtis, was actually delighted with the climate, which brought back happy memories of the Virginia winters of her youth. Living in South Florida for half a century, she'd forgotten how much she missed the smell of burning wood on a cold night and the feeling that the planet was steadily, almost palpably, on the move, tilting its way through the seasons and years, around and around the sun, circle after circle after circle . . . In fact, except for a persistent queasy feeling low down in her stomach—a vague yet deep discomfort which, for several months now, she'd been expecting to disappear any day—April was in every way thrilled with her new life in Oregon. Every day, no matter how chilling the rain, she slogged her way through the mud to the tallest Douglas fir tree on their property, not quite a quarter mile from the cabin, and, standing at its base, her fingers resting gently upon its damp bark, stared slowly up at the trunk, taking it in inch by inch, all the way to the top, an exercise that took her as long as a minute and a half and left her ecstatic with wonder, marveling that anything alive could grow so impossibly tall; could, starting as a tiny seed in the ground, shoot its way higher and higher—100 feet, 150 feet, 200 feet, and higher still—pushing into the sky as if it might grow forever, oblivious to any laws or limits.

And both she and Curtis were delighted to learn that there were others in Oregon who shared their reverence for the great fir trees. With keen interest, they followed the occasional newspaper stories about the Oregon Arborillas, a radical environmental organization whose members engaged in various activities which delayed, obstructed, and, in some cases, actually prevented the logging of old-growth fir and spruce trees. Their most celebrated and familiar tactic was the climbing of old-growth trees that were about to be logged. By skillfully and courageously hauling themselves high up into the great trees (each of which had been alive long before the first white axeman set foot on the continent), then ingeniously rigging up small wooden platforms upon which they could camp for days, the Arborillas not only delayed the cutting of the trees, but provided a fine media spectacle and drew attention to their cause.

But also attributed to the Arborillas were a number of extralegal and illegal activities—known, collectively, as "ecotage"—the most common of which were the removal or rearranging of survey stakes, the spiking of trees, and the sabotage of logging equipment. And although no evidence had ever been found linking such actions to the Arborillas, the organization's spokespeople refused to condemn or discourage the practice of ecotage so long as trees were without standing in a court of law.

"You know, I think I'd like to join up with those Arborillas," April admitted to Curtis. "I wonder if they could get an old lady up to the top of a fir tree?"

"I don't know about no tree climbing," said Curtis, who still vividly remembered his jaunt up the banyan tree when Rhapsody was a rebellious ten-year-old. "But I wouldn't mind to try a little bit of that *ecotage*. Take on The Machine, head to head. Get in my licks while I've still got the strength."

On the handful of spectacular days when the gray vanished from the sky and the winter sunlight came slanting through the trees, bathing everything in a dreamy soft Rembrandt gold, April and Curtis hiked into the forest bordering their land, and climbed a trail to the clearing at the top of Chintimini Hill, where, when they looked to the east, they could gaze upon the snow-covered Cascades jutting high above the horizon, as awesome and breathtaking a sight as they'd ever seen.

"Goddamn," Curtis whispered to April the first time they saw the majestic peaks of white. "Not even The Machine gonna hurt those mountains."

In early March, Curtis and April had a chance to escape the gray skies and drizzle when they traveled to Los Angeles for Curtis's first rehearsal and recording sessions with Rhapsody. But, despite the abundant warmth and sunshine, Curtis found L.A. to be everything he'd dreaded, only worse. Hurtling down the freeway and staring out the tinted limousine window on his way from the airport to his grandson's home, all Curtis could do was cling tightly to April's hand and shake his head, thinking that The White Machine had already consumed all there was of this city to consume. Everything was asphalt and steel, sprawl and waste. What was left of the Earth was mere token (and Curtis knew tokenism when he saw it): a pittance of endangered soil and greenery. He shuddered to think that he might well be looking at the future here. The concretization and plasticization of the country. The Whitening of the entire planet. If so, then he had to believe that a nuclear holocaust might, indeed, come as the ultimate ironic blessing. The White Machine mercifully stopping Itself when nothing else could.

Once they'd arrived at Rhapsody's estate—the limousine creeping past the crowds of fans standing vigil, as always, at the gate—Curtis refused to venture from the grounds. The state-of-the-art recording studio was right there, in the basement, and when he and the band weren't busy working on the album, he spent his time wandering about the enormous walled-in property with Rhapsody and April, soaking up the fabulous sunshine, inspecting the orange and grapefruit trees, and the tropical shrubs and flowers, and occasionally kneeling with April to pull some weeds or hand-prune some flowers or plants. (Even the soil felt insubstantial to him, as if a good wind might blow it all away, uncovering yet another stretch of hot white freeway.)

Of course, Curtis found the mansion itself—all fourteen thousand air-conditioned square feet of it—to be appallingly obscene, and told Rhapsody so.

"Don't worry," Rhapsody assured him. "I've got plans. I don't need this shit anymore, so I'm gonna sell it after the tour."

"You might *have* to sell it after they hear your new songs," Curtis warned him.

In fact, Curtis was delighted with Rhapsody's most recent compositions. The tunes were catchy as ever and the rhythms, for the most part, as terrifically danceable. But the lyrics were no longer just clever; they were angry and disturbing: the sort of lyrics, Curtis feared, that might instantly alienate a large percentage of Rhapsody's fans, as well as the—up to now—fawning media. And Curtis had no doubts that the media could destroy his grandson's superstardom as quickly as they had created it.

But Rhapsody wasn't the only one Curtis worried about during his L.A. visit. He worried, too, about April, who, for the past few weeks, had seemed to him to be slightly out of sorts, often tired and dragging, and ready to fall asleep before Curtis had even begun his evening saxophone sessions. And not only was she slinking off to bed much earlier, she was sleeping much later.

He'd hoped the L.A. sunshine might revive her; but now, in addition to her lack of energy, he noticed that she didn't have her usual good appetite and spent much of every mealtime just picking at the food, rearranging it on her plate, and, here and there, taking a nibble.

"You're looking too thin and weak," he finally scolded her. "You got to start eating better; got to get your protein."

"Oh no," April assured him. "When a woman gets to be my age it doesn't take much for her to put on weight. Just look at my stomach." She stretched her dress tight, from hip to hip, so that Curtis could see for himself. "See there? Pooching out worse than ever. At this rate it won't be long before I catch up to you."

But her flippant denial merely alarmed Curtis. He was certain, after all, that whatever she said about her pooching belly, she was eating less and less, and sleeping more and more. Troubling trends, each made all the more troubling by the fact of the other. And so he suggested that when they returned to Oregon she think about seeing a doctor.

But, like Curtis, April hadn't seen a doctor in years, not only because she'd stayed in perfect health, but because she believed the only thing doctors were interested in was prescribing medicines that might effectively annihilate the bad germs, but at the cost of annihilating the good germs along with them. A body, she'd long ago concluded, was just like a garden. If over the years you kept a garden healthy—feeding, maintaining, and strengthening it with natural nutrients—it would take care of itself. No need for pesticides (the garden equivalent of medicines) which created as many problems as they solved.

In any case, she wasn't yet worried enough to see a doctor. And Curtis, suspicious as he was inclined to feel toward modern medicine (which he thought of as just another cog in The White Machine) wasn't yet ready to press his point.

Meanwhile, he stayed busy helping Rhapsody perfect his arrangements. Every song on the new album was recorded and rerecorded, mixed and remixed, mastered and remastered dozens of times, until Rhapsody was satisfied that a single change in any of the tracks—the addition or subtraction of an instrument, the shifting of a harmony, or the displacing of a single lyric—would only diminish the overall quality of the production.

"He's a perfectionist!" Curtis proudly told April after they'd returned to Oregon. "I never would have thought it. The same little boy who couldn't stand to practice his scales."

Already there was much speculation in the press about Rhapsody's long seclusion following his near-tragic accident, and about the possible changes in his voice and personality. Some asserted that he now sang with a rasp or a whisper, and that he was no longer as feisty or irreverent as "the old Rhapsody" had been. There were even stories suggesting that he'd been "born again," or that he had spent the past months worshipping in a Tibetan monastery.

And his soon-to-be-released album, *Rainbow Rhapsody,* was the subject of rancorous rumor and debate in myriad newspaper and magazine articles. (Which was, of course, precisely what Rhapsody wanted: the more mystery and intrigue, the better.) The Seattle papers, in particular, devoted many columns to Rhapsody's new album and tour, for it had been announced that the Seattle concert would be a "free for all"—a make amends concert for Rhapsody's earlier aborted visit—and would be held outdoors, in Puget Park, where it could be attended, free of charge, by anyone who cared to battle the anticipated record crowds. One of the major networks had even purchased the rights to live coverage of the event after Rhapsody agreed contractually—it was widely reported—to refrain from using a number of specified obscenities that might offend the Saturday afternoon TV audience—an agreement which, quite naturally, fueled the rumors that the accident had "mellowed" the superstar's once fiery personality.

It was Rhapsody's strategy to keep his fans in the dark; to keep their curiosity waxing steadily as the concert date drew nearer. The less certain they were about what to expect of him, the more attentively they would watch and listen to the first few songs. And so he planned to win them over right away. First soften them up with the old songs and humor. Get them dancing with a good beat. Lull them into a false sense of familiarity. And then, when he was certain that he had them in his palm, he would jerk the ground from under their feet, and the sky from over their heads. "A fucking ambush," he told Russell Kirkland.

Kirkland had seen enough of Rhapsody in action to feel confident that, no matter how controversial his message might be, when the music stopped, the throngs of fans would be on their feet, applauding wildly, screaming and begging for more. Beyond that, he and the other musicians were beginning to believe that they were about to embark upon a vital, possibly even historic, mission. A mission which, with all of Rhapsody's charisma and influence, they might actually succeed at. A mission to save the planet.

♪♪♪

Back in Oregon, the month of April was mired in a relentless, round-the-clock-drizzle. It was hard for Curtis and April to believe that there was really any sunshine or blue beyond the gray, which seemed to have spread itself evenly and thoroughly from the ground to the heavens, so that the sky appeared to be, at once, nowhere and everywhere.

Curtis and April's cabin was surrounded by a landscape of miniature lakes and slippery mud, dripping trees and rotting tulips and daffodils. Wet as everything was, and sick as April had come to feel, she stayed inside, huddling under wool blankets and trying to keep warm and rested. But, no matter how many hours she rested and slept, she could not shake her exhaustion. Worse, she had developed a nagging cough. And for the first time in her life she was horribly constipated, and spent more and more time straining in the bathroom with distressingly insignificant results.

She finally agreed to try a laxative—which, when it did nothing to help, only confirmed her suspicions that medicines were not the answer—but still refused to see a doctor, not only because medical intervention ran contrary to her theory of health, but because she was secretly terrified, now, of what a doctor might find.

At night Curtis spooned up close to her, trying to recharge her with his warmth and strength.

"Ooh," she whispered, snuggling back. "You sure feel good."

But she was always too tired, now, to make love. And, to Curtis, her body felt only faintly occupied, and insubstantial: as if he could crush the life from it with one hard squeeze.

As the date for the final two weeks of concert rehearsals in L.A. drew nearer, Curtis felt a deepening ambivalence, an almost schizophrenic confusion, about April's deteriorating condition. On the one hand, he could not shake his profound distrust of doctors and all their medicines and technology, or, as he saw it, their White Poisons and White Machines. On the other hand, it was clear, now, that April was truly suffering. She'd been miserable for weeks and showed no signs of improvement.

And yet, every time Curtis reluctantly suggested that she make an appointment to see a doctor, she swore she was feeling better. "Give me a few more weeks," she insisted. "The illness has got to work its way out. That's all."

Three weeks before the Seattle concert, Curtis called Rhapsody to inform him of April's illness, and to let him know that he would be unable to fly to L.A. for the final rehearsals, or to otherwise prepare himself for the show. "It look like I'm gonna have to watch this one on the TV," he told his grandson.

"Damn," Rhapsody said. "This one is the *big* one. We need you!"

"I know," Curtis said. "I'm sorry."

"Well, what's wrong with her?" Rhapsody demanded. He could hear April coughing in the background. "What does the doctor say?"

"I just made her an appointment," Curtis lied.

"Just made her an appointment? She's so sick you're gonna be missing this concert—the big one—and you just now made her an appointment?"

"I'll call you," Curtis promised. "Just as soon as she starts to feeling better."

That night, as he snuggled up close to April in bed, Curtis said, "If you won't call the doctor, I'm gonna call him for you."

"Okay," April agreed. "One more week. And if I'm not better I promise I'll make an appointment."

It was a week and a half later, four days before Mother's Day and three days before the Seattle concert, that Curtis heard April moaning loudly in the bathroom and rushed in to find her slumped on the toilet, her face in her hands.

"Get me to the hospital," she sobbed without looking up, her fingers still covering her eyes. "I'm afraid I'm going to die."

The Rainbow Concert

♪

SEATTLE WAS READY FOR RHAPSODY WALKER, AND THIS TIME HE WAS ready for Seattle. Over half a million people were expected to attend the concert, and it was predicted that over 100 million people worldwide (one out of every fifty-five people on the planet) would be watching the live broadcast. A week ahead of time Rhapsody's fans had begun staking out campsites in front of the stage. And the day before the show the park was already half full, and crawling with newspaper, magazine, and TV reporters.

Early Saturday morning, traffic along Interstate 5 came to a standstill, and thousands of motorists, many of whom hadn't even planned on attending the concert, simply parked their cars on the freeway shoulder and joined the mass trek to Puget Park.

It was a fine, cloudless spring day in Seattle, the Northwest air crisp and dry and sweet-smelling. Throughout the city, particularly in Puget Park, the rhododendrons and azaleas were in full bloom, and with every mild gust of wind there came a shower of cherry tree blossoms, the pink petals floating and swirling through the air as delicate as butterfly wings. And, of course, the crowd itself (with half the people dressed Rhapsody-style: wild-colored t-shirts beneath buttoned down overshirts) was as spectacularly colorful as the springtime blooms and blossoms. As colorful as a great, kaleidoscopic rainbow.

Just before two-thirty the audience rises en masse as Rhapsody's band takes the stage to a thunderous and sustained roaring, and a sea of waving hands. Huge as the crowd is, everyone feels as though he has a ringside seat, for powerful speakers and giant video monitors have been placed at regular intervals throughout the park so that nobody, no matter how far from the stage, will miss a single word or gesture.

After a quick wave of acknowledgment, Sanchez on drums and Kirkland on bass thump out an upscale beat and are joined by Shadow Jackson on electric guitar, Mookie Perry on congas, Billy Davis on keyboards, Willie Veal on alto sax, and Hoop Granger (the former sax man for Hermanos) on soprano.

From the opening drumbeat heads are bobbing, shoulders dipping, and legs pumping. As the volume steadily increases, the level of excitement rises in direct proportion, exploding, at last, into screams when a small, specially trained, chestnut mare leaps onto the stage carrying the superstar on her bare back. Rhapsody slips expertly from the horse's back—a move he's repeated a thousand times on the orange grove—and hits the stage dancing. He is dressed to the hilt in a black and turquoise western shirt with silver sequins glittering across his shoulders and chest. From his black ten-gallon hat to his turquoise and diamond boots, he is pure caricature. A Madison Avenue country-western fop.

While the horse is led from the stage, and Rhapsody grabs his microphone from its stand, the roaring of the crowd reaches its peak; it can grow no louder. He prances across the stage, lifting those turquoise boots high, waving to his frenzied fans (more of them by far—three-quarters of a million—than have ever assembled in one place) and winking at the TV cameras.

Then, with a backward slip and slide, and a half-pirouette, he faces

Sanchez and Kirkland and swings up his arms; the music halts, in mid-note it seems, and the musicians scramble into action. And by the time Rhapsody brings down his arms the band has not only changed the beat, but their instruments and their entire demeanor. Kirkland has traded his electric bass for a stand-up, Shadow Jackson has switched his electric guitar for a pedal steel, Willie Veal has brought out a harmonica, Billy Davis has moved from his synthesizer to the piano, and Mookie Perry and Hoop Granger are strumming acoustic guitars. And they are all grinning, nodding, and playing in an easy, blithely mindless three-four tempo.

Rhapsody turns to stick his microphone back in its stand and hitch up his pants. Then he whips out a can of Red Man chewing tobacco, and, after holding it up for all to see, pops off the top, scoops out a plug, and wedges it between his cheek and teeth. "How y'all doing?" he drawls into the microphone, his first public words since the accident.

The crowd responds to the white country accent with yowls of delight, the volume of their collective scream no louder, just higher-pitched.

"That's good," he says. " 'Cause I got some tunes I'd like to play for y'all."

While hands are clapping above heads—for everyone knows what the first song will be—Willie Veal, harmonica in mouth, swaggers up in a bow-legged cowboy parody to hand Rhapsody an acoustic guitar.

"Now, if it's all right with y'all, here's what I'd like to do," Rhapsody says, taking the guitar and strapping it over his shoulder. "I'd like to dedicate these first two tunes to Dr. Brock, a good old boy and gen-u-ine country and western fan who saved my life and helped to patch up my throat, and who, honest to gosh, lives right here in your fair city."

While the crowd cheers for Brock, and the band continues to play in the background, Rhapsody turns his head to spit a stream of tobacco juice, and Kirkland hops back just in time. " 'Scuse me, boy," he drawls to Kirkland, then turns back to address the crowd. "Before me and the boys play I want y'all to listen up. Now y'all know I been reading them newspapers, too. And I know there is some been saying that after the accident old Rhapsody Walker lost his voice, and the only thing he got left is a whisper. Or that he went and got himself born all over again. Well shoot, folks, that ain't nothing but hogwash. Truth is, as y'all can see for yourselves, I'm just the same old Rhapsody." He pauses here to lift his hat and scratch his head. " 'Cept that when Doc Brock sewed my throat up, it seems he accidentally got his surgical thread mixed up with his gen-u-ine Hank Williams guitar string which, being a dedicated fan of Hank's, he bought at a souvenir store in Nashville and for seven years carried in his shirt pocket for good luck and inspiration. Now the boys in the band all keep telling me they believe that guitar string in my throat is making me talk and act like old Hank himself, and that I'm *not* the same old Rhapsody." The band members all nod vehemently to the audience, and Rhapsody shakes his head, grinning. "But I know they're all just pulling my leg." He strums his guitar, now, then stops and looks back up, wide-eyed. "Ain't they?"

With the band still playing, Rhapsody joins in on his guitar, then, with his finest Roy Rogers half-faced white grin, sings "Roses for My Keen-Nosed Gal." At every chorus, with Rhapsody's encouragement and direction, the entire crowd sings along in a bawdy, group drawl—"Now I know you were blessed with the keenest of noses"—everyone swaying back and forth like giddy, drunken, cowboy sailors—"So I'll gargle for you, but I can't poop roses."

When the song ends and the applause, screams, and whistles begin to diminish, the band modulates to a new key—same easy tempo—and Rhapsody says, "The next tune I'd like to play for y'all is a brand-new one called 'Country Cliché.' This is the one I promised you, Dr. Brock." Still grinning, he sings into his microphone:

My baby treated me bad
Took all the money we had
Flew to Honolulu
To live with a guru
She found in a magazine ad.

Tomorrow the rent payment's due
The job at the factory fell through
But I won't despair
I'm gonna pull up a chair
And do what them songwriters do.

I'm gonna write me a country cliché, a country cliché
'Cuz I need a hit in a very bad way

Radio please won't you play
My country cliché.

In every dream her face appears
Her pillow is soaked with my tears
It hurt so today
When the man called to say
Our new bedroom set's in at Sears.

I don't know just where we went wrong
I tried so hard to get along
But I'm not denying
It might be worth the crying
If I could get rich off this song.

And write me a country cliché, a country cliché
'Cuz I need a hit in a very bad way
Radio please won't you play
My country cliché.

Now you can write a hit song too
Just don't put in too much that's new
And stick to the rhymes
You've heard ten thousand times
So we can sing all the words first time through.

So if your true love leaves you cold
And looking at Playboy *gets old*
Don't think it's the end
Just pick up a pen
And turn your depression to gold.

And write you a country cliché, a country cliché
When you need a hit in a very bad way
Say is that check on the way
For my country cliché.

As soon as the song is over, while the roars of approval are still going strong, Rhapsody disappears backstage for half a minute. He returns with a twisting jump (changed, now, into his familiar black- and white-legged tight pants and rainbow-striped t-shirt beneath a buttoned-down white and black long-sleeved shirt), and lands in a full split on the downbeat of his most popular, most irresistibly danceable song, "Black and Blue." He pops up from the split and dances his way across the stage, moon-walking backwards and forwards and skittering sideways, to grab and swing his microphone, his black and white knees lifting high, his mostly white fans dancing then singing with him:

My skin is black, your soul is blue
My music's hot, your dancin's cool
So down you go, and up I come
The Black and Blue ain't never done. . . .

The crowd is completely his—has been his from the moment of his horsebacked entry, and probably before that—but he's not taking any chances. After "Black and Blue" he and the band perform a medley of three more old hits: a reggae tune called "Buy My Love with Love, My Love," a blues tune called "Baby Blues," and a jazzy rock tune called "Skip a Beat."

And then it's time. His fans are deep and secure in their happy delirium. If they're not ready now they never will be.

Without warning, a blast of smoke rolls across the stage and is, for several minutes, so thick it conceals everything; even the TV monitors show nothing but a white screen.

When at last the fog lifts, the Rainbow Band, to the crowd's delight, is in place, each man standing at attention in front of his microphone, dressed to do battle: Rhapsody looking dapper in an officer's uniform, complete with medals, Kirkland, Billy Davis, and Mookie Perry in camouflage fatigues, Willie Veal and Shadow Jackson in white sailor's suits with white hats, and Sanchez and Hoop Granger in navy blue sailor's suits.

It had come to him late one night in L.A. After a grueling day of practicing and recording with the band, he'd spent three hours after dinner wrestling with the lyrics to one of his new songs, "Worst Case Scenario." Unsatisfied and exhausted he'd switched on his bedroom TV and sprawled back on his unmade bed. He didn't care what was on—anything to short-circuit his thought processes, to quiet or distract or override that insistent and obsessive voice in his head that seemed as if it would be unsatisfied until every word of the song was in its proper place.

He was still wide awake after the eleven o'clock news, when a bizarre old movie musical called *South Pacific* came on. The setting was a South Pacific island during World War II. There were white faces and sailor's hats aplenty, and a fat native black woman called Bloody Mary who chewed betel nuts and collected shrunken heads, and whom the white sailors sang to with joking adoration and suggestiveness, when, clearly, what they were *really* wanting was a shapely young white "dame," which is what they proceeded to sing about in a number called "Nothing Like a Dame."

This was all rather baffling to Rhapsody, who finally had to conclude that the movie was actually not a savage parody of white lunacy and obtuseness. He hoped to God that fifty years from now—if there was anyone alive to listen fifty years from now—his ideas and music would not seem this irrelevant and out of date.

There was a blatant, cheery naiveté about the music. And, worse than naiveté, the film seemed to contain an intentional vision of self-congratulatory vacuousness, of high-spirited empty-headedness, or, as one of the female characters proudly called it, "cockeyed optimism." (There was something Rhapsody found terrifying about all this: somehow it made the "worst case scenario," about which he was writing, seem more insidiously plausible. Maybe even likely.)

It was while the cast was concluding "Nothing Like a Dame" that it came to him in a flash: the smoke, the uniforms, the choreography, and even the substitute lyrics. Everything. A moment of pure gestalt. Like some daffy epiphany from a demented white God. He grabbed a pen and paper and scribbled it all down in one sitting, before the movie had ended.

And now, as the band members continue to stand at attention, Rhapsody, followed one at a time and in turn by the rest of the Rainbow musicians, each at his own microphone, begins to sing his new lyrics to the jaunty, peppy, pre-recorded background music of "Nothing Like a Dame":

We got submarines and bombers, we got land-based missiles, too,
We got thirty thousand warheads that can turn the world to stew

We got frigates and destroyers, we got carriers galore,
What ain't we got? We ain't got war.

We got neutron bombs and choppers, we got laser rays and tanks,
We got carbines and bazookas that can blast you from the ranks,
We got hand grenades and land mines that can blow you straight to hell
What ain't we got? You know damn well!

The next two lines, Rhapsody sings a capella, in a goofy-sweet falsetto:

There ain't nothing to put on a dirty camouflage—suit for,
What we need is what there ain't no substi—tute for.

Here, they pull their microphones from their stands, form a chorus line, and, kicking their legs high, their timing worked out to perfection, sing in unison:

There is nothing like a war
Nothing in the world
There is nothing we adore
That is anything like a war.

Then, right back to alternating voices with another verse:

We got mustard gas and nerve gas that can kill you while you cough
We got deadly sprays like napalm that can burn your flesh right off
We got cyanide and periquot and chemicals to pour
What ain't we got? We ain't got war!

Again, Rhapsody in his treacly falsetto:

Lots of things in life are deadly, but—brother
There is one particular thing that is nothing whatsoever
in any way, shape or form like any—other.

Back to the chorus line and high kicking:

There is nothing like a war
Nothing in the world

There is nothing we adore
That is anything like a war.

Next, the fourth and final verse:

We got men in special forces, we got war games we can play
We got covert operations from the boys at CIA
We got army, navy, air force, and the zealots in the corps
What ain't we got? We ain't got war!

And now the finale, in bold, rousing unison:

Nothing thrills like a war
And nothing kills like a war
Or excites like a war
Or delights like a war

And nothing feels like a war
Or appeals like a war
Or employs like a war
Or destroys like a war

There ain't a good man here with an honest chin
Who couldn't be cured by putting him in
A fun-filled, glorious, homicidal, world-destroying WAR!

A roar goes up from the crowd—laughs and cheers mixed with tumultuous applause—while another cloud of smoke billows over the stage. And, minutes later, as the ovation diminishes and the smoke begins to lift, a reggae beat starts up, and soon everyone can see that the musicians, except for the superstar, are back on stage. And, in front of and arching over the band is a giant paper rainbow, flapping crisply in the spring breeze, its apex at the stage ceiling and its ends hidden inside two large brass pots, one at either side of the stage.

While the reggae beat grows louder, and the TV cameras focus in on the brass pots, the crowd ripples and surges toward the stage in anticipation. Until, with a deafening crash of Sanchez's cymbal, and a dynamite-like explosion set off by a button on Billy Davis's synthesizer, a thick blast of smoke gushes from the pot at the left end of the rainbow, and billows into a cloud that hangs, spreading, above the stage. Meanwhile, the blast seems to have ignited the paper rainbow, which is sizzling steadily from left to right like a great, arching fuse, past the apex, now, and curving down toward the pot at the right end of the rainbow.

And just before the flames and sparks reach the gaping brass mouth at the rainbow's end, Rhapsody springs from the pot like a jack-in-the-box, and lands dancing to the reggae beat. His new pants are a rainbow of thin vertical stripes, accentuating the loose-limbed movements of his legs; while his new t-shirt (no buttoned-down overshirt to half hide it) is lavender, with a rainbow split apart at its apex, and a mushroom cloud rising up through the jagged gap. *Save the Rainbow* is printed in rainbow lettering at the top of the shirt. *Before It's Too Late* is printed below the stem of the mushroom cloud. And just beneath, in smaller black lettering that is too small to be read from more than ten or fifteen feet away, is printed *Coalition for the New Abolition.*

Rhapsody snatches his microphone from the stand, and in his finest reggae accent sings a brand-new verse to the old standard:

Somewhere over de rainbow
Blackbirds cry
Don't be killing dat rainbow
Don't let de rainbow die.

Somewhere over de rainbow
Blackbirds scream
Don't be feeding dat rainbow
Into de White Machine.

The scream of a siren interrupts the song, and as the pitch and volume continue to rise, Rhapsody rolls his eyes skyward and dips his shoulders, slowly tilting back his head. Nervous laughter peals through the crowd—no telling what tricks old Rhapsody is up to—and then the audience is rocked by another explosion from the wall of amplifiers, this one much louder than the first. Half the people reflexively duck; many cover their ears and scream, while the superstar flings his arms up and out, and Sanchez smashes his cymbal. And then a great, palpable hush, a ringing silence, floats over the park.

He speaks softly into his microphone, almost a whisper, "And the worst part is you know it could be the truth." Then he raises his voice. "You know it could happen any second! Before the next rainbow spreads itself across the sky! Before you can turn for another look at your friend or lover! Before you can suck in your next breath!"

Sanchez starts in with a soft but funky beat, Rhapsody's head and shoulders bobbing in time. "Any moment, Jack. Before your next thought. Before your next heartbeat." He's dancing, now, gazing back up at the sky, while Kirkland thumps away at his bass, and then the rest of the musicians join in. And while the music blasts and throbs about him, Rhapsody barks out the lyrics, rap style:

At any moment comes the bomb
No time to say the famous psalm
The Lord's your shepherd? That's a joke
If all he's got's a flock of smoke.

Willie Veal plays an alto sax lead while Rhapsody boogies and bounces around the stage, then skitters back to his microphone:

Old Jesus say to turn your cheek
The Kingdom of Heaven is for the meek
Swords to plowshares, enemies loved
Stones unthrown and hawks turned dove.

But peace through strength was our reply
A bomb for a bomb, an eye for an eye
And when the world is blind and burning
Won't be no cheekbones left for turning.

Now, Billy Davis plays a synthesizer lead while Rhapsody dances and claps, the crowd dancing and clapping with him, then hustles back in time for the chorus:

At any moment comes the bomb
No time to say the famous psalm
The Lord's your shepherd? That's a joke
If all he's got's a flock of smoke.

All the musicians go at it, here, in a spectacular weaving of simultaneous leads. And then Rhapsody raps out the final verses:

It's time to get our act together
We hanging by a fragile tether
One false move, just one mistake
And that thin sweet Thread is sure to break.

So let's be smart and raise our voices
Tell the world just what your choice is
Clear your throat and tap your toe
Then raise your voice and just say NO!

"No!" each of the band members screams on the following beat.

"Just say NO!" Rhapsody gestures to the crowd.

And the response comes back loudly and nearly in unison, "No!"

"Just say no!"

"No!"

"Just say no!"

"No!"

"Just say no!"

"No!"

"Listen," Rhapsody hisses, holding up a hand to silence the mass chant. "I know you scared of the Russians. Right? They been bad before and they gonna be bad again, and Jesus was talking pretty when he say to turn the other cheek and love your enemy, because he didn't know nothing about the evils of communism. Am I right?"

The crowd—same crowd that has just been chanting "No!"—now screams in agreement, an irony which is not lost on Rhapsody, who understands that if the audience continues to respond to him but not to his message, then his cause will be lost, his mission fated for failure.

As Kirkland and Sanchez once again set the rhythm, each musician adds his own layer of sound to the musical cake, and Rhapsody careens about the stage, never missing a beat—never letting up or slowing down—then hikes the mike to his mouth:

It's better to be dead than red
Dead than red

Dead than red
It's better to be dead than red
The children must be saved.

Americans believe it's true, the Russians are no good
They can't be trusted, and would make the world theirs if they could
So if we want our freedom, and our rights to vote and speak
We'd better build more bombs so they don't think our will is weak.

It's better to be dead than red
Dead than red
Dead than red
It's better to be dead than red
The children must be saved.

We'll build bombs by the thousands, and by the megaton
We'll build them 'til those commies learn there's no place left to run
They'll see that if they try to fight we'll blow them to the sea
And if we blow ourselves up too, at least we'll all die free.

It's better to be dead than red
Dead than red
Dead than red
It's better to be dead than red
The children must be saved.

And if one day the bombs are dropped, the more we got the better
'Cause that's the way to keep the world from turning any redder
And if your kids are sad to hear their time on earth is done
Just wipe their tears, remind them that they'll go out number one.

It's better to be dead than red
Dead than red
Dead than red
It's better to be dead than red
The children must be saved.

"Man, that's some crazy stuff!" Rhapsody cries when the crowd has quieted. He paces back and forth as he shakes his head, the microphone tilted to his chin, the cord snaking after him. "But you *know* it's the truth. We ready to blow our own children straight to hell to save them from the Russians. Well listen to me, 'cause I got something to *say* about that! Listen close now, 'cause we gonna think this through together. All right?"

The crowd screams its assent.

"All right! Now, I know we scared of the Russians. But tell me: what's the worst thing could happen if we go on like we *been* going on? If we go on like we got no choice but to build more bombs to keep the world safe from *all* the people and *all* the nations we believe is evil and dangerous? What's the worst could happen?" He pauses for only a moment. "You know the answer, don't you? You remember how close we came a few months back, even if you don't *want* to remember. The worst that could happen is *the worst that could happen!* Blam! Boom! *All gone!* Forever and ever. Gone for an eternity. As gone as the dinosaurs. But even *more* gone. Because there ain't ever gonna be nobody to uncover *our* bones or piece them back together. Never! Nobody to draw our pictures or talk about all that we done or could have done. Never. Nothing at all. Because in a few ticks of the clock, maybe any moment"—he glances to the sky—"we gonna take the past and future right down the tubes with us, and then we gonna tie those tubes tight. An irreversible operation, Jack; the ultimate birth control; an abortion to end *all* abortions!" He's rapping, now, inspired by the possibilities of his grand mission, by the seeds of conversion he hopes he is sowing over the airwaves and scattering round the world. "Oh yeah, if you truly opposed to abortion you better forget about the pregnant mamas, because in a few ticks of the clock we gonna have us one final *mass* abortion, a nuclear curettage at the hands of the a-to-mic doctor, the womb of the future scraped clean forever and ever and ever, amen." Not just rapping, but preaching—and to the largest congregation ever assembled—a singsong, gospel-style chanting. Of course, he'd written much of his sermon beforehand and memorized the key phrases. But the way he's preaching now, it all sounds utterly spontaneous, a geyser of emotion suddenly tapped and set free, gushing up from the black depths and into the light of day—the light of this specific, electric moment—so that many of the viewers, even those watching on TV, oceans and continents and thousands of satellite miles away, are already hooked by the spectacle of the superstar in his pulpit; by his charismatic presence and the hypnotic, anguished, incendiary rhythms of his seemingly impromptu homily. "And if all those unborn children of the future could talk to you right now, right here, you think *they* would understand why you feel so good and righteous about being prepared to take their world from them? You think you could look them in the eye and explain it to *their* satisfaction? Explain that you got no choice? That you doing it for their own good? Doing it to save them from evil?" He screams now into the microphone, gesticulating wildly, "Well what in all the world could be *more* evil? What in all the world could be *worse* than stealing life from all the children of the future? What in all the world could be worse than *destroying* the world? I want you to tell me, now! *What could be worse?"*

"Nothing!" the Rainbow musicians shout back to him.

"And what could be more evil?" He cups his hands behind his ears.

"Nothing!" comes the answer, right on cue, from the faithful in his assembly, although it is suddenly clear to him that there is a break in the solidarity of this group communion, not quite a mutiny, but a visible secession from the collective mania. A number of faces seem to be distracted. Heads are turning, casting about for confirmation.

"And what could be more sinful?" he presses on, slightly shaken but undaunted, focusing on the majority that still seems to be with him.

"Nothing!"

"And what could be uglier?"

"Nothing!"

"And what could be sadder?"

"Nothing!"

"And what could be crazier?"

"Nothing!" Despite the diffusion of restlessness, tens of thousands of fists are jabbing toward the sky, now, like angry exclamation points punctuating each response.

"And what could be more tragic?"

"Nothing!"

"And what could be more brutal?"

"Nothing!"

"And what could be more inhuman or ungodly?"

"Nothing!"

He again cups his hands behind his ears as if he can't quite hear. "Nothing, you say?"

"Nothing!"

"You sure?"

"Nothing!"

"You ain't just saying that?"

"Nothing!"

"But wait a minute," Rhapsody says, holding both hands up high as he skips across the stage. "What about the Russians? You *know* the worst that could happen if we go on like we *been* going on. But what's the worst that could happen if instead of building more bombs we start taking apart the bombs we already built? If we start to dis-ass-emble the Machine? What's the very worst the Russians could do to us if we had no bombs at all?

"Well, listen to me and I'll tell you. We know and they know that they can't drop enough of their bombs to wipe *us* out without wiping *themselves* out, too. Nuclear Winter, Jack. It's like we all standing in the same puddle of gasoline. Don't matter *who* drops the match. We *all* gonna go up in the flames. We know that, and so do they! And so the very very *worst* they could possibly *want* to do to us—*if* they completely crazy and evil—is to try to slowly take over the world and make us their slaves. Divide and conquer. Nuclear blackmail. Am I right?" He raises his voice, and again cups his hands behind his ears. "I said, am I right?"

The response comes back in an appreciable testimony of screams.

"Then listen to me. Because I *came* from slaves." His voice actually trembles, preacher-like, when he says the word, *came*. "And because the slaves I *came* from kept on slaving and suffering and enduring I'm here right now, standing in front of you. And I'm alive and kicking. And I am forever grateful, Jack. They lived for me. They suffered for me. And they *died* for me. And unless you completely crazy, you *know* it's better and smarter and braver to take a chance that you gonna live and slave and die for the sake of your children, than to take a chance that you gonna wipe out every human being forever and all time, including your children, *for the sake of your children!*

"And if it *still* scares you to think about being a slave to the Russians, I got to tell you that as far as I been able to tell, there ain't *no way* the Russians could be any meaner or crueler, no way they could be any worse, than some of your ancestors was to some of my ancestors. But my ancestors survived your ancestors, and in my heart I still sing their praises. I'm proud, every day, of the suffering they endured for me. And here I am, Jack. And here you are, too. All of us. Alive and kicking. Hallelujah! They suffered and saved us, and now *we* got to risk suffering to save our children. To save *all* the children that's ever been or going to be.

"And unless you completely, stark raving mad and your brain is solid white and socked in, you *know* the risk of abolishing the weapons is better than the risk of doing what we been doing; going on like we been going on. You know it! And if anybody ever tries to tell you different—if anybody tries to tell you we got to build *more* bombs instead of less—just tell him to think long and hard about the worst thing that could happen if we go on building more bombs. Tell him to think about this next song."

While the rest of the group stands watching, none of them even leaving the stage for a quick drink or smoke, Rhapsody sits at Billy Davis's acoustic piano and bangs out a long progression of chords, then, repeating the progression, sings:

In the worst case scenario, when the hard rain starts to pour
There'll be no one left to win or lose, no one to keep the score
So if you kick ass down in Macon, or fight gang wars in the barrio
You should save your strength and fight to stop the worst case scenario.

And in the worst case scenario, all our flesh will burn the same
It won't matter what your job is, it won't matter what your game.
So if you drive a truck in Memphis, or sail yachts on Lake Ontario
You're just cruising down the same path toward the worst case scenario.

And in the worst case scenario, when the blast lights up the night
All the food will turn to poison, there'll be death in every bite
So if you feast on steak and pork chops, or eat millet like a sparrow
Your last supper can't prepare you for the worst case scenario.

And in the worst case scenario, when we let the warheads fly
It won't matter if you're cool or hip, or square or dull or shy
So if you trip the life fantastic, or you walk the straight and narrow
You're just pissing in the same wind toward the worst case scenario.

And in the worst case scenario, it won't matter who was right
It won't matter who was evil, who wore black or who wore white

So if you build bombs for your country, or for God or Queen or Pharaoh
All your righteous claims can't save you from the worst case scenario.

And in the worst case scenario, when the night lights up like day
There'll be no time left to dance or sing, no music left to play
So if you're into rock or reggae, or play Mozart on the stereo
You should contemplate this final song, the worst case scenario.

Rhapsody finishes the song with the same progression of chords he started it on, then, wasting no time, hurries back to the microphone at center stage.

"It could happen any moment!" he cries, looking at the sky. "It might already be too late." He lifts the microphone from its stand. "But it might *not* be. And if it's not too late it's going to be up to you and you." He points the mike at the crowd. "And you and you and you." He sweeps it from one side of the park to the other, then aims it, as if it were lethal, at the TV camera. "And you! Ain't no risk we could take that's any bigger than the risk we taking right now, every time we take a breath. Every time we blink our eyes. So I want you to listen, now, 'cause I'm gonna tell you what we got to do. Listen to me careful, now, 'cause here's the plan.

"See now, I figure if the worst that could happen happens, my singing and dancing won't do me no good. My album sales won't do me no good. My millions of dollars won't do me no good. And neither will my mansion. Or my jet or helicopter or all my limos. And so the first thing I'm gonna do is take all my money and use it to start up a new organization called the Coalition for the New Abolition. And I'm gonna sell my mansion and my limos, my jet and my chopper, and give all of that money to the Coalition. The CNA. An investment for the future, Jack.

"Now let me tell you . . . " He holds his arms straight out at his sides and turns directly to camera one. "If you like this t-shirt I'm wearing then you better get ready to watch your TV sets." The cameraman immediately obliges him by zooming in for a full-framed close-up of the shirt. "Because in a few weeks, the Coalition for the New Abolition will start advertising on TV, and I'm gonna be selling you as many t-shirts as you want so *you* can help broadcast the message with me. And all the money I make, every penny, will go right back into the Coalition. And if you think you seen a lot of commercials for McDonald's and Coca-Cola, then, man, you ain't seen nothing! Because if I sell enough albums and t-shirts, I'm gonna have a commercial on every TV station every hour. Gonna spread the message far and wide. And you all gonna help every time you buy a t-shirt and every time you wear one or give one to a friend to wear. And you gonna help every time you buy an album and every time you play it or give it to a friend to play. Oh yeah, together we gonna be changing some minds. Gonna be putting the heat on our leaders, Jack! Gonna be putting a fire to their toes.

"Now I know there is some of you thinking old Rhapsody has gone too far; old Rhapsody is sounding too po-lit-i-cal." A startling number of heads nod. There are even a few screams of agreement and a smattering of shouted requests for some hit tunes from his old albums. But it is too late to change course; he's already looked and leaped, and now all he can do is attend to his landing. "Oh yeah! I know there is some of you thinking that a popular rock and roller ain't got no business sticking his nose into such things.

"But if that's what you thinking, then you thinking wrong. Thinking crazy. Because, man, it *is* my business, and it's *your* business, too, political or not. Because there's a gun aimed right at my head, and I mean aimed point blank, Jack! A gun aimed at my head and at *your* head, too, and a finger on the trigger. And it's up to all of us to wake up and stop pretending it ain't there. Because it *is* there, and there ain't *nothing* in the world that's worse. Nothing in the world! And it ain't about to go away unless you ready to stand up and say, 'No!' "

Rhapsody suddenly leaps across the stage toward Shadow Jackson, who, with a hot guitar introduction, launches into the next song. It's got a hard, driving rock beat, and for a minute Rhapsody dances in front of Jackson and his guitar, then turns and bounds past Sanchez and Kirkland to the front of the stage to sing:

Come on people, there's hell to pay
There's demons on the hill
If we keep turning our backs this way
The Reaper's knockin'
If we don't stop him
No one ever will

And there ain't no doubt about it
It's time to stand up and shout about it
There's just one planet, there's nowhere else to go
It's time to say NO NO NO!
It's time to say NO NO NO!
It's time to say NO NO NO NO. . . .

Come on people, get your ass in gear
This madness can't go on
If you think the problem's gonna disappear
You must be dreaming
Your mind needs cleaning
You been asleep too long

And there ain't no doubt about it
It's time to stand up and shout about it
There's just one planet, there's nowhere else to go
It's time to say NO NO NO!
It's time to say NO NO NO!
It's time to say NO NO NO NO. . . .

Here, the Rainbow musicians showcase their talent with a round of hot leads, followed by a spectacular battle royal, each of them wailing away at once while Rhapsody flies about the stage, riding the music like a surfer rides the waves, his feet and hips, shoulders and head dipping and swinging with every screaming note and thumping beat, until he finally returns to grab his microphone:

Come on people stand up and fight
Our back's against the wall
This ain't no time to be polite
While we been sleepin'
The poison's leakin'
The Reaper's come to call

And there ain't no doubt about it
Time to stand up and shout about it
If we don't stop it, the whole damn thing could blow
It's time to say NO NO NO!
It's time to say NO NO NO!
It's time to say NO NO NO NO!

While a tumult of roaring drifts over Seattle, the band leaves the stage, and in the hectic interlude before their encore, Rhapsody grabs Kirkland by the elbow. "What do you think, man? Did we do it?"

"Just use your ears, Rhap Man," Kirkland says, reaching up to tweak the superstar's earlobes.

But for Rhapsody the roar of the crowd has become oddly equivocal, a great thundering of ambiguity: if they are only thrilled, it is not enough.

He gives the signal and the band hustles, with him at the rear, back to the stage. Kirkland, triumphant, raises his bass, one-armed, high above his head. And then the band coalesces about Rhapsody—Kirkland and Shadow Jackson flanking him—and they perform their final song, a slow, haunting melody with a sing-along chorus:

Where are the rainbows? Celebrate the rainbows
May you always see your fill
We can save our planet
If we all demand it
And celebrate the rainbows

Where are the flowers? Celebrate the flowers
May you always smell your fill
We can save our planet
If we all demand it
And celebrate the flowers

Don't think we don't need you
We need you
Don't think we can't hear you
We hear you
So raise your voice and help us spread
The message of our dream
Save the Rainbow, stop the White Machine

Where is the water, celebrate the water
May you always taste your fill
We can save our planet
If we all demand it
And celebrate the water

Where is the sunshine, celebrate the sunshine
May you always feel your fill
We can save our planet
If we all demand it
And celebrate the sunshine

Don't think we don't need you
We need you
Don't think we can't hear you
We hear you
So raise your voice and help us spread
The message of our dream
Save the Rainbow, stop the White Machine

Here, Jackson and Kirkland let their guitars hang, and the entire band, joined now by the backstage crew, loop arms over shoulders and sway back and forth—many in the crowd following suit, an uproar of arms and shoulders groping and stretching to lock together—as they sing the final two verses and chorus, a capella:

Here is the music, celebrate the music
May you always hear your fill
We can save our planet
If we all demand it
And celebrate the music

Here are the people, celebrate the people
May you always love your fill
We can save our planet
If we all demand it
And celebrate the people

Don't think we don't need you
We need you
Don't think we can't hear you
We hear you
So raise your voice and help us spread
The message of our dream
Save the Rainbow, stop the White Machine

Don't think we don't need you

We need you
Don't think we can't hear you
We hear you
So raise your voice and help us spread
The message of our dream
Save the Rainbow, stop the White Machine.

♪♪♪

Long after the band had been ferried away by helicopter, a fair portion of the crowd remained in the park, several of the long chains of arm-linked fans reluctant to let go; reluctant to descend from the high peak of rare group intoxication.

Back in his hotel room, Rhapsody was taking calls from all the major networks, each requesting that he appear for an interview: "Meet the Press," "Face the Nation," "The Today Show," "MacNeil-Lehrer," "Nightline," "Oprah," "Donahue."

"Maybe we're really gonna make some kind of difference," he said to Kirkland, who sat beside the phone, screening the calls. "Maybe we're really gonna do it!"

"Damn straight we gonna do it!"

And, swept up now in the hoopla of apparent success, the more Rhapsody thought about it, the more it made perfect sense. The only thing the peace movement had ever needed was a popular, powerful, visible, and articulate spokesperson. The Abolition had Frederick Douglass. The Civil Rights Movement had Martin Luther King. And, now, The New Abolition had Rhapsody Walker.

It was while he was sitting there beside Kirkland, almost serenely contemplating his lofty place in history, that the phone call from his grandfather came.

"Your grandma's in the hospital," Curtis told him. "She got a tumor in her stomach big as a grapefruit, and they gonna cut it out tomorrow morning."

Ashes and Acceptance

♪

EARLY SUNDAY MORNING, WHILE ROARING OVER THE SPECTACULAR Northwest landscape at thirty thousand feet, Rhapsody kept his eyes tightly shut and his stereo headphones turned up to as loud a volume as he could tolerate in an effort to drown out his thoughts. It seemed that when he wasn't worrying about, or prematurely grieving for, April, he was, to his horror, resenting her for having sidetracked him from his grand mission. He was certain, after all, that civilization was, at this very moment, hanging in the balance and believed that if there was anyone who had an honest-to-God chance to tip the scales in the right direction, it was he, Rhapsody Walker, and it was now, while the media's fascination with him and his urgent message was at its peak.

Before the phone call from Curtis, he'd been all set to appear on every major news program, sit face to face with celebrity newscasters, talk-show hosts, and government officials, and reiterate his fervent plea for the new abolition.

But after learning of April's condition he'd had to cancel his TV appearances, and feared that in two or three weeks, or however long it might take to deal with his grandmother's surgery and recovery, all the

Rhapsody-mania generated by the internationally-broadcast Rainbow Concert would begin to fade. The media, whom Rhapsody had clearly taken by storm and surprise, might even turn hostile, by then, to him and his call to disassembly. And government and military leaders would, no doubt, take the opportunity to warn the networks and newspapers to think twice about providing a forum for an ill-informed, black rock and roll singer whose anti-government, anti-military, rabble-rousing rhetoric posed a clear threat to national security.

In short, The White Machine would have a chance to gear up against him.

The more Rhapsody worried about his squandered opportunity—and not just his squandered opportunity, dammit, but humanity's squandered opportunity—the more he resented April for her illness. And the more he resented her for her illness, the more monstrously despicable and reprehensible he felt, and the louder he turned up his earphones.

Even on his brief limousine ride to the hospital, sunk deep into the plush back seat while he stared out his window at the nearly deserted Sunday morning streets of Chintimini—not ten minutes from his grandmother's bedside—he simply couldn't keep from sulking over the misfortune of her awful timing. He had a planet to save, for Christ's sake! A history and a future!

Good Samaritan Hospital of Chintimini was set atop a hill that sloped most sharply to the north and east. All around the hospital purple azaleas were in full bloom, and cherry blossoms swirled past Rhapsody's window and skittered across the parking lot like pink confetti. To the east, the white peaks of the Cascades were barely visible beneath the aching glare of morning sunlight.

Before he stepped from the limousine, Rhapsody slipped his black-lensed sunglasses over his nose and ears, then set his newly purchased Seattle Mariners baseball cap on his head and pulled the bill as low as he could, so that his mouth and chin were all that was visible of his face.

Curtis greeted him in the hospital lobby with a brief but intense hug. "Come on," he said, taking his grandson by the elbow, then guiding him past the admissions desk and down a corridor. "They operating right now, up on the third floor. Say they should be done before eleven . . . unless there is complications."

In the elevator Rhapsody pulled off his sunglasses and tipped back the bill of his cap, while Curtis stared above the doors, watching the floor numbers light up. He had deep pouches under both eyes, and Rhapsody thought he looked slightly dazed.

When they stepped out at the third floor, Curtis led his grandson to the waiting room, where they sat knee to knee on a small naugahyde couch. After shaking his head, pursing his lips, and rubbing his chin for what seemed to Rhapsody a good two or three minutes, Curtis finally spoke. "They tell us they got to take her blood and shoot her full of poison and X rays, and we smile and say, 'Okay, doctor, we understand.' They tell us they got to cut her open, and we nod and say 'Go right ahead.' They tell us we got to sign our names to a piece of paper so if they want to they can cut up her intestine and push it out through her stomach, and we hurry and sign it , and say 'Thank you very much, doctor.' Damn! It look to me like she ain't nothing but a prisoner; it look to me like we got nothing to do with her life no more but to turn it over to white doctors who don't even know us." He tilted back his head and blinked at the ceiling. "And, I can't help it, I'm afraid they gonna kill her."

"Listen," Rhapsody said, taking his grandfather's hand and squeezing it, surprised by its bulk and roughness. "All they're gonna do is cut out the tumor, sew her up, and she'll be good as new. You ought to just be glad they finally found out what was wrong. Because, man, that's the whole trick. Soon as they know what's wrong they can fix it. I know, because Mama used to all the time tell me how once a doctor makes the right diagnosis she's home free. Because that's the key to medicine. The right diagnosis."

"The right diagnosis," Curtis repeated.

"Sure," Rhapsody nodded and slapped his grandfather's shoulder. "The hardest part's already over."

It was before ten-thirty when the chief surgeon stepped into the waiting room, his blue mask at his neck and a circle of sweat at the chest of his smock. There was something about the set of his chin and the tightness of his lips that terrified Rhapsody.

Curtis, however, pushed himself eagerly from the couch and said, "You finished up early. Must be good news."

The surgeon, a middle-aged man with bushy black and gray brows and large angular ears, frowned. "No sir," he said. "I'm afraid it's not good news." He motioned for Curtis to sit back down, then sat beside him on the couch arm. "I'm sorry. She has ovarian cancer. And the problem with ovarian cancer is that by the time it's been detected it's usually too late to do anything. In your wife's case we weren't even close to detecting it in time. The tumor started out in her ovaries, but it's already engulfed her intestines and the lower part of her stomach. And the cancer cells have metastasized. To her liver and her lungs. Basically, we just took a look around and closed her back up."

"Goddamn," Curtis whispered.

But Rhapsody was already on his feet. "What do you mean you just closed her back up? You telling me you didn't even cut out the tumor? You didn't even try?"

"If we'd cut out the tumor," the surgeon said,"we'd have had to take half her organs with it. She'd have died on the table."

"How long?" Curtis asked.

"There's really no accurate way of predicting; but I'm afraid not long. Once her intestine becomes blocked . . ."

"We'll fly her to New York or Houston," Rhapsody cried. "Man, I know they got experts can help her."

The surgeon nodded. "If she were my wife or mother I'd probably want to do the same thing. But listen. Let her talk to Dr. Wade, the oncologist. He'll explain her options and she can tell you what she wants."

"That's right," Curtis nodded. "What *she* wants."

"I'm really very sorry," the surgeon said. "Please let me know if there's anything I can do." He glanced at his watch. "They should have her in her room within the hour. You can sit with her, but I suspect she'll be too groggy to talk until late tonight. If you'd like to be the ones to explain the situation to her, that would be perfectly appropriate. Otherwise, I can tell her tomorrow morning."

As soon as the surgeon stepped from the room, Rhapsody sat back on the couch with Curtis. They stared at the floor, saying nothing, scarcely breathing. There was a tightness and density in Rhapsody's chest, and he felt stone-like, almost immovable. But nothing else.

Later, they sit with her in her private room while she sleeps, the plastic pouch hanging from its stand beside her bed, the clear fluid dripping through a tube and into the back of her hand. Rhapsody sits across the bed from Curtis, who holds her hand, the hand without the tube running into it, rubbing each of her knuckles, then turning the hand over to trace the lines on her palm, probe the gardening calluses below the base of each finger, and carefully feel the softness and thinness of the skin stretched across her wrist.

She is sleeping still, in mid-afternoon, when Rhapsody finally badgers his grandfather into grabbing some fast food with him. And though Curtis doesn't want to leave her, not for a minute, it occurs to him that they will be needing to eat sooner or later, and that they might as well do it now, while April is sleeping. Sleeping better, in fact, than he has seen her sleep in months.

In the elevator Rhapsody tries his best to boost Curtis's spirits.

"You know they're working miracles, now, with cancer," he tells his grandfather. "All we got to do is find the right doctor. And, man, we'll fly in a fucking army of doctors if we have to."

But Curtis doesn't even answer him. Just stares straight ahead at the doors until they roll open. Rhapsody follows him through the lobby, then out the front door and into the parking lot. When they reach the pick-up truck, Rhapsody clambers through the passengers' door while Curtis slides behind the wheel.

"I swear to God, Grandpa," Rhapsody says, setting a hand on Curtis's shoulder. "We're gonna find a doctor who can help her."

Curtis jams the key into the ignition, but before he can crank the engine his hand goes limp, then his body gives a shiver, and he is, all at once, tipped over sideways, kicking at the door, and howling like a wild animal that's just had its foot caught in a steel trap. And, as he floats above his body and looks down at the old man who is stretched across the truck seat, writhing, kicking, and howling uncontrollably, all he can think is how, in his sixty years of playing the saxophone, this howling is the closest he has ever come to replicating his father's piano music.

Rhapsody

At first all that screaming scares the shit out of me, Jack. He's acting and sounding like his heart's just been shot full of holes and he's gonna die right now, right here, with his head twisting round in my lap and his tears soaking the legs of my pants. Makes me want to kick open the fucking door and run without stopping. But there's nothing to do but keep my seat, and when, after a minute, he's still screaming and kicking, I press one hand to the fuzzy gray top of his head, and with my other hand rub his back.

And that's when I understand—really understand—that it's beyond my control, and beyond the control of any doctor or medicine or machine: April, my grandma who raised me, is going to die.

Later, after he sits back up, Curtis tells me, "She never would have seen her fir trees if it wasn't for you. And I want you to know I will appreciate that for as long as I live." He runs his fingers over the hard cracked leather of the seat. "But when she's gone I believe I'm gonna have to get back to Florida. Back to the grove. Because as much as I like Oregon, it ain't yet familiar. And I *know* I'm gonna be needing all the familiar I can get."

In truth, April had, for months, secretly suspected she was seriously, deeply, even mortally ill, though it was only in retrospect that she understood this. And so it did not surprise her when the oncologist, Dr. Wade, informed her that her list of options did not include living out a long and normal life.

Earlier that morning he'd explained that her first option was to do absolutely nothing. He could send her home today with a prescription for morphine and the phone numbers of private nurses who specialized in the sort of terminal care she would be requiring. Or if she found it more comfortable in the hospital, she could stay right here where she was. Either way, she would not live long. At best, a few months.

Her second option—and the option he recommended as a professional physician dedicated to the preservation of life—was to pursue massive chemotherapy treatment. She would have to endure nausea, hair loss, weight loss, weakness, fatigue, and other less predictable side effects, but he could almost guarantee that he could extend her life by a number of weeks, months, or longer. And there was even an outside chance that she would respond abnormally well to the treatment, and that he might then be able to shrink her tumor to a point at which it could be surgically removed; although he readily admitted that the odds of such an outcome were stacked heavily against her.

Certainly, April admired Dr. Wade's directness. And when he spoke he looked her in the eye in a way that few white men ever had. Unflinchingly and yet unaggressively. With respect, and with caring. She trusted him, she thought, as much as it was possible to trust a stranger with your life.

And yet there was something unsettling about the alternatives he had given her. It seemed that in the end it all came down to a simple non-choice. A yes or a no to chemotherapy, and either way, the curtain would begin to close on her. The biggest event of her life, and her input amounted to nothing.

April

The decisions come easy.

Decision number one: Like everyone else, I've seen what chemotherapy does to people. Oh, it *might* be worth it if I were much younger, or if my chances were much better. But I'm almost sixty-eight years old. I've seen everything I'm going to see and done everything I'm going to do.

Not that I want to die: I love my new life in Oregon, and I'm going to miss all of its trees and mountains, and yes, even all its rain that keeps everyone away who would come running here if it were sunny like Florida; I'm going to miss Curtis so bad it makes me ache to think about it, and to think of him aching without me; and it's not fair at all that I'm never going to get to know my grandson any better, when it was just beginning to seem like maybe I would—when I was just starting to get *back* from him a little of the adult love and understanding and appreciation that I gave to him *and* George Gershwin *and* Porgy all those years. Hell no, I don't want to die!

But an extra three weeks or three months, or even an extra year—most of it sick as a dog—is not what I want either. True, you can't put a price tag on life, but I *know* I'm not willing to pay for an extra year of it with my own suffering and misery, and the suffering and misery of the man I love; and I don't care what he or anybody else says about that. I don't want to die, but if it's my time, then it's my time, and all I want is to get on with it the best I can.

Decision number two: I'll go home to die, because Curtis and I both hate to be in the hospital. Dr. Wade warned me that it would be harder at home, but I told him that as long as I was doing something as hard as dying, a little more hardness wouldn't make much difference.

Decision number three: I tell them that I don't want to be buried in a coffin. In the dirt, naked, would be fine; so I could give back to the soil some of what I took from it. But naked in the dirt is against the law, so I tell them I want to be cremated. That way they can spread my ashes at the bottom of my special fir tree, and I'll at least be giving *something* back to the soil.

Rhapsody

Two days after the surgery I call Kirkland to let him know what's happening, and when we finish talking about my grandma he asks if I've been watching the TV or reading the newspaper. I explain that I haven't had a chance, and he says it's probably a good thing, because there's been some strong reaction to the Rainbow Concert, lots of it negative: the politicians, every one of them, and most of the columnists and entertainment critics have been saying that what Rhapsody Walker is trying to do is naive and misguided at best, and unpatriotic and subversive at worst. And just this morning a national poll showed that although most of the people who saw the concert enjoyed it and would even pay to see it again, only nineteen percent agreed with my message while sixty-five percent disagreed and the rest weren't sure one way or the other.

"They still love you, Rhap Man," Kirkland tells me. "They just don't love what you're saying."

"Nineteen percent love what I'm saying!" I remind him. "That's a start."

He also tells me that Sleepy Newton, the hot new country-western singer, is organizing an event called "The American Vision Concert"—already scheduled to take place next month in Nashville—to counter the message of the Rainbow Concert.

But, man, I can't let myself be distracted by any of that, not now, so I try my best to put it out of my head and focus all my attention on my grandma, who—sixty-seven years old and dying—is somehow, impossibly, in good spirits.

Her first two weeks back home she swears she's not feeling too bad, and refuses to take any of the morphine Dr. Wade prescribed for her. The sun even stays out, and she has us push her bed right up to the window so she can stare out at her fir trees and all the jays and barn swallows that swoop and dive past. But she and Curtis are the real birds. A pair of big black lovebirds huddled in their nest. He spends hours sitting and lying beside her bed, staring out the window with her and holding her hand like they're on a date at a drive-in movie. Every fifteen or twenty minutes he lifts her hand to kiss it, then smiles at her, their eyes meeting like they are falling in love for the first time.

He plays his saxophone for her, all her favorite tunes, whenever she asks for it. He brings her soup, toast, and orange juice, and helps her to the bathroom every time she needs to go. At first, she makes him wait for her at the bathroom door. But, after she falls once while trying to stand up from the toilet, she lets him follow her in and wait with her while she sits and strains.

Man, and it's easy to see that the bathroom is the one place she doesn't want to be. But she can't seem to stay away for more than a few hours; says she feels like she has to go constantly. And when she does go, Curtis tells me she can't squeeze out more than a little bit, a few pebbles' worth, then has to lean against him, fatigued and trembling from the effort, all the way back to the bed.

And after those first two weeks things go steadily downhill. Every time she coughs, her forehead and eyes wrinkle up and she holds on to her chest. She can't eat her toast anymore, and even struggles to get a few sips of soup or juice down. And each trip to the bathroom is a terror. Working together, Curtis and I have to half carry and half drag her all the way to the toilet. And by the time she's finished squeezing out a drop or two, she is too weary to wipe herself. She has to stand, her full weight against me, while Curtis cleans her, puts cream and a new band-aid on the hemorrhoids that have split open from all the straining, then lets her robe drop back to cover her. She finally agrees to start in with the morphine, and though she hates the bitter taste, and seems to resent the taking of it, it does help her to sleep.

But the worst thing is that she won't let Curtis sit or lie beside her in bed, because every time he shifts his weight the mattress bounces, and even the slightest jostling now causes her great pain, whether she's doped up with morphine or not. She barks at him, once, when he does accidentally jostle her, and her pain and anger devastate him for half a day. He knows he's finished being her lovebird.

And it's then that I feel the emptiness coming back to my stomach.

And it's then that I understand how in the end it all comes down to the same thing. In the end, it all comes down to *this*. No fucking escape, Jack. The Law to end all laws.

And that's when I finally see the bigger connection. Not just her, and not just us, but everything. I'd forgotten my geology, Jack. I'd forgotten my fucking astronomy. The destiny of the Earth. Ain't nobody gonna save April, and ain't nobody gonna save the planet. Not Rhapsody Walker or anybody else.

I can see it all, now, stretched before me like a giant mural, each possibility lined up one after the other. Even if I *could* stop the bombs, there's the rest of The Machine to stop. Because the planet is under attack, Jack. From the ozone to the oceans, from the air to the soil. And even if I *could* stop the rest of The Machine, there's an ice age on the way. And, beyond that—the final picture of the mural—the explosion of the sun. The real superstar. The final rhapsody. A fire greater than any Machine—any number of bombs—is ever going to make.

Oh yeah, in the end it all comes down to the same thing. A whack on the throat or a cancer in the lungs. Death by Machine or Death by The Sun. Not a bit of difference. In the end it all comes down to *this* right here. To my grandma who raised me, suffering and dying before my eyes, and not a thing to do but let it happen.

Curtis

No more soup. All she can manage is a few slow sips of cold orange juice. And it look to me like her pain is harder and harder for her to take; so hard she finally just shuts her eyes, stops talking, and sinks into herself. And I want to tell her what I'm thinking and feeling about her, but I don't know how because I never before had to tell her with words. Used to be I could tell her with my body. Tell her with my body every way there was to tell her. But no more. Because her body don't work no more. So what I do is keep my saxophone by my side, and whenever I got to tell her something, I pick it up and play it to her.

April

I never knew that music was solid. It goes through me like solid bars of gold—hot when I'm too cold, and cold when I'm too hot. I can even feel it and see it meshing with the pain. Taking its place. And, best of all, I understand it, now. Each note as recognizably clear as a word, or maybe ten words, or even ten sentences. I knew I was loved, but not like this. I want him to go on and on, singing me everything he can. Sometimes I'm not certain if the music is still going on, or even if I'm awake, so I say, "Good," so he'll go on and on, because I'm afraid the music will stop, and I want him to go on and on, singing to me and filling the pain with gold.

Curtis

Every now and then, her eyes will pop wide open and she'll smile, and even squeeze my hand. "Good," she tells me. And, as she gets worse and worse, every time she smiles and I see that beautiful gap in her teeth it feels to me like she just done something big: like she just canned forty jars of orange marmalade or tomatoes, or pulled up every weed in her garden. And it's the same all the way around. With any little thing she does. Every sip of juice and every dribble of pee makes me want to clap my hands and cheer. And I can picture how, soon, it will even be the same thing for every breath she takes. It's like she's an infant and moving backwards in time, becoming less and less of what she has all along been, the woman I've loved for fifty years disappearing before my eyes.

Rhapsody

It slowly starts to hit me that there's something familiar about all this. And, man, it's weird, because I'm almost sure it's a *good* familiar. But I don't know what or why.

Her eyes are huge and yellow, almost electric. Her lips are dried and cracked, and all the Vaseline in the world doesn't seem to help. The orange juice stings her lips, now, so we water it down to a weak solution. She's talking more often, but when she does, it's like she's talking in riddles.

"Scratch my chin," she orders. And when I scratch her chin she says, "Not my eyes, you. My chin. My chin. Down there."

She wiggles her toes, so I scratch her feet and she nods, satisfied.

"They're back," she cries, her eyes popping open.

"Who's back?" I ask her.

"At the door," she says.

And Curtis looks from her to me to the front door and shakes his head.

"The first ones to see me are the first ones to know," she says. "G.G. is smiling, but where's Porgy Porgy?"

"Porgy?" Curtis says, and she shuts her eyes and sleeps.

She's stopped complaining about pain, so we decrease her dosage of morphine, hoping that will help her think straighter. But the smaller dosage seems not to affect her at all.

"Tip me up," she suddenly cries, though we were sure she was in the middle of a deep sleep.

"Tip you up?" I say.

"I need something," she says. "Please please please!"

"What do you need, baby?" Curtis says, taking her hand. "How about a sip of juice?"

"Just tip me up," she smiles. "So I can fill up like the bottle."

Then she closes her eyes and moans, her chin dropping and her moan turning into the final note of a fucking aria or some shit, her entire jaw trembling with vibrato as she sings it out.

There is something familiar about all this, but I'm not sure what it is.

April

The door doesn't have a door like a door, and behind it they wait so patiently I love them and become impatient. The pain jerks me back and I open my eyes and they are staring at me so worried I love them but they don't understand how it hurts and it's so good good good, keep it coming, like sex it almost hurts too much but I don't want it to stop. "Good good goooood" I say, then laugh, but they are still staring at me, looking even more worried, so I close my eyes, but they were already closed and I laugh again, and Porgy and Daddy and Cody wait so patiently and *un*worried I love them all on both sides because even when they can't see it and both have it that's all there is, waves of it, filling me up like the milk bottle I tip up when I'm a little girl with Mama, who's not here with G.G. And I can see how easy it is to go through the door because there is no door and it's right there, right here, where my head opens up, and it's so easy to get me open like with Porgy Porgy and G.G. squeezing through so tight but now I can see it would be so easy. "So easy," I say, I think, and I must have said it because Curtis says, "What? What's so easy?" And I tell him, "To get me open for passage." And he wipes the tears from my feet and it hurts so much. "Do something!" I cry. "Make it stop!" And Curtis floats over me. "How? Tell me what to do." And I tell him, "Don't." Because it's so good good good. "Don't don't don't!" And when he plays his saxophone it is so good I can't even tell which side of the door it's coming from, or which way it's coming through to fill me with gold.

Curtis

We can't get her out of bed no more, so Rhapsody rolls her over to her side every few hours and holds her in place while I pull out the dirty towel she been lying on, sponge her off, then slide a clean towel under her. And it's a good thing we keeping her so clean because her odor is stronger every day. Not a bad odor, just strong, and it seem to just pour right out of her. From her mouth, from her hair, from her skin, and it smell just the way she always smell, but a hundred times stronger, like it's all bleeding out from her, now.

But what's good is how my music seem to help. Whether she's sleeping or awake. When the music's going, her moans sound almost sexy, and I can almost imagine I'm making love to her. So I play my sax until I got no breath left. I play until my lips are rubbed raw. I play until I know I can't get it up again. And then I take a break and give her a sip of juice. Music and fruit . . . and who knows?

Rhapsody

Seems like I lost track of time long ago. The hours run into days run into weeks, and I can't imagine any of us can go on much longer. As much pain as she's in I'd have thought her heart would have given out by now. Man, and tired as I am, Curtis must be a hundred times more tired. Sixty-eight years old and it seems like it's been weeks since he had a decent night's sleep. He plays his saxophone halfway through the night and starts back in as soon as he's awake. Old and tired as he is, and I swear I never heard him play better. Him or anyone else. He starts with a familiar tune, then shifts it around and turns it inside out until he's found every possible combination of notes that's in it and played them all without repeating a single phrase. He'll go on like that with one song for twenty or thirty minutes, or longer, then give her a sip of juice, and start back in on another song.

But I know he can't go on much longer, and I know *I* can't go on much longer, so I finally tell him we better take her to the hospital and get some help. But he flat out refuses. "She told us she wants to die right here," he says. "So this is where she's *gonna* die."

The problem is that if she lives much longer, he and I might die right here along with her.

Curtis

I can't help but think that the only thing keeping her alive, now, is music and fruit: my saxophone playing and the orange juice. Her cheeks have fallen in, her ears are poking way out from her head and got three or four sharp angles to them and the skin hanging loose at the bottoms, like collars with the starch all gone out of them. And her arms have thinned out so much she look like she just come out of a Nazi concentration camp. But if I keep on playing and giving her juice, maybe she'll last as long as I do. Maybe we'll go together. Float right up to heaven, hand in hand, on my final note.

Rhapsody

I knew there was something familiar about this, and while I'm watching and listening to her struggle and moan, it finally hits me what it is. Déjà vu, Jack. The same as being there to coach Clara Fry through her birth. Being there to watch a life squeezed from a body. Participating in a process that's out of my hands. Beyond my control. And when I watched it back then, it seemed so damn hard I couldn't believe that everybody came into the world that way. And as I watch now it's almost exactly the same. Only she's going instead of coming, and the going seems even harder. Even bigger. And instead of squeezing a baby from her body, it's like she's squeezing *herself* from her body. And when she's finished there won't be two in the bed, there'll be none.

After that, it's still just as hard, but not so terrible or frightening. Nothing evil. In fact, it almost starts to feel like if I could see beneath her pain I would be seeing something good happening. And who knows? Maybe I'm just thinking wishful. Ignoring the facts. But, man, there it is. A feeling. Something good.

Curtis

Every time she takes a breath it's a struggle, now. And every time she takes a breath I'm scared it's gonna be her last. She hasn't opened her eyes or said a word since late last night. She just struggling with her breathing; sound like she trying to breathe and gargle water at the same time.

And I'm listening so hard to every breath, struggling with her, that I can't even bother with the saxophone. *No more music.* And her lips are so cracked and purple that even a drop of watered-down orange juice burns her, so I got to give her clear water. *No more fruit.*

Her eyes stay closed, but hang open almost halfway so you can just see a sliver of her dark iris. The whites of her eyes are yellow, like the white of an egg that's been fried in plenty of butter.

Her mouth hangs open, too, and her tongue keeps snaking out like she got no control over it. Even the gap in her teeth looks all different because it's set in a different face. A face with the flesh hanging on it so thin it look like you could scrape it right off with a fingernail.

April

I don't even have to breathe to breathe. Like a tree, I wait, and it all comes right to me, even when I float up through the door and look down on it all, in love with it all, from the highest branches.

Rhapsody

It goes on for hours, every breath an agony, until finally it sounds like there is more water than air passing into her lungs, and her body heaves and tightens in a final panic, and then releases into a perfect stillness, and while Curtis dives for her arm, already sobbing hard as he hugs and kisses it, I feel something at my shoulder and whirl around. Nothing there. But high up in the corner, where two walls come together to meet the ceiling, there seems to be a thickness to the air. A concentration of darkness and light, squeezed together. Like when you stare at the sun or at a bright light bulb, then look away fast. I glance around, now, to the other three corners, but there's nothing to see but the corners. And when I look back to that first corner it's just the same as the other three. Man, and who knows? A fucking revelation or wishful thinking? Black Magic or hocus pocus? Something good or something bad?

And either way it doesn't much matter. Because either way it's beyond my control. Same thing my mother taught me after Clara Fry's birth: it's out of our hands. Beginnings and Endings, both. Only thing *we* have any control over is what comes in between.

Curtis has moved down to her feet, now, and is hugging and stroking them as he weeps. I touch her arm, and its warmth catches me by surprise because her body looks and sounds so empty. Empty as a cocoon without a caterpillar. Nothing at all like when she's asleep.

Curtis

I never even realized that I knew what her feet looked like. I thought they were feet like anyone else's. Size seven and black, but nothing special. But now they suddenly so familiar I don't even want to let go. So soft and smooth and graceful. So full of her personality. And so *lovely lovely lovely!* The most familiar thing left of her and I don't want to let go. Not ever.

♪♪♪

When I pick up the ashes at the funeral home, they got them wrapped in a plastic bag and packed snug in a small white box. But soon as I get them home I pour them into her favorite clay pot. The one she been using to mix her planting soil in for such a long time that she couldn't stand to leave it in Florida, so packed it in her trunk, wrapped in newspaper, when we came to Oregon.

The ashes ain't ashes like I'm expecting, but a fine gravel—white, black, and gray—that feels good and clean and heavy in my palm. The kind of fine gravel you could pour from one palm to the other and back, and be so comforted by its feel and its weight you could just keep pouring all day long.

Rhapsody

It's just like I figured while I was watching her dying: in the end it all comes down to this right here. In the end it all comes down to ashes. Her ashes and the earth's ashes. Her death and the death of the planet—the explosion of the sun. Only now I'm not so worried about The End. Because now I don't even know if it's something good or bad. All I know is that it's beyond my control. Out of my hands. Nothing to do but accept it.

But what I don't have to accept is what comes *in between* the Beginning and the End. Because it's what comes in between that's up to us; what comes in between—the In and the Out; the Thread of Miracles—that we got to take responsibility for.

And so, after a month of watching my grandmother die before my eyes, I'm right back where I started. More eager than ever to get back to the fight. More eager than ever to ban the bomb and save The Rainbow—the new abolition and *the real rhapsody.*

Only I'm not in such a rush like I was. Not so panicked or desperate. Because it's not just a matter of fear, now, but responsibility; not just a matter of putting off The End, but turning it loose—pure acceptance,

Jack—and committing myself to The In-Between. And it don't matter, now, *what* percent of the people agree with me—don't even matter if I stay a superstar. Because no matter *how* super I am, there ain't nothing I can do about the ashes; and because no matter *how* super I am, I'll still have the same responsibility. Right up to The End, Jack. Whichever End that is, however soon It comes, and whatever It might mean. The best I can do, no matter how super I am, is to commit myself to The In-Between.

Curtis

Like I promised her, Rhapsody and I spread most of the ashes around the roots of her favorite fir tree, but I leave a handful in her clay pot to take back to the grove and spread under an orange tree and in her garden space. And after we've done the spreading I play "Summertime" on my saxophone. Same song I played at Feyla's funeral, Porgy's funeral, and George Gershwin's funeral. Same song I was playing fifty years ago when I first saw April in the flash of lights beneath the giant Christmas tree in the A & P parking lot.

My second time through the song Rhapsody surprises me by singing the lyrics—I didn't even think he knew the lyrics—and I got to admit it: the boy can sing. High notes and low notes. He gets 'em all and gets 'em good.

Afterward, he tells me we should record it and dedicate it to April. And it sounded so pretty, just his voice and my saxophone, that I'm half tempted. But I tell him I can't. Not unless he wants to come to Florida and record it at the grove. Without his roomful of equipment and his army of technicians. And when I tell him that, I figure he's gonna be mad at me. But he just squeezes my shoulder and says I'm right: it's music for the trees, for April, not for the machines.

The White Train

♪

IT WAS EARLY IN THE AFTERNOON, A FEW HOURS AFTER THEY'D SPREAD April's ashes, that Curtis saw the poster.

He had driven into Chintimini to pick up a load of groceries at the community co-op, and the poster was hanging just to the right of the screen door entrance, impossible to miss. Curtis froze, sucked in his breath, and stared at the words and the drawing.

STOP THE WHITE TRAIN was printed at the top of the poster in bold capital letters. Just beneath the lettering was a white train engine, outlined in black. And at the front of the train engine, pushing against it and apparently attempting to keep it from progressing, was a silhouetted line of people. A single-file, stiff-armed human chain.

And, finally, directly beneath the drawing were several paragraphs in smaller print, which Curtis quickly read.

> *Fifty years ago, the trains that rolled to Auschwitz were carrying people to the ovens. On July 1, the train that is scheduled to roll through Portland will be carrying the ovens to the people. And the responsibility for stopping this train of death will be yours!*
>
> *The White Train originates at the Pantex plant in Amarillo,*

Texas—the final assembly point for every hydrogen bomb built in the United States—and is destined for the Trident submarine base in Bangor, Washington. It consists of approximately fifteen heavily armored railroad cars, painted white to reduce the temperature inside. Within each of the white railroad cars are enough hydrogen warheads to destroy approximately fifty major cities.

Those of us who refuse to look the other way intend to place our bodies in front of the train when it passes through our community on July 1. If you wish to sit with us on the tracks, please join us on June 13 or June 21 from 10:00 to 4:00 for the protest orientation and non-violent resistance training. (If you are unable to attend either of the orientation and training sessions, we would still be grateful for your presence, on July 1, as witnesses.)

At the bottom of the poster were an address and a phone number to call for further information.

Curtis pushed through the screen door, shrugging. Kids, he told himself. Nothing but foolishness.

Grabbing a basket, he headed for the produce section and picked out corn, spinach, carrots, tomatoes, avocadoes, oranges, and nectarines. *The White Train.* In the dried fruit section he loaded a bag with raisins, then poured half of them back into the bin. Don't want to overdo it, he thought. I'll be leaving soon enough. Another week, maybe. By the Fourth of July. *Passing through our community on July 1. The White . . .*

"Cancer," he whispered, his hands trembling as he dropped a loaf of oat bread into his shopping basket. Maybe it had started back when she inhaled the poison spray that killed little Porgy along with the baby still inside her. Maybe there had been asbestos in their walls or attic, or in their basement bomb shelter where she kept all her canned goods. Maybe it was the DDT the city had sprayed for years to keep the mosquitoes under control. Or maybe . . .

Too late, he thought. Done. White Poison and White Death. The final gleanings from the White Machine. *The White Train.* He grabbed two small cartons of peach yogurt from a refrigerated shelf, then headed for the check-out counter.

The young woman who rang up his groceries and asked to see his co-op membership card smiled at him. A sweet sincere smile. But he didn't even see it. Just accepted his change from the small white hand, lifted his bag, and hurried out the door to rip the poster from beside the entrance and run with it to the truck, the grocery bag bouncing at his chest.

When Curtis drove into town for groceries, Rhapsody, more unwilling than ever to risk a public appearance, stayed home, sitting at the piano and worrying about his grandfather. Since April's death, Curtis had spoken sparingly; he seemed intent upon keeping all his grief to himself. And when Rhapsody pictured his grandfather returning, next week, to the orange grove to live out his life alone—sixty-eight years old and no one to share his grief with—he had to worry.

He desperately wished that Curtis would agree to join his band. Tour with them across the country. Play out his grief to adoring audiences. Maybe find that he still had plenty of life in him. Possibilities and purposes. A commitment to The In-Between. But Curtis had made it clear that all he wanted was to return to his orange grove and be left alone.

A lemming, Rhapsody thought, shaking his head. Him of all people.

He was still sitting at the piano, mindlessly fingering the keys, when he heard the pick-up pull in. He hustled outside to help carry in the groceries; but when Curtis stepped from the truck, instead of grocery bags he handed Rhapsody a poster.

"Look!" he told his grandson, his voice scarcely louder than a whisper. "The White Machine. A chance to take it on, head to head. A chance to stop it in its tracks."

As he looked over the poster, Rhapsody shook his head, incredulous. "July first. That's perfect! Unbelievable! Man, because I *know* I can get the band here in time. I'll put out a press release today. Announce it as another free concert." He thumped the poster with the back of his hand. "And with all the people who are gonna show up—whether they agree with me or not—the police won't stand a chance; and neither will the White Train. Hah!"

Curtis frowned, but Rhapsody was already rereading the poster. STOP THE WHITE TRAIN. It would be a great symbolic victory. The perfect opportunity to demonstrate to the critics and pollsters that he had more than enough supporters to make an impact. And, even more important, his grandfather seemed eager to be a part of it.

But when Curtis stepped from the truck with his bag of groceries and headed for the front door, he said, "Goddamn, boy. It look to me like you ain't even thinking straight."

"Why?" Rhapsody said, following his grandfather inside. "What do you mean I'm not thinking straight?"

"What I mean is that the ones who work The Machine ain't stupid." He set his grocery bag on the kitchen counter and began unloading and putting up the food. "If they hear there's gonna be a big crowd they just gonna reschedule the train. A week earlier or a week later. And then what you gonna do? You gonna have fifty thousand people standing on a empty train track. And most of 'em won't even care, 'cause they gonna get what they came for. They gonna get you!"

"Right," Rhapsody said. "You're right."

"Sure I'm right."

"So what do we do?"

"We show up is what we do," Curtis said. "Forget the band. And don't even mess with the TV or newspapers. Just show up. That's all we gonna need."

The groceries had been put away, and Curtis now headed back through the front door with Rhapsody right behind.

"We're gonna need numbers is what we're gonna need," Rhapsody pointed out. "Because what if there aren't enough people there to stop the train? What if the police haul us all away and the train goes on through? Who wins then?"

"It ain't *gonna* go through," Curtis said, leaning through the opened truck door. "Because the only way they gonna get *me* off the tracks is to shoot me dead and cut my chain." He backed out of the truck with a thick steel chain in one hand and a huge padlock in the other. "And I believe they'll have to think twice before they decide to shoot a sixty-eight-year-old man for non-violently resisting."

The last three days of June they spent preparing for the protest. Curtis picked up a chain and padlock for Rhapsody, and a pair of sleeping bags so that the two of them could keep warm on the tracks, overnight, in case the engineer of the White Train tried to wait them out—a victory by attrition.

Although Curtis still wouldn't or couldn't talk to Rhapsody about April, every morning and evening he trekked to the fir tree she'd loved, sat in her ashes, his back against the trunk, and played his saxophone while the sun was rising or setting, the changes in light and temperature somehow helping him feel her presence. And during June's final sunset he decided that if he took his saxophone to the protest and played, chained to the tracks, she would be right there with him, giving him strength.

According to the poster, the White Train would be passing through Portland the afternoon of July 1. But when, on the morning of July 1, Rhapsody called the number at the bottom of the poster to ask for directions to the protest site, he learned that the train had been delayed by peace activists in Denver and Missoula, and was now scheduled to arrive in Portland that night between nine and ten.

And so it was not until late in the afternoon that Rhapsody and Curtis loaded the old pick-up with their food and gear—two thermoses of orange juice, two bags of Red Chile Kettle Chips, four ham and cheese sandwiches, a gallon jug of water, and their locks, chains, overcoats, and sleeping bags—then rumbled down the long dirt driveway, Curtis at the wheel.

It is an idyllic Oregon summer evening, the sky blue and cloudless, the temperature in the high seventies. To the west, the summer sun still hangs high over the coastal mountains. To the east, the white peaks of Mount Jefferson and Mount Hood flash above the horizon. All along the interstate, the farm fields are lush with strawberries, beets, mint, squash, and row after row of knee-high corn, while bright yellow batches of scotch broom sweep the nearby meadows and hillsides.

With Curtis driving slowly as ever, they enter the Portland city limits at eight-fifteen. And when, twenty minutes later, they reach their destination, the sun is finally dipping toward the coastal peaks.

The protest site is an asphalt lot beside the train tracks, two blocks north of the Portland Coliseum, where, nine months earlier, Rhapsody had given his final pre-accident performance. Dozens of cars, trucks, and vans are parked about the lot in scattered clusters, and batches of the protestors mill and mingle close to the tracks, most of them crowded between two tall phone poles with green-capped street lights hanging from skinny metal arms.

"Think we need to get out yet?" Rhapsody asks, not wanting to greet the crowd any sooner than he has to. "Nobody's even on the tracks."

"Could be another train coming through first," Curtis says. "Better sit tight until we can see for sure what's going on."

The majority of protestors, as far as Rhapsody can tell from his seat in the truck, are white, and in their twenties, thirties, and forties. Maybe as many as a hundred of them. Maybe more. And the number seems evenly divided between men and women. Most are dressed casually, but a few of the ladies are wearing dresses or skirts, and a few of the men are wearing coats and ties. Many carry simple posters or placards: *Choose Life! Accept Responsibility!* or *Say No!*

Just after the sun sets and the street lights flicker on, a small fleet of police cars and vans pulls up and parks. No flashing lights or sirens. No movement, even, behind the windows. Almost spooky.

A woman wearing a blue dress gives a signal, and perhaps a third of the protestors surge toward the tracks and quickly sit between the rails, two abreast, facing south, the direction the train will be coming from. The remaining protestors stand in an orderly, attentive fashion, all facing the track, five to ten yards back.

"Looks like it's time," Curtis says, kicking open the door. "Let's get!" Standing by the truck, he loops his chain and lock over his shoulder, straps his saxophone to his neck, then grabs a thermos of orange juice and his rolled-up sleeping bag.

Rhapsody, meanwhile, carries the Kettle Chips and the two remaining sandwiches, as well as his lock and chain and sleeping bag. And as they approach then pass the protestors who are standing back from the tracks, there is a rumble of recognition, then a smattering of cheers, whoops, whistles, and applause.

A nice change, Rhapsody thinks. Though these people recognize him, even by street light, and are obviously excited to see him, they are not the sort who would ever mob him. Not a teeny-bopper among them.

He waves, proudly holding up his chain, and is at once halted by the woman with the blue dress.

"Wait a minute, there!" she says, more of a command than a greeting.

Rhapsody stops and turns to face her.

"Oh my!" She smiles, folding her arms. "I didn't realize . . . what a surprise! And an honor."

"Thank you," Rhapsody says.

"Thank *you,"* she says, "for coming. Your support has *got* to help us, and we appreciate that very much."

"Let's get," Curtis hisses, edging impatiently toward the tracks.

"Hold on," the woman says. "You didn't have a chance to attend our orientation and training, did you?"

"No problem," Rhapsody assures her. "We're fast learners."

"I'm sorry." She reaches out, now, to touch his shoulder. "But it's our policy that unless you've attended the most recent training sessions, you shouldn't sit on the tracks. Of course, we would be thrilled to have you join our group of witnesses." She lifts her hand from his shoulder to point at the protestors who are standing back from the tracks.

"Witnesses?" Curtis frowns.

"I don't understand." Rhapsody holds up his lock and chain. "We're all set to chain ourselves to the track."

"I can see that," the woman says. "But we don't use chains. That's why it's so important to attend the trainings. Over the years we've come up with some strict guidelines."

"Goddamn," Curtis growls. "I don't even believe it."

"Listen." The woman brushes blonds bangs from her forehead. "I really am sorry. But we happen to be committed to non-violence both philosophically and tactically, and that sort of commitment has a number of implications. For instance, we have to be concerned not only about your safety and the safety of all the protestors, but the safety of the police officers, and of the security and railroad personnel as well. We have to be concerned about the security of a train that is carrying enough warheads to annihilate sixty million people. And we have to understand the position of the armed guards riding the train who have been given the responsibility of shooting anyone who might represent a threat to all those warheads.

"I could go on and on," she goes on. "I could explain why we believe it is essential for us to avoid any sort of conflict mentality in our methods of protest. I could explain why we believe that physically stopping the train is useless if we fail to change the spirit and reasons behind the train's delivery of weapons. I could explain that we think of our protests as an ongoing dialogue between ourselves, the railroad and security personnel, the media, and everyone else involved. That we think of each protest as a single event which constitutes a small part of a long-term commitment."

"A long-term commitment," Rhapsody repeats, nodding.

Curtis, however, has stopped listening. His chain is looped over his shoulder, and he is squeezing the links in his hand.

"I could go on and on," she says again. "But that's what I do in our training sessions, and our training sessions last six hours. Please!" She fixes her gaze upon Curtis. "Try to understand. We've worked too hard to risk losing all the trust we've built."

"And *that's* what you worried about, ain't it?" Curtis is staring back at her. "You worried that if we really *do* stop the train and make some people mad, *y'all* are gonna take the blame."

"What we're worried about," the woman says evenly, "is the ethical consistency of our methods. Our means. Because we believe, as did Gandhi, as did Martin Luther King, that means are ends in the process of becoming."

"Well, it don't make no difference to me *what* you believe, or *who* all believes it," Curtis says. "All I know is that you ain't even half serious about stopping this train."

"That's not true," the woman says. "And if you knew the depth of our commitment—if you knew how much of our time and effort we've dedicated to this cause—I suspect you would be ashamed of yourself for even suggesting that we aren't serious."

Rhapsody moves up close to his grandfather and lowers his voice as he hisses, "Come on, now, Grandpa! They're just looking at it different from how you are. They're looking at it as a long-term thing. A commitment."

"A commitment? Hah! Look to me like if they was committed they would be chaining themselves to the track and throwing away the keys. *That's* committed. Look." Curtis points his thermos of juice past the lady in the blue dress to the sitters on the track. "Every one of them could be committed for the next fifty years, and it ain't gonna do nobody a bit of good. The police just gonna haul them off the track, and the train gonna go right on through with all the bombs. And so much for their goddamn commitment." He turns to the woman in the blue dress. "How would it be if we was to drive a ways up the track, another five or ten miles maybe, and tell everybody we got nothing to do with you. Tell 'em you chased us away because you didn't like our methods."

"And chain yourselves to the track?"

"That's right. And *you* won't have to worry about taking the blame."

The woman shuts her eyes and rubs her forehead with two fingers. "You know, it can take a long time for an engineer to stop a train. Now what if you chain yourselves to the track, and the train can't stop in time because the engineer wasn't expecting you the way he is expecting us? Is that what you want? Is that fair to the engineer? Or to your friends and relatives? And what good, ultimately, will come of it?"

Curtis turns away, squeezing his chain links tighter.

"And what if the train hits you and your chains, and derails with all those warheads? There are a thousand questions you should ask yourself, and that's one of the things we help you do in our training sessions."

"She's right, Grandpa," Rhapsody pleads. "We got to think it through better. Maybe we ought to take that training, and we can sit on the tracks next time."

"Ain't gonna *be* a next time," Curtis says. "Because I'm gonna be in Florida by the next time. In fact, it look to me like maybe I should have been in Florida by *now*." He turns and stalks off, his thermos in one hand, his sleeping bag tucked under one arm, his chain rattling over his shoulder, and his saxophone swinging like a pendulum from his neck strap.

"I'm sorry," Rhapsody tells the woman, then hurries to catch up with Curtis and walk briskly alongside him.

As he hustles just to keep up with his old grandfather, Rhapsody notices the moon rising, huge, yellow, and almost full, above the coliseum. "Shit, Grandpa," he says. "I understand how you feel. But we already came all this way. Let's at least be witnesses; stand with them and watch it. That's better than nothing, isn't it?"

"You do whatever you want," Curtis says. "I've witnessed all I need to witness." He reaches for the truck door. "I'll be waiting right here."

Rhapsody

I hate to see it turn out this way, but what else can I do? No way I'm gonna sit and sulk with him in the truck. Not when we've just driven a hundred miles to get here, and got nowhere to go except a hundred miles back. And not when there are this many people who are taking responsibility. This many people who are in it for the long run. In it for The In-Between. A genuine commitment, Jack.

I unload my chain and sleeping bag, and the potato chips and sandwiches, then nod at him before hurrying off to stand with the group of witnesses.

Right away, hands touch my shoulders. Gentle, not aggressive. Not touching me just to touch the superstar, but to welcome *me*. If every crowd was like this I could forget about disguises.

It's dark enough now to see plenty of stars, and the moon has turned from yellow to white as it floats up higher and smaller, like a bright eye ready to witness from the sky.

Curtis

I was nothing but a fool to think a bunch of white kids would ever be serious about it. They serious about stopping the White Train just as long as they don't dirty their hands or get themselves hurt. As long as they can keep everything under control—everything according to the rules *they* made up.

I been sitting in the truck for a few minutes, munching my chips, when doors start slamming, and the police—maybe twenty-five or thirty of them—head for the tracks. The sheriff and the lady who kept us off the tracks greet each other like old friends, and for a few minutes they talk, all smiles. And *that's* how committed she is to stopping The

Train. *That's* how serious she is about taking on The Machine.

For a minute I think about sneaking on down the track with my lock and chain, and teaching them all—him too—a lesson about real commitment. But it's too late. Ain't enough time, now, and the fight's gone out of me, anyway. The end of the story already been written: only thing that's ever gonna stop The Machine is The Machine.

Rhapsody

The police, two to a protestor, are already pulling people off the tracks when we spot the train, its headlight rolling back and forth like an evil yellow eye hunting through the dark, looking for something to pin in its light. And as it rumbles closer I can feel its weight in my chest and legs, and then I can see, behind the engine, all the white cars, the moonlight reflecting off the armor. Two of the cars—one directly behind the engine, and the other at the end of the train where the caboose ought to be—are taller than the rest, with high cabs in the back, and tiny windows. "Turret windows," the man next to me explains after I ask him. "That's where the armed guards from the D.O.E. ride with their machine guns."

Between the guard cars I count twelve white bomb-carrying cars, which aren't box-shaped, like regular train cars, but wider at the bottoms than at the tops. Makes them look even more deadly. Like they can slice right through the darkness, unstoppable.

But the closer the train comes, the more it slows, until, finally, the brakes start to squeal. And, maybe twenty or thirty yards back from the track-sitters who haven't yet been hauled off by the police, the train does stop; and right away I cheer and raise both fists over my head. But everyone else, instead of cheering or raising fists, joins hands and starts to sing, "We Shall Overcome," and the man beside me quickly reaches up for my hand.

For a minute I almost resist. I think of Curtis watching from the truck, and I feel like a chump. A big black sucker. Especially with all the white hands and voices. But it's not my show for a change, it's their show—it's our show—and so I sing right along, my voice blending with the others', lifting and floating through the night while the police keep working to clear the tracks.

Curtis

Soon as the train stops I slide out of the truck. And I can feel The White pulling at me—so evil I can smell It, floating right to me like a evil fog, the train cars thick with It, inside and out. The same White my daddy tried to beat back with his piano; same White that choked my sister's spirit then crushed her body; same White that killed my children; same White that turned my mango grove into concrete and poisoned my trees and water; same White that worked its way inside my wife, my April, and spread through her like a slow White Plague until there was nothing left of her. White Death, shining off the outside and pushing from the inside, hungry for more. Hungry for it all. And the kids on the tracks just melting before all that White. Just going limp as they dragged away, and the engine rumbles and smokes, all the Evil ready to roll forward, nothing to stop it.

I reach back into the truck, grab my saxophone, and strap it round my neck for protection.

Rhapsody

Soon as the track is cleared the train starts up. The last car has rolled past, and we're all still holding hands and singing, when somebody down the line shouts, "Oh God, what the hell's he doing?" And I see him, maybe sixty or seventy yards down the track, running right alongside the guard car with the turret windows, lit by the moon and white reflection, his saxophone bouncing from his neck.

And before I know it my legs are pumping in high gear, and I'm already past the line of singing, hand-holding witnesses, and the police, who are only now reacting, giving chase, the closest one a good twenty yards back, screaming, along with all the witnesses, for me to stop.

But I can't stop because there's no time; I'm gonna have to do all my thinking on the run. Do my thinking now, while up ahead Curtis grabs hold of a metal rung at the rear of the guard car and—sixty-eight years old!—hoists himself up, smooth as any acrobat, like he's been hopping trains all his life.

The train is steadily picking up speed, but not enough to keep me from catching up to him, one long car at a time. Not when I'm running harder and faster than I've ever run, knowing that any second, even now, one of those invisible guards might be poking his machine gun through the dark window above Curtis's head, taking aim, and blasting away. And even if they can see, in the moonlight, that he's nothing but a harmless old man, and *don't* blast him away, even then the train's just gonna keep picking up speed until he finally loses his strength and takes a high-speed fall. And so there it is. No turning back. I've got to catch him. Pull myself up beside him and help him to hold on until they get word to the engineer to stop the train and let us off.

Just one car back, now, and I can hear him swearing and screaming, even over the great rumble of the train, and can see him as he swings back his old saxophone then bashes it against the white metal, again and again, the bell busting right off, valves flying everywhere. And there's nothing to do but keep running, my eyes fixed on those deadly narrow windows above his head.

The train continues to pick up speed, not so easy, anymore, to overtake. I shout to him as I close in, but he just keeps swinging back his saxophone like some crazy old lumberjack, hammering away at the white car, metal against metal, sparks flying through the night.

It's only when I've passed him and am running slightly ahead, still shouting and waving my arms, that he looks over his shoulder and sees me. His face is pure black—darker than the night—against the white metal background. His old saxophone is broken and twisted. I wave for him to jump down before it's too late, but he just shakes his head, then watches over his other shoulder when I drop back behind him. As soon as he sees what I'm going to do, he edges over to give me room. I'm not quite running at full speed, but, man, I'm winded as hell, and the police are catching up fast—one of them almost close enough for a flying tackle. It's now or never, Jack. I grab hold, tight, to a white steel rung just below and beside Curtis's waist, and the train seems to lurch forward, ripping at my hand and arm with its full weight and force—a million tons of it, tearing at every muscle from my fingertips to my shoulder—and whipping me back just behind the corner of the car, where there's nothing for me to see but white metal sliding up my face as I drop straight down, not even a chance to hear the end of Curtis's scream.

The In-Between, Not the End

♪

EARLY OCTOBER AND NOTHING BUT HEAT AND HUMIDITY. HE wonders how he had ever tolerated this climate. The glass door is a heavy one, but he's getting better with doors all the time. Already sweating in his suit—no boots this time—the brown bag squeezed between his thighs, he wheels himself on in, and sees, as he knew he would (for he has timed his entrance to the minute), that the game, the first of the series, has begun—one out, bottom of the first inning—and nearly everyone is watching it on the wide-screen TV high over the bar. Unnoticed, he wheels his way to the same table in the corner, adjusts his white beard and his pillows, and waits.

"Remember me?" he asks, as she comes shuffling up, same loose limbs and voluptuous neck, even the same blue jeans and t-shirt. And still no wedding or engagement ring.

"Sure I remember," she says with an easy grin. "Mr. Black Santa Claus. You even earlier this year." Only then does she notice the wheelchair and the reason for it, and he is relieved when she appears more puzzled than shocked. "I don't remember *that,* do I?" she says.

Rhapsody shakes his head.

"You feel like telling me what happened?"

He shrugs. "It's a dangerous job. Donner went left and Blitzen went right. A mid-air crack-up."

"Ho ho ho. Still the joker," she says, shaking her head and lightly touching his shoulder.

And his knees feel instantly weak, even though his knees are gone.

With her hand she gestures to the TV. "So . . . does Santa Claus have a favorite team?"

"L.A.," he says. "But that doesn't matter; because the real action comes *in between* the innings."

"In between the innings?" She puzzles over his answer for a moment, then shrugs and asks what she can bring him.

"How about a chili dog?"

"One chili dog." She writes it on her pad.

"And a Heineken Dark."

A smile works its way into her cheek. "Don't even tell me. No ID."

"That's right," he says.

And she nods. "Okay, Mr. Santa Claus. You win."

"Good," he says. "But remember, now: you've got to watch in between the innings." He points to the television. "One out to go."

"You talking crazy," she says, squinting from him up to the TV.

"Just sit for a minute. You don't want to miss the real action, do you?"

"I'm gonna have to miss it," she says. "I got about six orders up."

"Okay, look. There it is." The first baseman snags the throw from the shortstop, and the umpire's arm shoots straight out. "Third out, and here comes the in-between. Sit." He touches her elbow, then pulls out a chair. "Sit!"

She sits.

For a moment the screen is blank. And then comes the footage of the blast—not your typical World Series commercial fare—the mushroom cloud rising. A close-up of a wooden shack bursting apart. Trees whipping in one direction—bending like tall grass stalks in a strong wind—then back in the other direction. And all the while, a voice-over: a recording from the radio broadcast of last year's nuclear crisis, with the word *inequationable* mixed in every few seconds. A final mushroom blast. Then silence. And, as the cloud is fading, a piano and saxophone start up softly, the volume steadily increasing and the beat becoming familiar. The camera focuses in on Rhapsody's face as he sings the two replacement verses of his reggae "Over de Rainbow." Meanwhile, the camera is pulling back and to the side, showing Rhapsody in profile, sitting in his wheelchair at the piano, an old man standing beside him playing a brand-new tenor saxophone. As soon as the second verse is over, the camera zooms in on Rhapsody's rainbow-and-mushroom-cloud t-shirt. "Please." It's the voice of the superstar. "Wear my shirt. Help spread the message. Show the world you are *committed."*

The camera pulls back to show Rhapsody still at the piano, the old man at his side.

"Because superstars fade."

Now the old man, Curtis, speaks. "And bodies grow older."

Then they speak together. "But real commitment only deepens."

"And," Curtis says, "when you vote next month—"

"Remember to vote for The Rainbow," Rhapsody says.

"And against The Machine," Curtis adds.

They slap hands, a perfect high-five, and the picture freezes in mid-slap. Then, over the picture, the phone number and address for placement of t-shirt orders is flashed, and, below that, the message, *Paid for by the Coalition for the New Abolition.*

A few of the patrons sitting at the bar whoop and slap hands, while others shake their heads, but *she* has been gawking at him—trying to stare right through the phony white beard as if she had X-ray vision—ever since the camera pulled back and focused on the superstar, legless, in his wheelchair at the piano.

"Damn," she hisses. "The Santa Claus suit and the beard; no ID; the fifty-dollar tip."

"I got a different tip for you this time," he tells her, then pulls one of his rainbow-and-mushroom-cloud t-shirts from the brown bag on his lap and hands it to her.

Behind the bar, a man with a black bow tie signals to her, scowling.

"Hang on just a minute," she tells Rhapsody and, leaving the t-shirt on the table, hurries back to the kitchen to take out a trayful of orders.

When she returns she sits in the chair across from him and leans forward, wide-eyed, her arms folded on the table, her fingers interlocked upon her new t-shirt. "Okay," she says. "I ought to have a few minutes now if I'm lucky, so tell me what in the world you doing here."

"My grandfather owns an orange grove. Just west of town. We came back for blossom time. And to tie up some loose ends before we get back to Oregon."

"Oregon? I thought you lived in Hollywood or somewhere. What's in Oregon?"

"Battle lines," he tells her without hesitating. "From the fir trees to the train tracks. An In-Between still worth fighting for." He runs his fingers through his beard. "Although we been running out of fuel for the fighting faster than I ever expected we would. You got any idea how much it costs to buy commercial time for the Series?"

She shakes her head.

"Too much. Especially with album sales slower than what I thought they'd be. But it doesn't matter. There's plenty of other things we can do cheaper than commercials. And, if we have to, plenty of other groups we can join up with. In fact it might even be best that way. A coalition of coalitions. A network of commitment." He shrugs, allowing himself a glance at her neck, then gestures to the t-shirt beneath her hands. "At least *those* are selling the way I'd hoped."

She nods. Holds up the t-shirt by the shoulders. "I been seeing them around."

"And what do you think of the message?"

"I don't know," she says. "Some people say it's a good thing you been doing, but there's a lot of people saying it ain't none of your business."

"But what do *you* say?"

She frowns, taking a moment to study the shirt. "I say they crazy with all the bombs and shit. But I don't know."

"Listen," he says. "I'm gonna be in town a few more days. Maybe we could take some time to talk about it. It's important."

Her eyes narrow, and she lets the t-shirt fall to her lap. "Why? Why it's so important to talk about it with *me?*"

Looking up to the TV, he watches the left fielder chase a fly ball to the warning track. "Cupid," he finally says, still staring at the TV. "I couldn't help it. From the minute I saw you when I walked in last time."

She laughs. Lets her face fall into her hands. "I don't believe this."

"Are you working tonight?"

"No," she quickly says. "But I already got plans."

"How about tomorrow night?"

She takes a few seconds to think. "No plans tomorrow night. But I got a three-year-old at home, and I can't afford to be paying no baby-sitter two nights in a row."

He almost offers to pay for the baby-sitter, but changes his mind. "I could come to your place," he suggests.

She laughs again, then looks him up and down. "I guess if I had to I could always outrun you."

"Don't be too sure," he says. "My reindeer can pull this wheelchair even faster than they can the sleigh." He pats the tops of his wheels. "So tomorrow night? How about seven o'clock?"

"Eight," she says. "But you got to promise to come *without* the beard. Mr. Black Santa Claus."

"Rhapsody," he corrects her, extending an arm across the table.

And, shaking his hand, she introduces herself, "Daphne," then writes down her address for him. "Now what about your chili dog and beer?"

"Well," he says, patting the top pillow that's stuffed in the belly of his suit. "My stomach felt empty when I came in here, but I'm really not hungry anymore. And besides, I got a car waiting outside."

"All right, then. I guess I'll see you tomorrow night."

"Right. Tomorrow night."

Pushing her chair back, she stands, t-shirt in hand, and winks at him. "I still don't believe it," she grins, then whispers, "Rhapsody Walker."

He watches her disappear into the kitchen, her hips and elbows swinging, then wheels himself across the floor to the heavy glass door, pulls it open, easily, with one quick jerk, and maneuvers his way out into the brightness and heat of the day, the brightness and heat of The In-Between, feeling giddy as he gulps a deep breath—In and Out—and notices the vague scent of blossoms that has tinged the city air.